CORNERING CARMEN

DRAGON LORDS OF VALDIER BOOK 5

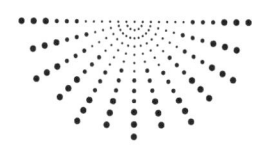

S.E. SMITH

ACKNOWLEDGMENTS

I would like to thank my husband Steve for believing in me and being proud enough of me to give me the courage to follow my dream. I would also like to give a special thank you to my sister and best friend, Linda, who not only encouraged me to write, but who also read the manuscript. Also to my other friends who believe in me: Julie, Jackie, Christel, Sally, Jolanda, Lisa, Laurelle, Debbie, and Narelle. The girls that keep me going!

And a special thanks to Paul Heitsch, David Brenin, Samantha Cook, Suzanne Elise Freeman, and PJ Ochlan—the awesome voices behind my audiobooks!
—S.E. Smith

CORNERING CARMEN: DRAGON LORDS OF VALDIER BOOK 5
Copyright © 2012 by Susan E. Smith
First E-Book Published December 2012
Cover Design by Melody Simmons
ALL RIGHTS RESERVED: This literary work may not be reproduced or transmitted in any form or by any means, including electronic or photographic reproduction, in whole or in part, without express written permission from the author.
All characters, places, and events in this book are fictitious or have been used fictitiously, and are not to be construed as real. Any resemblance to actual persons living or dead, actual events, locales, or organizations are strictly coincidental.

Summary: Carmen is mortally wounded and wakes to find herself on board an alien warship headed for a distant world and an alien determined to make her want to give love a second chance.

ISBN: 9781481273084 (kdp paperback)
ISBN: 978-1-942562-04-7 (eBook)

{Romance (love, explicit sexual content)—Science Fiction (Aliens)—Royal—Contemporary—Paranormal (Shifters)—Action/Adventure—Fantasy.}

Published by Montana Publishing.
www.montanapublishinghouse.com

CONTENTS

Synopsis	vi
Prologue	1
Chapter 1	9
Chapter 2	12
Chapter 3	20
Chapter 4	25
Chapter 5	32
Chapter 6	40
Chapter 7	48
Chapter 8	56
Chapter 9	64
Chapter 10	73
Chapter 11	82
Chapter 12	89
Chapter 13	96
Chapter 14	105
Chapter 15	113
Chapter 16	123
Chapter 17	136
Chapter 18	144
Chapter 19	152
Chapter 20	164
Chapter 21	173
Chapter 22	181
Chapter 23	190
Epilogue	195
Additional Books	202
About the Author	207

SYNOPSIS

Carmen Walker has spent the last three years of her life focusing on avenging the murder of her husband, and she's closing in on his killer. To meet with her informant, she catches a ride on the business jet her sister is co-piloting to California, but plans change when one of the women is kidnapped when they land, and Carmen is mortally wounded. She wakes on board an alien warship heading to a distant world.

Creon Reykill is credited with ending the wars between the Valdier, Curizan, and Sarafin worlds, and building a strong alliance with their former enemies. But that victory came at a cost. Creon has given up hope of ever finding his true mate, believing his soul is too dark to ever be gifted with one.

That all changes when a female unlike anything he has ever seen before is brought to his world. The moment he sees her, he knows she belongs to him. His dragon will do anything to claim her, his symbiot will do anything to protect her, and he would do anything to chase the shadows from her eyes, for just her presence has brought light to his darkness.

Can a dragon-shifting warrior with his own demons help heal the broken heart of a human woman who wants to give up everything—including her life—for revenge?

PROLOGUE

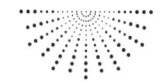

Florencia, Colombia, three years earlier...

"Carmen, remember to watch your back," Scott said as he brushed a kiss across her lips. He had a bad feeling about tonight. "I don't like it. This meeting is too important for the drug cartel to ignore. If the governor of this region gets the support he needs, the cartel will lose their hold on this area."

Carmen smiled at her husband of four years. They may have only been married for a short time, but he had been the love of her life since the first day of kindergarten when he stood up for her against another little girl who was picking on her. She wound her arms around his neck and buried her face against it, inhaling his wonderful scent.

"I will," she whispered. "I have a good reason to be extra careful now," she giggled.

Scott pulled back and looked down into Carmen's glowing face. His eyes widened as her meaning sank in. His face tightened with sudden concern. He should never have accepted this last assignment. He cursed under his breath as his mind ran through everything that might happen.

"Shush." Carmen grinned up at him. "Tonight should be easy. You and your team are covering the governor and his wife. My team will cover their son. We meet at the airport and get them all on the plane. After that, the assignment is complete, and we go home. We've covered every scenario," she added as his arms wrapped around her tightly.

"When...when did you find out?" Scott asked hoarsely, moving one of his hands down to rest on Carmen's still flat stomach.

"This morning," she giggled again. "I had Maria get me a home pregnancy test while she was out."

Scott wrapped his arms back around Carmen and held onto her as if she was the most precious thing in the world. She was to him. He had fallen in love with her the moment he stared into her dark brown eyes when they were both five years old.

She had been standing in the playground with her fists raised and a stubborn, fierce expression on her face. He had stood there watching as Sally Mae took a step back as Carmen advanced on her. Sally Mae had been pulling on Carmen's pigtails, and she'd had enough of it. When one of Sally Mae's second-grade friends pushed Carmen down, Scott had enough. He went in swinging. No one messed with the little girl with eyes the color of dark chocolate, hair the color of the sun, and the prettiest face he had ever seen.

Sally Mae and her friends had beaten him up, but it was worth it. From that day forward, he and Carmen had been inseparable. When they reached high school, he had asked her to be his girl forever, and she had agreed.

Their parents had worried at first, but finally accepted the amazingly special feelings that Carmen and Scott had for each other. Scott had promised both his parents and Carmen's he would wait until they married before he acted on his feelings. When Carmen's parents were killed in a car accident during their senior year of high school, it had sealed his determination to care for the girl of his dreams. They had married days after graduation and embarked on the life of adventure they had talked about for years.

Now, as Scott looked down into Carmen's excited eyes, he wondered if he had made the right decisions. He should have called it quits six months ago. Carmen had wanted to accept this last assignment, but he should have said no. Yes, it would give them the extra money they needed to set up their own business back home, but the fear that something might happen to her flooded him with a need to protect her unlike anything he had ever felt before.

"I love you, Carmen Walker," Scott said quietly. "Tonight is the last time. Tomorrow we go home and start a new life," Scott murmured as he pulled back. "I don't want you to go with the team tonight. I want you to wait for me here, where I know you will be safe."

Carmen shook her head, laughing. "Are you getting all protective on me, Scott Michael Walker? Because if you are, let me remind you…" Carmen's voice faded away as Scott pressed his lips against hers.

"Yes, I am. I'm also the boss of this operation in case you don't remember," Scott said thickly. "Stay in the car at least. The rest of the team can make sure José is safely on board the plane."

Carmen softened when she saw the fear in Scott's eyes. "Okay," she agreed, lovingly running her hand over his cheek.

~

Later that night the teams headed out. Each team would take a different route and use several different vehicles to transport the governor of the local province in Colombia and his family to the airport. There had been increased threats against him from the local cartel group, and Scott was taking every one of them seriously. He gave strict commands to the teams to not take any risks.

Scott came up to Carmen as she was about to get into the vehicle with Governor Alvaro's ten-year-old son, José. He pulled her to one side and pressed a hard kiss to her lips. His eyes glittered with determination as he gazed down at her.

"If there is any trouble, if you get even the slightest itch that something is wrong, you get the hell out of there," he said grimly. "You do whatever you have to do to remain safe, Carmen. You are my life. I love you."

Carmen smiled up into Scott's light green eyes. "Ditto for you. I love you so much. Stay safe"—she laid a protective hand over her stomach—"for the both of us."

Scott pressed another hard kiss on her lips before pulling away and yelling for everyone to get moving. He looked back at Carmen one last time before he moved toward the vehicle with the governor.

∽

Carmen looked out at the darkness that surrounded the vehicle. The ride to the airport was thankfully uneventful. They had made several cutbacks before turning to come in from the north. Carmen was the only one who knew how they were approaching. Scott had made sure only the team leader of each vehicle knew the route in order to reduce the chance of a leak.

The black SUV pulled up to the gate. Marcus, one of their advance team members, opened the gate with a nod. He gave the signal that Scott and the others were already there. Scott was standing near the plane when they pulled up. Carmen slid out first, looking around. She nodded to the other two men in the car that it was clear. She smiled down at the frightened face of the little boy who had ridden in silence in the back seat.

"You will walk with me?" José asked in a small voice.

"Sí," Carmen said gently in Spanish. "Come on, let's get you to your parents."

She reached her hand out and squeezed his in encouragement when he placed his smaller hand in hers. "It's almost over," she whispered with a wink.

His tentative smile broke her heart. A child should never have to feel this kind of fear. Scott had warned her that the cartel might target the boy in an effort to get back at the governor's crackdown on them. Carmen would make sure they never got to him. Children were the essence of innocence and should be protected at all cost.

She was halfway to the plane when the SUV they had just exited exploded, throwing all of them to the ground. Carmen instinctively rolled her body over José and covered his head. She heard the sounds of automatic gunfire in the distance above the sound of the jet's engines revving up.

She shook her head to clear the ringing in her ears. Carlos and Enrique were struggling to get up next to her. She forced her body up, pulling José with her. She made sure she shielded him as she pushed him toward the plane. Carlos was firing behind them at several vehicles that burst through the gates and were approaching at a high rate of speed.

Carmen saw Scott returning fire at the approaching vehicles, even as he ran toward her. Carmen gasped as she felt a bullet pierce her thigh. She collapsed with a cry. Enrique swooped in, grabbing José up and running toward the plane with Carlos covering his back. Carmen rolled, gripping her leg with one hand while she fired her semiautomatic 9mm handgun at the vehicles.

Gunfire erupted again, and Carmen jerked as one of the bullets hit her in the arm, knocking her backward onto the pavement. Her head turned when she heard other bullets hitting something else not far from her. A cry of denial ripped from her as she watched Scott's body jerk as a series of shots cut through him. He collapsed about eight feet from her. Carmen fought through the agony searing through her body, determined to get to the man she loved. She made it to within three feet of him before a set of polished shoes stood in her line of vision.

The figure bent down, gripping her uninjured shoulder, and turned her over until she was staring straight up into the black eyes of Javier Cuello. Carmen's eyes moved away from his cold ones, trying to find Scott. Her only thought was to get to him.

"So much beauty," Javier said softly, brushing a strand of white-blonde hair back from Carmen's face and turning her head toward him. "I heard about the young American security team that was protecting the governor and his family. My informants did not lie when they said the woman was of exceptional beauty," he said, chuckling when Carmen tried to turn her head again.

Javier looked over to where Scott was lying, fighting for breath. "He means something to you, sí? The others, they do not care so much for you. They have left you all alone." He tsked, shaking his head and running his thumb over her bottom lip. "Perhaps I should keep you as a prize."

Carmen's eyes glittered with fury. "Go to hell. You are a coward and a bully," Carmen choked out hoarsely.

Javier chuckled. "A bully?" he responded, laughing out loud as he looked at his men. "I have not been called a bully since I was a child," he said, turning to look back down at Carmen with a cold smile. "No, little American, I am not a bully. I am a cold hearted murderer."

A sob escaped Carmen as she followed Javier as he stood up and walked over to where Scott was lying. Scott looked up at Javier before he turned his eyes to Carmen. She saw love, acceptance, and regret in his eyes.

"No!" Carmen tried to scream out. "You get away from him! You get away from him!" she sobbed out, struggling to move.

Javier nodded to one of his men to hold Carmen down as he used his foot to nudge Scott. "You do not need to worry. I will take very good care of your woman," Javier grinned as he pulled a handgun out of his pocket. "For a very, very long time," he added before he pulled the trigger.

Carmen's screams pierced the night. Tears burned, but refused to fall as she watched the man who meant the world to her jerk once before remaining still. A cold enveloped her body and soul as she stared into Scott's sightless eyes. Her fingers gripped the knife she had unsheathed at her side. Her eyes moved back to Javier, who shook his head in distaste before he slid the handgun back into his pocket.

"Now, I have taken care of the competition," he said casually, moving to squat down next to Carmen again. "Now, you will be mine."

"When hell freezes over," Carmen said in an emotionless voice as she raised the knife she had clutched tightly in her fist.

She buried the knife as far as it would go in Javier's thigh. He fell backward with a strangled curse, grabbing the knife sticking out of his leg. One of his men drew his gun and fired it into Carmen several times, while several other men pulled Javier away from her.

She smiled as she listened to the faint sounds of Javier's screams as they moved him back to his vehicle. In the distance, she heard the sounds of sirens, but none of it mattered to her. She used the last of her strength to reach her good arm out to where Scott lay near her. She needed to touch him one last time. A sob caught in her battered body, even as the flashing lights swirled around them.

I need to touch him... one... last... time, she thought hazily as her fingers tenderly skimmed his cheek before darkness swept her away.

CHAPTER ONE

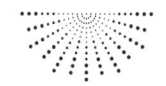

*A*board the Valdier Warship *V'ager*: **Present Day**

Carmen stood frozen on the transporter platform. A part of her wanted to rebel against leaving the alien warship she had woken up on weeks before. She was afraid that once she was off the warship, all chances of finding a way home would be gone. She looked over at her sister. She knew deep down Ariel was relieved at the strange turn of events in their lives. Ariel believed that Carmen would have to give up her thirst for revenge now.

That will never happen, Carmen thought sadly. *If it is the last thing I ever do, I will return to Earth.*

Carmen didn't remember the actual moment she was brought aboard the warship. She had been dying. The man who kidnapped Abby, the artist who had been traveling with them, had pulled a knife on her. She didn't see him pull it until it was too late. She had been distracted by the sounds of some wild animals they had spooked. Or at least, she had thought they were wild animals. Carmen wasn't sure what category men who changed into dragons would be classified as in the scientific world. Personally, she really didn't give a rat's ass. Her biggest concern was to get back home.

At first, a part of her was furious that she would die before she had finished what she had promised Scott. Even as that fury washed through her, another part of her was relieved that the intense pain she had lived with for the past three years was about to end once and for all. She had given in to the sense of peace that enfolded her in its tight arms, ready to join Scott at last.

When she awoke almost a month ago in the medical unit aboard an alien warship, fury flooded her. She had cheated death again. She had spent the first week taking her rage out on the men on board the warship in the hope they would just put her out of her misery. After the first week, though, she had to reluctantly admit she had grown to like the oddball aliens. They had an off-the-wall sense of humor about them.

And, they're good fighters, she thought, glaring at a couple of the men looking at her in a way that made her uncomfortable.

She knew they only went to the medical unit to make her feel good. She might have given them a few new bruises, but she had never really hurt any of them. Well, except for the couple of guys the first time when she was still in the medical unit. Ariel, Trisha, and she had taken them by surprise and used a couple of less than fair blows to knock them out. That was when the anger had been at its zenith. Afterward, it was almost fun when one of the warriors would come to the door of their rooms anticipating her response.

She used that time to practice and develop her skills. She learned from the men she fought, enjoying their greater strength and agility. It helped her get back into shape, made the time aboard seem to fly by, and honed her fighting skills. She figured she could use all the skills she could learn when she got back to Earth. She would need them to get to Cuello when she found him.

Carmen shook her head and focused when she heard Trelon tell the man behind the transporter to beam them down. She needed to learn all she could if she was going to escape. It was best to keep her memories where they belonged for right now, in the past. Everything lit up around her, and she felt a sense of disorientation before everything blurred.

CHAPTER TWO

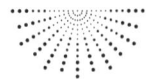

Creon Reykill was not in a good mood. In fact, he was in a really foul mood as his older brother gripped his arm, turning him in the direction of the transporter room located in one of the wings of the palace. It was the absolute last place he wanted to go.

He hated weepy females. He hated whiny, crying, clinging, fragile females. Give him a sturdy Sarafin or Curizan female any day. Not that there weren't a few Valdier women who could compete for his attention, but at least he didn't have to chance running into a Sarafin or Curizan female he had bedded again unless he wanted to. The Valdier females all wanted something from him, namely a high position, the comfort of the palace, and him waiting on them hand and foot.

Clarmisa was a perfect example of everything he hated about weak females. He ended up having to leave the planet before she would return to her clan. She had driven him out of his mind with her whining: the food was too cold, the rooms too small, the servants too rude. Then, she started her clinging. She was too weak to walk without him holding her hand, or she was frightened by the shadows in the corridors. He didn't know why she had targeted him. He finally had enough the night she sneaked into his living quarters. She had broken down in a torrent of tears after he ordered her out of his rooms. She was damn lucky his symbiot hadn't killed her. The only thing that saved her was probably its distaste of even touching her.

Creon felt his dragon shudder at the thought of touching the beautiful but empty Valdier princess. He could feel his own skin crawl as he remembered her touching his chest with her soft fingers. He had taken a long, hot shower before he packed his bags and took off again for the Sarafin star system. He had only returned a few days ago. He had been searching for information on his oldest brother Zoran's kidnapping. He knew the Curizan weren't behind it. He was best friends with Ha'ven, the Curizan leader.

One of his informants had mentioned a possibility that Vox, the leader of the Sarafin, might know something. Creon was friends with the huge cat-shifter. They were a wily species that were as fierce as they were cunning. He had saved the big son of a bitch during one of the battles in the Great Wars. While Vox was recovering, he and Creon had talked. They learned there was more behind the wars than they had been led to believe, but certain factions within their governments were feeding them false information. A friendship was formed, and they had worked together behind the scenes with Ha'ven to expose the plot to bring down each of their respective governments.

"I still do not understand why I need to be there," Creon muttered to Mandra as he walked next to him. "Isn't it bad enough I had to deal with Clarmisa sneaking into my bed? Why do I have to deal with this weak species Zoran is bringing back? Surely you can handle it?" he groaned.

Mandra glared at his youngest brother. "You owe me! After you left I had to deal with her and her father. He wanted to demand you claim her as your mate. I had to finally threaten to challenge him if he didn't get the hell back to his clan," he growled back. "I can deal with one whiny, weepy female, but not two. Trelon said he needed help with the two sisters. We talked yesterday about how delicate and fragile they were. As soon as we get them settled, we will have mother and the healers take over their care."

Creon groaned silently. He hated dealing with situations like this. Give him a good fight, some undercover work, even an assassination attempt on his life, but never, ever a needy female. He sighed as he followed Mandra into the transporter room. He paused to look around, hoping the females had already arrived and by some miracle they had missed them.

He walked over to a small group of warriors he recognized from being on his brother Kelan's warship. They must have come down earlier. He was surprised that they were still here. Usually once the warriors arrived, they disappeared to find a willing female or two.

"Welcome home," Creon said easily. "I am surprised you are still here. I thought for sure you would have hurried to one of the pleasure houses by now," he joked, slapping Jurden on the shoulder.

If there was one thing he excelled at, it was putting others at ease and getting information. Trelon had been tight-lipped when they had talked to him. Creon liked to deal with all the information he could get. If the females needed a healer right away, he wanted one on hand to take care of them as soon as possible.

Jurden grinned at Creon. "It is good to be back, Lord Creon. We are waiting for the human females to transport down. I keep hoping that I can be the one to capture the short-haired one. She is unbelievable!"

Creon frowned. Why would a warrior as fierce as Jurden want a weak, alien female? He listened as the men joked about being the one strong enough to capture the alien female's heart. They laughed about how Tammit still bragged about his encounter with her.

What in the gods' names are they talking about? Creon wondered with a shake of his head. He looked at Mandra with a confused shrug. *Surely they must be talking about someone else.*

There was no way they could be talking about the females from the planet his brother had landed on. He had seen and talked to Zoran's mate. She was as gentle and delicate as his mother's flowers. She looked like a gentle breeze would knock her over.

Creon turned to say something to Mandra when the body of his brother, Trelon, and three females appeared on the transporter platform. Creon looked on in disappointment as three small figures appeared next to Trelon. The one closest to him looked like a child. The other two females were similar in coloring, but that was about all they had in common from what he could tell with a quick glance. He started in surprise when he heard Trelon bellow out for him and Mandra to grab the females. Trelon had grabbed the smallest one up over his shoulder and taken off at a run for the door. Creon turned in time to see the female with the long white hair planting her booted foot in his brother's face.

Creon turned to grab the female with the short hair. Yells of warning from the men behind him came too late. He reached for the female's arm, only to feel his body leaving the ground and going airborne for a brief moment. It was only his years of training that prevented him from landing on his back. He twisted at the last minute, landing on his feet with a snarl.

The slender figure turned on him and struck out for his throat. Creon fell back a step as he moved away from the blow that would have left him gasping for air if it had landed. He felt his dragon roar out and push against his skin in a fierce battle to break free. Black scales, the color of the darkest night sky, rippled over his arms and up his neck as he fought for control.

What in the hell is the matter with you? he exploded as he ducked another blow meant to incapacitate him and spun around to circle the figure.

Mate! his dragon panted. *My mate! I capture my mate.*

Mate? Creon asked, confused as he felt a booted foot connect with his stomach as he lost his focus. *You think this she-demon who is trying to kill us is your mate?* he wheezed as he tried to suck in air as her next kick connected with his groin.

Creon blocked blow after blow, trying to keep from getting his ass kicked while trying to gain control of his dragon. The damn thing was refusing to listen to him as it fought to escape and grab the female who was moving with lightning-fast moves. He finally had enough of it and let out a loud, frustrated roar as he finally got his arms around her slender form.

He was afraid to hold her too tight in case he hurt her. That was his first mistake. She took advantage of the close proximity to inflict more damage. He felt her head connect with his left eye in a blow that brought tears to his eyes. The second mistake was thinking if he pulled her head closer she couldn't hit him with it again. He yelled out as her small teeth clamped down on his ear in a vicious bite that had him releasing his hold. That was his third mistake. That left him vulnerable to her knee which found its way to his groin before connecting with his mouth.

Creon saw stars as he let go of the seething white-haired savage. He fell back several steps, trying to catch his breath as he put both hands on his knees to steady himself so he wouldn't fall on his ass. He spit the blood from his busted lip out as he drew in a deep breath, willing away the pain.

Go! Why you wait? Mate get away. Chase her! Chase her! His dragon bounded around inside him.

Chase her? I'm going to strangle her! I just don't know if I'm going to do it before or after I kill Trelon, Creon growled out, painfully straightening up.

He glared at the men trying to hide their laughter. "I think you need to explain where in the dragon's balls my brothers got these females, and whose stupid idea was it to think they were delicate?" Creon growled out, wiping the blood from his mouth and wincing as he felt first his eye, then his ear.

"That little savage almost emasculated me!" Creon snarled when the men burst out laughing. "Not to mention nearly biting my ear off."

Jurden grinned. "Now you know why we were waiting. Aren't they magnificent?"

Creon felt his ear again, grimacing at the touch of blood that came away with his fingers. "Just bloody magnificent," he replied sarcastically. He turned away from the men, snarling. "And will you bloody shut the fuck up! You are not helping my pain level at this moment."

"My lord?" Jurden asked, confused.

Creon flashed a pained look at the men looking at him like he had lost more than a fight. "Not you." He grimaced again, heading toward the door. "My stupid dragon thinks that she-demon is his mate," he grumbled as the doors closed behind him.

∼

Carmen turned in a circle. She was in some type of long corridor. Floor-to-ceiling windows reflected the brilliant light of the planet.

When she had finally escaped from the man trying to grab her, all she could think about was finding a place to hide and regroup. She had run out of the room like the hounds of hell were after her. In a way, she felt like they still were. The moment that man had touched her, something inside of her reacted to him. It...frightened her. Carmen muttered a curse under her breath. This was stupid. The only feelings she had left inside her were for revenge.

She walked along the corridor until she came to another set of narrow stairs leading upward. She looked behind herself briefly to make sure no one was following her before she turned and took a tentative step forward. Soon she was moving up the stairs, staring in wonder at the ceiling murals and the carvings on the walls. She ran one hand along the white stone that glittered with tiny crystals that glowed as her hand moved over them.

Carmen rounded the corner at the top and stopped in disbelief at the magnificence of the atrium filling the top floor. The ceiling was clear glass, reaching almost thirty feet up. Plants of all sizes, shapes, and color grew in wild abandon. Carmen turned, trying to see everything at once, but there was too much to see. Glowing flowers hung down, and vines with pulsing greens, purples, and pinks wound around tall statues of dragons and other creatures Carmen had never seen before.

She walked along the narrow paths, stooping under the hanging vines, touching flowers and gasping when they suddenly closed. In the center of the atrium was a raised pool. Small fountains in the shape of birds poured water back into the pool. At the end, the huge shape of a dragon lying on his back with water pouring out of his mouth and over his belly formed a small waterfall.

Carmen walked over to stare down at her reflection in the surface of the water. Grief flooded her as she stared into eyes that used to shine with excitement. Now all she saw was bleakness and pain. She reached out her hand, splashing the surface until she couldn't see her image any longer before she sat down on the edge of the pool. She tilted her head to look up at the ceiling, unwilling to look into her own eyes again. Through the clear glass she could make out the images of real dragons soaring overhead.

Wrapping her arms around her waist, she rocked back and forth. "Oh, Scott, I wish you could hold me again," she whispered in a soft voice. Even as softly as she spoke, the sound seemed to echo above the sound of the water. "I'm so scared. I don't know what to do."

She sat for a long time, letting one plan after another flow through her mind in an attempt to figure out how she could get back home. She discarded one after another as she realized she had no idea where she was, much less how to fly a spaceship.

Her hand moved to the knife she always kept with her. It had been Scott's hunting knife. It was the knife she was going to use to kill Cuello with when she found him. Her fingers ran over the handle before she wrapped them around it and pulled it out.

She kept the blade as sharp as a surgeon's scalpel. Raising her hand up, she let the tip cut along her palm just deep enough to draw blood. She needed that small reminder that she was still alive, that she still had a chance to complete the one last task she had set for herself.

Carmen started when she heard the sound of claws rasping against stone. Rising slowly, she sheathed the knife at her waist and looked around. Plants moved to her left, so she moved to the right, trying to keep the edge of the pool between her and whatever was coming toward her. She stumbled backward when the shape of a huge, golden dragon appeared. Colors swirled through the golden body, changing as the light from above reflected on it.

"Get out of here," Carmen said in a low, stern voice. "Go on! Get out," she repeated.

She didn't have the same touch with animals that her sister did. Ariel could look at a mountain lion and the damn thing would start purring and trying to be a lap cat. Carmen would look like lunch to the damn thing. She had seen similar creatures on board the warship. The men referred to them as their symbiots. They seemed to have some type of symbiotic relationship with the living creatures. All she cared about was if that thing was here, then that meant its other half might not be far away. As far as she was concerned, that spelled trouble.

"Go on. Scat!" Carmen said, beginning to feel a little nervous as the creature took another step toward her.

It raised its massive head up in the air and looked as if it was sniffing something. Carmen watched as its head lowered until it stopped at her side. She followed the golden creature's line of sight and cursed when she saw it was focused on her hand. Blood pooled on the ends of her fingers from where she had cut her palm. Carmen clenched her fist in an effort to keep the blood from dripping, but she was too late. A small drop clung stubbornly before falling to the pristine white stone floor.

Carmen's head jerked up as she felt the shift in the air as the creature responded to the blood. She jerked in surprise when a line of gold shot out from it, winding around her injured hand. She burst into action, fighting to break the hold on her.

The more she fought, the more gold swirled around her, encasing her in its tentacles until she was held immobile by it. She refused to cower. If this was the way she was meant to die, then so be it. Her eyes glittered fiercely for a moment before she closed them and drew a picture of Scott into her mind.

Memories of his light brown hair curling at the ends after he got out of the shower shimmered and formed. Carmen embraced the memories, pulling them to her until she was wrapped in his warmth and love again.

She remembered his dancing green eyes as he teased her out of being mad. She remembered the way he made tender love to her in front of the fireplace at the small house they had purchased in their hometown. She remembered him holding her like he would never let her go when she found out her parents had been killed in a car accident. And, she remembered the look of sheer wonder when she told him… Pain and grief filled her suddenly to the point she wondered if the creature would even have to bother with killing her. She felt like she was dying again right there.

A low keening sound escaped her as the grief became more than she could keep inside. She opened her eyes and stared into the dark, golden flames burning in the creature's eyes. She looked at it with a silent plea for mercy.

"Please," Carmen whispered. "Please. I don't want to live anymore. It hurts too much. Please give me peace," she quietly begged the creature.

CHAPTER THREE

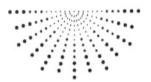

Morian stood back in the shadows with her fists pressed tightly to her lips. Her heart was breaking for the fragile human female. She had known the moment the young girl had entered her sanctuary. The plants reacted differently to the changes in their environment. This was the one place she retreated to when loneliness and pain took hold of her. Working with the plants and soil gave her a sense of peace when she needed it.

She missed her mate. While he had not been her true mate, she had loved him and still grieved for his passing. She had thought to join him in death at first, as this was the way of the true mates of their world, but something told her it was not her time.

When her oldest son Zoran was kidnapped, she had been frightened she would have to live through the loss of one of her children as well. Instead, his abduction had turned into a blessing from the gods and goddesses. He had discovered his true mate with a female from the distant world where he had sought refuge. In addition, it appeared the journey had blessed all her sons with their true mates, if Creon's symbiot was any indication.

She had watched from the small office she kept up on an upper level of the atrium as Mandra's symbiot played with the female with the long, white hair. She thought of leaving her sanctuary to meet the girl when this one appeared. Even from a distance, she had known instinctively that the girl wanted to be alone. Morian had given her that space, but she was curious about these beautiful, fragile creatures that had captured her sons' hearts. She had sneaked down one of the many paths and followed her. Her whispered words had pulled at Morian. The girl tried to appear so tough on the outside, but inside she was hurting deeply.

Morian waited to see what Creon's symbiot would do. If this girl was her son's true mate, it would do everything in its power to help her. Morian bit her lip as the golden symbiot let out a low sound of anguish at the girl's pain. Its colors shimmered in a rapidly moving mixture that reflected its distress.

The girl gasped as the sound built until it echoed through the enormous room. The golden form surrounding her shifted again until it was in the shape of a large creature with long, drooping ears. It was an unusual shape for a symbiot, one Morian had never seen before, but the girl must have recognized it. Morian watched as the slender figure fell to her knees and wrapped her arms around the shape, clinging to it, and whispering quietly.

"I'm sorry," Carmen's faint voice echoed soothingly. "I'm so sorry. It's okay. I shouldn't have asked that of you. It's just, sometimes..." Her voice faded before she spoke again. "Sometimes the pain is too much for me to handle. Soon, though, soon everything will be all right. Once I return home, everything will be all right," she added with a determined smile.

Morian pulled away as she sensed another change in the atrium. She looked at the young girl soothing her son's symbiot, and a feeling of fear for the girl swept through her. Something told her it would not be a good thing for the girl to return to her world. Turning, Morian moved to stop her new visitor. She needed to warn him that all was not as it seemed.

∽

Creon cursed under his breath again. He had been looking for the white-haired savage for the past couple of hours with no luck. He had found his brother Mandra instead—unconscious! The other she-demon had knocked him out with a planter and escaped out of one of the windows leading into the gardens. Once he was sure his brother would be all right, he had left him to deal with the other female while Creon hunted for her sibling.

I cannot believe we thought they would need a healer! Creon thought disgruntledly. *What we need is a cage for them. I will throw her ass in one of the old cells under the palace for a few days and see how she likes that! Or maybe I'll just tie her up and deliver her to Trelon so he can take her back to her world.*

Creon frowned. Neither one of the ideas gave him the satisfaction he thought it might. In fact, the idea of anyone taking the female anywhere caused a fierce wave of rage to burst inside of him.

"Maybe I'll just tie her up to my bed," Creon muttered under his breath.

Yes, yes, yes, yes, yes, his dragon answered hopefully. *You tie. I bite. We both get mate.*

Shit! Creon thought as he felt his cock swell at the image of the white-haired she-savage tied up in his bed.

The image continued to form in his mind until he had to stop and adjust the front of his pants so he could walk without it hurting. He had to admit, his body was saying a *yes, yes, yes* to the idea. That pissed him off even more. He didn't have time for this. He needed to figure out what in the hell was going on and find out who was behind his brother's kidnapping before it started another war.

Creon was still grumbling under his breath when he suddenly felt a small hand grip his arm. He jerked back out of instinct and moved to draw the weapon he always kept at his side. He frowned heavily when he saw his mother standing in the shadows, looking at him with a worried expression on her face. He opened his mouth to ask her what was wrong, but she shook her head quickly and pressed her fingers against his lips to silence him.

Creon followed her glance when she looked toward a thick set of bushes, but he didn't see anything out of the ordinary. He started again when she pulled on his arm and indicated that he was to follow her.

His frown turned dark as his eyes continued to search for what had upset his mother. If there was a threat to her, he would kill whoever it was without mercy. He followed her down a path that opened up to the hidden staircase leading to her private office. They moved in silence.

Creon continued to look around carefully, trying to find the threat. He paused halfway up the stairway, searching the thick foliage for anything unusual. His eyes widened when he caught a glimpse of white hair near the center pool. He shifted slightly, letting his dragon come forward to improve his vision. Within seconds, the sharp details of the female who had attacked him in the transporter room came into focus. She was kneeling on the ground next to…

"My symbiot," Creon growled out softly.

"Come, I need to speak with you," Morian said, pulling on Creon's arm. "Please. It is about the girl."

Creon's head swung around to glance up at his mother who was waiting impatiently for him. She was biting her lower lip and seemed very worried. Creon turned his head to stare at the slender figure again. Was something the matter with the girl? Was she injured? Had he unknowingly hurt her when he grabbed her or blocked some of her blows? He let his eyes move down over her figure, really taking a good look at her.

She's too thin, he thought with growing concern. *She looks like she hasn't been fed properly in a long time.*

There was something else about her. The way she was clinging to his symbiot confused him. He ran his hand through his hair in frustration. There was something he was missing; he just couldn't seem to think straight. It was in her body language, the way she was holding his symbiot, the fragile look of her.

Creon shook his head. That didn't make sense at all. He had felt her strength when she fought against him. She didn't give up, and she was fast, really fast. She used moves he had never seen before mixed with moves he had personally trained some of their warriors on. She was also very good at disappearing. It had taken him hours to narrow down where she had gone, and even then he hadn't been sure she was up here.

A soft groan escaped him as another fact sank in; she was clinging to his symbiot, and it was wound around her. His eyes narrowed on the thick gold bands on her delicate wrists. His eyes shifted to her throat where more gold glittered. His symbiot had claimed her. His dragon wanted her, and he…

Creon closed his eyes and drew in a deep breath, trying to calm the raging need to go to her and gather her close. He wanted to protect her, possess her, and claim her for all to see. Opening his eyes, he turned to look up at his mother who was staring at him intently.

"She is my true mate," Creon said with quiet conviction.

"Yes," Morian responded softly. "But, there is more to her than meets the eye. Come with me. There is something you should know."

Creon felt his eyes move back toward the figure far below him. She was sitting on the ground now with the head of his symbiot in her lap. His symbiot was in the shape of some unusual creature that the girl seemed to find comforting. His dragon seemed to sense something in his mother's voice because it wanted to go to the girl and wind itself around her.

My mate. Something happen to my mate? his dragon asked fearfully, pushing against his skin again to break free. *Let me go to her. I protect.*

We will protect her, Creon said, trying to calm his dragon. *But first, we need to know what has happened. Mother would not be so worried if our mate was all right. If she is in danger, then we will do what we have to do in order to protect her. Even if that means locking her up until we know she is safe.*

He knew his dragon did not like the idea of locking their mate up, but until he knew what danger she was in, there might not be a choice. He climbed the steps after his mother. He had always been good at discovering others' secrets. He was even better at protecting them.

CHAPTER FOUR

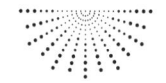

*C*armen drew in deep, calming breaths using the meditation techniques that she had learned after Colombia. Kevin Arbor, their boss with Security International, had demanded she receive counseling after Scott died. The therapist, Connie Wong, had taught them to her. Connie explained it would help her deal with the panic attacks and depression she was suffering from after such a traumatic experience. Carmen had learned them simply so she could remain focused on the one goal she had left in her life to complete… to kill Javier Cuello.

"It will be all right," Carmen repeated out loud. "You just need to figure out how to get off this world and back home. You can do it. You can do whatever you set your mind to. Do not stop; do not give up," Carmen said quietly to herself while she focused on breathing. "You have to have a plan, that's all."

She continued to run her hand soothingly over the huge golden creature that was an almost exact replica of Harvey, her old, droopy-eared basset hound that she had growing up. Granted, it was a much larger and shinier Harvey than the original. Still, the shape was comforting to her as she stroked the soft, shiny surface. She felt a small smile curve her lips as she looked down into the eyes of the creature.

"Do you have a name?" she asked quietly. "If not, I'll call you Harvey. He was a dopey, lovable dog I had when I was little. He was the only animal that liked me more than Ariel. He followed me everywhere." She spoke in a hushed voice, feeling suddenly calmer than she had since… since Scott had died.

Carmen looked down, startled as a wave of warmth flooded through her. Her eyes widened as images of her old basset hound floated in her mind. Her smile grew until she could feel tears burning her eyes. The gold creature's tail thumped back and forth in response to her surprise and smile.

"I don't understand any of this," she whispered with a shake of her head. "This world, you, the warriors I've met, and the man…" Her voice faded as an image of the man from the transporter room formed in her mind.

A shiver went through her body as the image became clearer. The tall warrior had been more than a match for her. He had reacted with a grace and style that sent waves of heat through her. His lithe body had twisted around as if flowing in a graceful dance when she had tossed him over her shoulder.

Carmen had reacted out of fear and the instinctive need to escape a predator. There was no doubt in her mind that was exactly what he was, a deadly predator. Every line of his body screamed he was lethal. His golden eyes had flared with a heat that reached out to something deep inside her that she thought had died three years ago when he had stared at her in fury. His long, black hair flowed around his dark muscular shoulders that were clearly displayed under the black leather vest he wore. His black pants had been stretched tightly across thick, muscular thighs. She had feared that if she couldn't get away from him immediately, she might never escape.

"Is he your other half?" she asked, biting her lower lip in worry as she looked around.

The new wave of warmth the creature sent through her confirmed what she had been dreading. If this creature was the man's symbiot, then she needed to escape from it as well. Unless—Carmen looked down into the droopy, sad eyes—unless it could help her.

"I need to find my sister and get back home. Can you help me escape?" she asked in a slightly pleading voice. "Please. We have to return home immediately. It has already been longer than I expected. I have to find someone. It is important that I return to my world as soon as possible. Can you help me?"

A part of her felt guilty about asking for the creature's help, but she knew how powerful they were. She had observed them when she was sneaking around the ship trying to learn everything she could about the species that had kidnapped her sister and friends. She knew Abby trusted them. She had fallen in love with the one called Zoran. She would not fault or deny anyone their chance at love. She had been given her chance. She would not leave without Ariel, Trisha, and Cara unless they wanted to stay. If that was what they wanted, then she would go alone. She felt sure that Trisha would want to return to Earth. She would never leave her dad behind.

Paul Grove had been like a second father to her and Ariel their whole life, even before the death of her own parents. They had spent as much time at Trisha's house as she had spent at theirs. Well, when they weren't trying to hide her and keep her.

Carmen had always loved the quiet little girl who was a little over a year older than her. She couldn't count the times she had talked Trisha into hiding at their house so she could have two big sisters. Paul and her parents had finally given up and let the girls take turns staying at each other's house on the weekends. Even as they grew, their special friendship had survived. It would have broken her heart when Ariel and Trisha went off to college early if Scott and Paul hadn't been there.

When her parents had been killed, Paul stepped in, taking guardianship of her during her last year of high school. He had taken her with him during some of his training exercises, showing her how to survive in the wilderness. He had also shown her how to let the peace of the mountains take away some of the pain she was feeling. She had worked with Samara—another girl who worked part-time for Paul and who was the same age as Carmen herself—with the horses that Paul kept on his ranch. Samara was barely bigger than Cara and almost as hyper. She had a firecracker temper, though. Probably from having to deal with four older brothers who liked to boss her around.

Carmen was so lost in her memories that when Harvey suddenly stood up, she had to shake herself to bring everything back into focus. When she realized she wasn't alone anymore, a dark scowl twisted her pale features into a hostile mask.

"Not you again!" Carmen bit out sarcastically. "Wasn't getting your ass whipped once enough?"

She glared up fiercely at the tall man who had sent her running in a panic. She would never let anyone know she was scared, though. She also wouldn't let him or anyone else stop her from her mission. He needed to learn that right off the bat. She wouldn't let her body rule over her head. She rose to stand defiantly before him, her body taut with tension.

"I need to return to my planet immediately," she added with a determined tilt to her chin as she faced him. "As in yesterday."

∽

Creon had listened in disbelief to his mother's fears for the slender female down in her garden. She had told him of the girl's desire to end her life. That something was hurting her. Tears had formed in her eyes as she told him of the whispered words of fear the girl expressed and about the painful cry that had been torn from the girl when his symbiot held her. The pain had been so intense, his symbiot had absorbed some of it and was in distress.

"I have never seen anything pull a cry like that from a symbiot before," Morian had said desperately. "The sound of it resonated with such pain and grief, it tore at my own heart. Your mate is hurting. I do not know if she is ill or what, but you must help her."

Creon had looked doubtfully at his mother until the image of the slight figure clinging to his symbiot surfaced in his mind. Fear swept through him at the thought of his mate in pain. He needed to link with his symbiot so he could see what was wrong with her. If he needed to chance putting her through the transformation where the added healing qualities of his dragon would help her, he would. It would be dangerous, but if there was a risk of her dying anyway, he would have no choice. Creon knew that if there was something wrong with her and she did not make it, he would not live. Even without fully claiming her, their lives were intertwined together, whether they wanted them to be or not.

"Are you sure?" he asked his mother quietly.

"Yes," Morian replied, looking carefully at her youngest son.

He had suffered so much during the Great Wars. He was also the reason the wars had ended peacefully. Out of all her sons, she had worried the most about him. He had always been the quietest one of the five boys she had been blessed with. He had also been one of the most lethal in his protection of Valdier and their people. Not that her other sons would not have done what was necessary, but Creon had sacrificed a part of who he was to ensure the successful end to the wars.

"She is a she-demon," he had responded with a slight curve to his lips as he touched first his ear, then his eye, before his lip. "It is hard to believe anything could be wrong with her, but I will make sure she is well," he had added as he turned to walk back down the stairs.

"Creon," his mother called out softly.

Creon paused at the door and looked back at his mother. "Yes."

"Look beneath the mask she wears as protection, and you will see the true girl underneath," Morian advised quietly. "And be prepared for a fight unlike anything you have ever had to deal with before. She will not give in easily."

Creon's lips pulled up into a smile even as a hard glint came into his eyes. "I am well versed in the art of war, *Dola*. And I never lose," he replied in a steely voice.

Morian watched as her son descended the steps and moved toward where the human girl sat. Her eyes followed the fierce figure until he stood over the smaller one sitting next to his symbiot. As the girl rose, she saw the defiant stiffening of her body and the stubborn tilt of her chin.

Morian shook her head in concern. "I hope you are right, my son. For this is a battle that could take your heart as well as your life if you lose it."

Creon rolled his shoulders to ease some of the tension in them and grimaced as he felt a new bruise. The meeting in the garden with the white-haired savage had gone about as well as the one in the transporter room. He finally had to tie her up and haul her ass out of the atrium kicking, screaming curses, and vowing to do more than emasculate him when she got free. His symbiot had been very protective of the female, but at the same time worked to help him capture her.

She had looked at his symbiot with such a look of betrayal it had taken off almost immediately after he locked her in his suite of rooms. The sounds of glass breaking against the door as he pulled it closed showed her temper had not calmed down during the time he had carried her over his shoulder to his living quarters.

The one thing he discovered was she was not hurt physically. At least, that was what he hoped from the information his symbiot was able to tell him during the brief contact it had with her. She had removed the wristbands and necklace that it had formed on her, tossing them out the window before it could make sure of her health.

Right now, he needed to get down to the conference room. He was supposed to meet with his brothers to go over the information he had learned so far. The newest information from Ha'ven was too disturbing to share yet. At least, until he could verify it. He was supposed to meet up with Ha'ven in a couple of days. Until then, it was best to keep what he suspected to himself.

He wanted to tell his brothers about what he had learned from his trip to the Sarafin star system. He had met up with Vox, the leader of the cat-shifting race. Vox said that several of his most trusted warriors had approached him about a member of the royal family of Valdier requesting a meeting with him. Vox had put off the meeting as he was about to embark on a quick trip to one of Valdier's spaceports to broker a deal for more crystals and sniff out some troubling information about one of his councilmen who had disappeared suddenly while at the spaceport. Vox was concerned, as the man was one of his most trusted friends.

Taking a deep breath, he refocused on his current situation. He had to attend the meeting downstairs, but he needed to make sure his mate was safe first. He glanced at the closed doors where his mate could still be heard yelling dire threats of murder and mayhem.

A good ass-whipping might be in store for his older brother while he was down there. It wouldn't change anything, but it would make him feel a little better. He rolled his shoulders again and motioned for the two guards who had been standing to the side, waiting for his instructions. Both of them were staring warily at the door as if expecting some insane beast to suddenly burst through it.

"Guard her with your life," Creon instructed before he grimaced. "Dragon's balls!" he muttered as another string of unladylike curses sounded through the door followed by another crash. "Just…make sure the door stays locked and she doesn't get out," he ground out in exasperation.

The guards nodded their agreement to Creon before positioning themselves in front of it. Both winced when a small thump hit the door, followed by a bellowed demand to be released immediately or else. Creon shook his head in resignation before he turned and strode down the long corridor. It was going to be a very, very long day.

CHAPTER FIVE

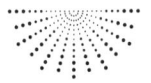

Creon could hear Mandra's voice before he entered the conference room. From the sound of it, his older brother was in a foul mood. Creon entered the room just as Mandra was threatening to beat Zoran's ass.

"You brought those females here! I should kick your ass good for that," Mandra growled out in a low voice.

"I second that!" Creon said, walking into the room and moving on silent feet to sit down at the beautiful rosewood table with a holovid display mounted in the center. "I'll help you, Mandra, with total enjoyment."

Creon couldn't help but cast a dark look at Trelon and Kelan as he sat down in one of the plush dark leather seats. He rubbed a weary hand over his forehead before he sat back to watch his two older brothers clash. They were locked arm-in-arm, their muscles straining as each pushed against the other.

"I can't find that damn female anywhere," Mandra snarled out. "I should kick your ass for bringing her back!" he said, looking darkly at Trelon as well.

Trelon raised his hand in defense. "Don't blame me! I have enough on my hands. I can barely catch the one I have. She never sleeps, never shuts up, and has dismantled everything on Kelan's warship and in my home at least a dozen times, trying to see how it works."

Kelan looked at Mandra and Creon with a long suffering look on his own face. "The female called Trisha is demanding I take her home to her father. She is a stubborn little thing. She refuses to give up the idea."

"How are you doing, brother?" Kelan asked, turning to look at Creon. "Did you ever find the short-haired she-demon? She was a pain in the ass on board the *V'ager*. She fought every male she could, and damned if they didn't all fall in love with her for it."

Creon face turned ridged with tension at the thought of other males fighting with his mate. "Yes, but she is not happy with me right now. She insists on being returned to her planet immediately. I had to restrain her so I could lock her up," he said tersely.

Zoran looked at Mandra and Creon in confusion. "I thought you two were going to find mates for the other two. Surely there are males who will take them," Zoran said.

Creon was on his feet, growling dangerously at Zoran before he could stop himself. His dragon fought to get loose at the idea of giving Carmen away to another male. Black scales rippled uncontrollably over his skin as he fought for control.

Zoran glanced back and forth between Mandra and Creon, watching in amazement as both of his younger brothers fought for control. He had never seen either of them like this before. It took a moment before he realized what had happened.

"You too?" Zoran asked quietly, looking between the two. "Both of you have claimed the females?"

Creon returned to his seat and stared moodily out the window with his arms crossed over his chest. No, he had not claimed the one called Carmen yet. He had finally learned her name after he downloaded the reports from the *V'ager*. He had read about her exploits on board. How she antagonized the men on board to get them to fight her. How she had barely been alive when she was brought aboard. Even with the advanced technology the Valdier had, Zoltin had written that he'd almost lost her more than once. She had been stabbed several times in the chest and side. The sound of Mandra talking about the long-haired sister broke through his thoughts.

"Yes," Mandra was saying. "The problem is, every time I get near her, she attacks me! Now, I can't even find her. She broke my nose and took off. She is hiding somewhere, and I haven't been able to locate her yet."

Creon's head jerked up. "She broke your nose? When did she do that? I just thought she knocked you out," Creon said with a frown, trying to remember his brother's condition when he found him unconscious. "Your nose didn't look broken."

Creon wondered if all the creatures on the planet Zoran landed on were like this. Females weren't supposed to know how to fight. What was the purpose of having a planet full of male warriors if the females were just as vicious as the men could be?

Kelan grunted as he stood up and walked over to the small bar to pour a drink. "What are we going to do with them?" he asked dejectedly. "How can such a fragile, delicate species do so much damage and be so stubborn?" His voice faded away as all of them contemplated the sudden changes to their lives.

∼

Several hours later, Creon stood outside the doors to his living quarters. He wondered vaguely if he had any more glass objects for his mate to smash. His symbiot stood at his side, looking at the door as well. Both of them were a little wary of what they would find.

"Have you heard anything recently?" he asked one of the guards standing by the door.

"No, my lord," the guard replied. "There hasn't been a sound for the past hour or so."

"I don't think there is anything left for her to break," the second guard said with a sympathetic look. "I also had no idea there were that many ways to curse someone either," he added with a small grin of appreciation.

Creon ran a tired hand over the back of his neck. Standing here wasn't going to make the task ahead any easier. He might as well face his mate's fury. He had a feeling she wasn't going to like it when she found out it was his rooms that she occupied.

He nodded his thanks to the two guards before he quietly opened the door. He was surprised that the floor wasn't littered with broken shards of glass. He pushed the door open a little further and listened. All that greeted him was silence. He nodded to his symbiot to go ahead of him. He stepped inside, closed and locked the door with a swipe of his hand. The hidden panel in the wall glowed briefly to show it was locked.

Creon glanced around. Against the wall near the door was a small basket he had picked up during one of his many journeys. It was filled to the top with bits and pieces of broken pottery and glass. Next to it was a small broom that the servants used when cleaning his living quarters. The female confused him. His mother worried that she was fragile and in pain while all he saw was the fierce hostility and defiance.

His symbiot paused by the door to his sleeping quarters and looked in. It turned to him and shook its massive body before it bounded into the room. Creon walked slowly forward until he stood in the doorway of his sleeping quarters. Curled in a small ball in the middle of the bed was his mate. In the soft glow of the moon, he could make out her white-blonde hair. Strands fell along her cheek and curled at her neck. He could see the steady rise and fall of her chest as she slept.

He stepped closer to the bed, carefully sitting down on the edge so he wouldn't disturb her. Gently lifting a strand of her soft hair, he tucked it behind her ear, marveling at the soft texture of it. She shifted in her sleep, tilting her head until her cheek rested against the palm of his hand. Creon clenched his other hand in an effort to control the feelings bombarding him. It was as if his entire body was suddenly alive and tuned into this beautiful creature.

Unable to stop himself, he ran his thumb over her jaw until it rested on her lower lip. Her lips parted in a soft sigh. A small smile pulled on her bottom lip. Creon leaned down to brush his lips against hers. Need unlike anything he had ever felt before overwhelmed his senses. He wanted her, needed her in a way that pulled at the very essence of his soul. He pulled back slightly, determined to wake her, when she suddenly whispered in a soft husky voice.

"Oh, Scott, I've missed you," Carmen murmured in her sleep. She turned over restlessly before sighing out, "I love you. Coming home soon."

Creon's eyes darkened until they burned fiercely. The name of another man on his mate's lips sent shafts of jealousy through him. He pulled away quickly as he felt the change sweeping through him.

Unable to prevent his dragon from taking control, Creon rushed to the open doors leading out onto the balcony and launched himself over the railing. He shifted as his body fell toward the ground. Large wings unfolded and caught the air under them, allowing him to glide just a few feet off the ground before he pushed off and lifted higher, soaring over the walls of the palace.

He remained invisible to everyone, including the guards. The only one who could see him was his symbiot, which had divided. One part lay curled up next to his mate while the other part flew up until it dissolved around him in midair, forming armor around his dragon.

He flew for miles, trying to escape the burning heat erupting inside him. He had passed the thick forest and headed upward into the mountainous regions. He often flew long distances at night. Normally, it was to escape the dark thoughts that plagued him during the long, lonely hours. Tonight he did it to cope with the burning anger that his mate wanted, loved another.

We take her anyway. She learn to love us. She is ours, his dragon roared out in anger. *We keep. Man from her world not keep her safe. He not deserve her.*

Do you think I don't know that? Creon growled back. *Zoran, Kelan, and Trelon brought the women back against their will. Our mate was mortally wounded and would have died back on her planet. But that does not mean she could not have belonged to another.*

She here now! She is ours. I no give back, his dragon said determinedly. *I want my mate! She mine. You not send her away.*

No, I will not send her away, Creon said tiredly, pulling his dragon in enough so that he could guide him to a small ledge on the side of a mountain. *She has been accepted by all of us. My symbiot is very protective of her. You want her; I need her.*

Creon's dragon landed on the narrow ledge and turned with a shiver, looking out over the vast terrain. The darkness did not interfere with his vision. He saw as well in the dark as he did during the day. A light breeze blew over the tall trees, most of which were over a thousand years old. In the distance, he could make out the shimmering of moonlight reflecting off the water of a nearby river. He was above the tree line and little tufts of snow still lingered on the rock face he had landed on. The cold did not bother him either. His body ran warm, and in dragon form, his scales helped to insulate his body from the outside elements.

Creon moved in a circle on the narrow ledge before lying down and tucking his wings up tightly against his sides. He was slightly smaller than his brothers in dragon form, but in some ways he was more lethal because of that. He could move in areas they couldn't, and his unique black scales reflected his surrounding environment until he was practically invisible.

He laid his head down on his front claws and stared blindly out at the surrounding darkness. It matched his soul right now. For a brief glimpse, he thought he had found the shimmer of light that would make him feel complete again. It had been a false hope. His true mate loved another. He had never heard of such a thing before. In all his life, in all the archives he had secretly read, never had he heard of the gods and goddesses gifting a Valdier with a true mate that loved and hoped for another.

He would have to look at the archives again. He refused to believe it was possible. Even the gods and goddesses could not wish to punish him for things he had no choice in. His thoughts turned darker as he thought back to the Great Wars. He had killed many during the wars. On all three sides—Sarafin, Curizan, and Valdier. He had done what he had to in order to protect his people.

When he found traitors within the Valdier who were working with a small group of Curizan and Sarafin royalty in order to bring down all three governments of their respective star systems, he, Ha'ven, and Vox had worked together to eradicate them. One of the traitors had been his lover, Aria. He had thought he loved her. He knew she was not his true mate. He knew it would have been a difficult life trying to balance the three parts of who he was to be with her, but he had been willing to try.

He would never forget when Vox had approached him with his suspicions. Ha'ven had been wounded—almost killed—in an assassination attempt shortly before being captured by an unknown group. The only ones who knew where Ha'ven was going to be and when were Creon and Vox. Creon had rescued Ha'ven and dragged his ass out of the dungeons of hell, literally. Ha'ven had been taken to Hell, an abandon mining asteroid on the outer regions of the Curizan star system. There he was being tortured in the hopes of discovering information about the Curizan, Valdier, and Sarafin warship movements.

It wasn't until Vox had mentioned that there had to be a leak somewhere within their inner groups that a sense of dread swept through him. Vox learned a short time later that one of his warriors had betrayed them. Vox tortured the man until he revealed he had given the information to a female named Aria whom he had taken as a lover. She was one of the top operatives for the group behind starting the war. Only she knew where Ha'ven had been taken.

Creon did not confront Aria with the information at first, unwilling to believe she could betray him like that. Instead, he and Vox set up a bogus mission and set a trap. Only the two of them and Aria had the information. He told Aria of his plans to transport a Curizan royal they had captured to a new holding facility. A small group of hired mercenaries appeared at the planned transfer. Before the last one died, Creon had his proof that his lover was the one giving out the orders.

He felt like he had betrayed his people. Hundreds, if not thousands, of Valdier, Curizan, and Sarafin warriors had died because of the greed for power by a few members of the royal houses. He had fallen in love with one of them and unknowingly given them inside information. Creon felt the death of each warrior who had died during battle as a mark against his soul.

It had been a clear night when Aria came to him that last time. It had not been much different than the night he was staring into now. The moons had risen several hours before, and she lay across their bed draped in nothing but the moonlight. She had been beautiful. Her dark hair spread out around her, and her full breasts were taut and inviting. But looking at her for what she was in that pale light, he was able to see the coldness in her eyes and the cruel twist to her mouth as she talked of her love for him. He had killed her slowly, extracting every bit of information from her before he gave her the peace of death. His dragon had burned her remains. He would leave nothing of her to remind him of her treachery.

The next morning, he and Vox had gone after Ha'ven. They had killed everyone on the asteroid. It took a long time before Creon could even begin to forgive himself for what happened to his best friend. While Creon could never truly forgive himself, Ha'ven had never held it against him.

CHAPTER SIX

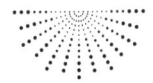

Carmen jerked awake, startled. It was the first time in over three years that she had slept through an entire night without having a nightmare. Even when she had been on pain medication and antidepressants, she had still been plagued with them. Her hand reached out to steady herself, only to find she wasn't alone in the bed. A smaller version of Harvey lay next to her.

"Where did you come from?" Carmen asked, puzzled, looking around in confusion as she tried to remember where she was.

She blew out a puff of air. "Oh, that fink! He better plan on taking me home today!" she said, scooting off the bed. "I need to find my sister and make sure she and Trisha are all right, not to mention poor Cara."

Carmen swayed for a moment. "First, I need a shower. I feel like my head is full of cotton balls. Then caffeine. God, I hope they have coffee here," she muttered as she opened several panels in the wall, looking for something she could wear.

She gave a sigh of relief when she found several large shirts. They would swallow her, but she didn't care. As long as she was covered, that was all that mattered. She reached in and pulled out a pair of leather pants. They were way too big, both in the hips and in length.

She would have to fashion a belt and roll them up, but they would work in a pinch. No underwear, but it wasn't like she hadn't gone without them a time or two when she and…

Carmen bit her lip to stop her thoughts. She would not go there this morning. She was feeling too vulnerable as it was without bringing up memories. She walked into the large room located on the far wall. She had found the bathroom after her failed attempt to break every dish in the place. Truthfully, she had gotten tired of throwing the dishes at an inanimate object. After she had explored for a little while she had finally decided she needed to clean up the mess she had made. It went against everything inside her and the way she was raised to leave the mess. Her mom would have taken a switch to her backside if she ever saw Carmen breaking dishes the way she had in her fit of rage at being locked in the room yesterday.

Carmen walked into the bathroom, admiring the beautiful colors in the stone. A huge pool that reminded her of some of the ancient Roman baths sat in the center of the room. There was a toilet, what looked like a long, shallow sink, and a shower area that was big enough to hold a compact car. On the back side of the shower was a garden. It really only consisted of the two end walls and the ceiling. The two long sides were open. Why anyone would need such large areas for bathing was beyond Carmen. She had been happy with her little shower stall. It was a hell of a lot easier to clean.

She set the clothes she had gathered down on a small table and began undressing. She didn't look in the mirror that covered one whole wall. She knew what she would see. She was losing weight again. It was hard to force herself to eat. She just didn't have any appetite anymore.

Well, she thought with a twisted grin. *I do, but not for food.*

The grin faded as a new image popped into her mind, and it wasn't Javier Cuello. The image was of the tall, dark-haired man who had fought with her and locked her in these rooms without saying a word. Of course, she didn't give him much of a chance.

Her face burned with embarrassment as she remembered some of the things she had said, not to mention her language. She had been in rare form yesterday. Between the fear, the anger, and feeling like her life was out of control, she had let it all out in one big temper tantrum that would have made any two-year-old proud, minus the inventive language.

Carmen let her clothes fall into a nice neat pile on the floor. She would wash them out and hang them to dry when she was done. She stepped into the huge shower area and turned in a circle. There were no doors to it. There wasn't even a shower curtain.

She looked up at the ceiling that had to be at least twelve feet high. She could see a series of holes where the water could come out. She was about to give up and just jump in the Roman bath when a soft, warm mist started, then became slightly heavier. A startled giggle escaped her as it surrounded her in a light rain. She closed her eyes and enjoyed the warm spray as it fell over her.

∽

Creon was still tired. He had not slept much the night before. His mind and his dragon refused to believe his mate could belong to someone else. He was determined to confront her. He would let her know that she would have to accept that she would never return to the male from her old world. Her place was now on Valdier at his side. Once the transformation was complete, she would not have a choice. Her body would be too different for her to be able to safely return to her world.

We die without our mate, his dragon added. *That good reason not to let mate go.*

Like you think I haven't already thought of that, Creon bit out sarcastically before he let out a puff of hot breath. *I'm sorry. I should not take my frustration out on you.*

I no care. I ignore you as long as you get me my mate, his dragon snorted.

Creon fought the desire to roll his eyes. His dragon had a one-track mind now. It wanted to mate, and it would not stop until he did.

Like you no want to fuck your mate too, his dragon smirked.

That was the other drawback to having three parts of himself, the other two knew exactly what he was thinking and feeling. He shifted uncomfortably inside his dragon. Yes, he wanted her. He wanted her desperately. His body was clamoring to take her hard and fast at first, then long and slow. He wanted to place his mark on her for all to see. He remembered Kelan's words about how half the men on board the V'ager were in love with her. He could understand why. She was a fierce fighter and strong. Even though physically she appeared delicate and fragile, she had a strength about her that made her seem as strong as any Valdier warrior.

Creon swept over the walls of the palace. He stretched his wings out as far as they would go and glided, turning in a slight arc until he was lined up with the balcony leading into his bedroom. The same balcony he had thrown himself off last night. He touched down lightly on the stone railing, transforming as he landed. Back in his two-legged form, he hopped down and walked swiftly through the doors. His eyes swept back and forth, taking in the disheveled sheets. A smaller version of his symbiot lay sleeping in the middle of the bed. It raised its head, sending images of Carmen to him. A wicked smile curved his lips when he heard the sound of water falling. Perhaps it was time to introduce the white-haired savage to her new mate.

Creon quickly shed his clothes and walked into the bathing room. He stopped long enough to appreciate the beauty of his mate. His eyes roamed her lithe form. She was turned sideways with her head tilted back and her eyes closed, a small smile curving her lips. He ignored the fact that the smile more than likely would disappear, but his desire for her only grew as his eyes swept down her slender frame. His own lips turned down when he noticed the shape of her ribs outlined under her skin. He would take care of that soon enough. He would make sure she had plenty to eat. Her short hair was slicked back from the water. He liked how it curled at the ends. She turned, letting her head drop forward. He started forward in curiosity when he saw she had something across one shoulder. The colorful image seemed to glow.

He stepped into the shower with her and reached out to touch the delicate wings of the flying creature painted across one shoulder blade. He thought for sure she would erupt into violence at his touch. Instead, she froze as if just the touch of his fingers against her skin held her immobilized.

"What is this?" he asked quietly.

Carmen kept her head down and turned slightly. She had been lost in the magic of the shower and didn't realize she wasn't alone anymore. A shiver went through her body the moment the man behind her touched her. A part of her wanted to cover up and another part was curious about what would happen. Her body seemed to come alive all of a sudden. It had been so long since she had felt alive, she wanted to feel it for just a brief moment longer.

"It's a phoenix," she replied in a low husky voice.

Creon traced the edges of the beautiful creature painted on her skin. He had seen others with such images on them, but never one as beautiful as this one. The intricate lines ran from the top of her shoulder down to her hip.

The creature had a delicately curved head with small feathers rising upward. It reminded him of the woman standing in front of him. There was a look of sadness in its eyes, as if it had experienced too much pain and suffering.

The back of it curved down in a smooth line until he reached the tail feathers that were long and flowing, reaching down to touch the slight curve of her ass and wrapping around her hip. It was painted in glorious shades of reds, pinks, and soft purples. The artist had taken the time to make each individual feather unique. It was clearly a labor of love for the artist. It was as if the creature on his mate's back had captured a part of her essence for all time.

"It is beautiful, like you. What is so special about this creature?" he asked in wonder.

"The phoenix is a mythical creature from my world," Carmen said, lifting her head to stare straight ahead. "It lives eternally, going through a never-ending cycle of death and rebirth until it grows old," she whispered.

He leaned forward so he could hear her softly spoken words and slid his arms around her waist. He tilted his face just enough so he could feel her warmth against his lips. He heard the pain in her voice. This creature symbolized something very important to her.

"What happens when it grows old?" he pushed quietly.

Carmen turned in his arms and raised her face to his. The water from the shower clung to her long eyelashes like tears. She looked deeply into his dark eyes, as if assessing whether she should stay or try to escape.

"It builds a special nest, then stands in the nest and is consumed by fire," her eyes darkened with sorrow. "From the ashes of the old phoenix a new one is born to live another lifetime."

Creon raised his hand to gently cup his mate's cheek. "I feel so much pain inside you. It tears at me. Let me help you. Let me take away your pain," he said hoarsely. "Let me shoulder it for you so that you can rise again."

Tears burned Carmen's eyes. She stiffened, refusing to give in to the desire to let someone else take her burden from her. She had made a promise she would never forget. Her hand moved down to her flat stomach. She clenched her fist against it. She had risen three times from the ashes. It was time to return to Earth and build her final nest. Only when she was done, she would not be reborn, but would seek everlasting peace instead.

"No," she responded, pulling away from the temptation.

Carmen quickly stepped out of the shower and grabbed the towel she had laid out, wrapping it around her. She tucked the ends between her breasts to hold it on before grabbing the clothes that she had brought into the bathroom with her. She needed to get out of here. She needed to go home. She had things to do, people to see, someone to kill. She had to find her sister, Trisha, and Cara.

Without turning around, she spoke just loud enough for him to hear her. "I have to speak with my sister, Trisha, and Cara. We need to be returned to Earth," she said in an emotionless voice before she walked out of the room.

Creon let out a small curse under his breath. His plan to claim her had changed when he saw the image on her back. He needed to know what was hurting her. His symbiot had examined her thoroughly while she was sleeping. It had sent him the information as soon as he arrived back. She had numerous old scars that his symbiot had healed. It had been concerned about how close many of them had come to her vital organs.

By the time he walked into his bedroom, Carmen was dressed in one of his shirts and a pair of his pants. His shirt went almost to her knees, and she was busy rolling the legs of the pants up. He couldn't resist the chuckle that escaped him.

"You look like a child playing dress up in my clothes," he observed.

Carmen flashed him a dark look. "I don't have any other clothes except what I was wearing, and those are dirty. I'll wash them and return yours as soon as I can put them back on. I am assuming from your comment that this is your apartment. Since I hope to be out of here by later today, I won't ask for my own place to stay. I want to see my sister and friends, then I want transportation back home. I need to return as soon as possible."

"Why?" Creon asked, leaning back against the wall.

Carmen flashed a quick glance at him before turning her head again. She really wished he would put some clothes on. The towel he had wrapped around him didn't cover nearly enough to make her comfortable. Hell, nothing about him, dressed or not, made her comfortable. Her body was hypersensitive where he was concerned. She had never been with anyone but Scott. He was the only male who had ever seen her without her clothes on except for the doctors who had operated on her. Even her GYN had been a woman.

A wave of guilt flooded her as she realized that she could think of Scott, and it didn't seem to hurt as much as before. She clenched her jaw. She would not let her confusing feelings for the man standing across from her dissuade her from her path.

"I have things to do," she said, turning away. "I was supposed to meet someone."

"Scott?" Creon asked with a deep growl.

Carmen swirled around in shock and rage. "How do you know about Scott?" she asked fiercely.

"Who is this male?" Creon demanded, standing straight. "I will not return you to him. You are mine now. You cannot return to him."

Carmen paled. "I am not yours. I can never be yours. I will go back to my planet. With or without your help. I'll never give up."

Jealousy bit deeply at Creon. He would not let his mate be under the impression that she would ever return to the male she left behind. Her life was with him on Valdier now. It might take time, but she would come to accept it. Neither of them had any other choice.

He strode forward until he towered over her. He forced himself to ignore the distress in her eyes. Gripping her arms tightly, he pulled her against him and pressed his lips against hers in a fierce, possessive kiss that spoke of his claim.

Carmen erupted against him, fighting as he expected earlier. He didn't make the same mistakes as he had in the transporter room. He held her close against his body, not giving her an opportunity to use her legs against him. His hands kept her arms pressed tightly against her side. His mouth kept her from using her head.

Unfortunately, her mouth was still a lethal weapon, he thought as he felt the sharp sting and the taste of blood where her teeth bit down on his bottom lip.

He pulled back reluctantly. "You are mine, *mi elila*. We cannot survive without you. The sooner you accept this, the easier it will be for all of us."

Carmen refused to look at him. She kept her eyes glued to his broad chest. Everything inside her wanted to give in, but his words stung. She bit her lower lip until she tasted her own blood mixing with his.

"I can't," she whispered. "I have to go back."

"Why?" Creon demanded in despair.

Carmen did look up as the sound of anguish broke through her own grief. "I have to kill someone."

CHAPTER SEVEN

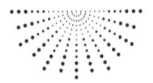

*C*reon stared moodily out the window. His mate's revelation that she needed to return to kill someone had taken him by surprise. She continued to confuse him. Every time he thought he was beginning to figure her out she would say or do something totally different from what he was expecting.

He was so confused, he did the only thing he could to help him understand the situation—he sought out his mother for advice. There were some things in a warrior's life that he excelled at and others when he knew he was totally over his head. In the case of understanding what to do with this female, he decided his best course of action was to seek help from another woman. That was why he was now standing in his mother's living quarters instead of charging off to meet with Ha'ven like he was supposed to.

"Creon, what is it?" Morian asked in concern as she walked into her living area from the library down the hall.

He turned to look at his mother. She was still very beautiful. Her hair was still as black as the midnight skies when the moons did not rise. Her eyes glowed with a soft, warm gold. Her skin had a few new wrinkles around her eyes and mouth. Most of them had appeared after his father's death. She moved with the natural grace of a Valdier princess.

When his father died during an accident while hunting, he had feared she would follow soon after. For several months her grief had been so tangible he felt like he could reach out and touch it. It had been several years since his father died, and at times he still felt the deep grief inside her. She missed her mate. He knew his father was not her true mate. They had married to forge a stronger relationship between two powerful clans, making them into one. Both of his parents had come from houses of royalty.

It was said his mother was a priestess for the gods and goddesses whose lifeblood flowed through their veins and whose blood gave life to their symbiots. His mother knew things that others missed. She could communicate with all the symbiots, and her love of the plants that lived on their planet was evident. If he didn't know better, he would swear that she could talk to them and vice versa.

"I need your help, *Dola*," he responded solemnly.

"Of course," she said, placing a comforting hand on his arm. "It is about Carmen?"

He nodded, not sure where to begin. He moved to sit down on one of the plush chairs near the window. He decided to tell her everything that had happened so far. Maybe she could see what he could not.

"She is hurting and refuses to allow me to help her," he said as he finished retelling her everything, including about the image on his mate's back and her desire to return to her world to kill someone.

Morian stared at her son's drawn face. It was obvious the young girl's pain was radiating outward until it was affecting Creon and his dragon. Perhaps it was time she visited the young girl herself.

"Perhaps she needs another female to talk to," Morian suggested. "I will go see her. There is a dinner planned for this evening. I had the seamstress make a few outfits for each of the women based on the information Zoran sent me. It will be a good excuse to spend time with her."

Creon let out a relieved sigh. "I would appreciate it. She is not talking to me again. Once I refused her request to see her sister and friends and take her home, she turned her back on me and refused to say another word. That worries me more than anything else," he said with a pained expression.

Morian opened her mouth to respond when a rapid knock on her outer doors stopped her. She was not expecting anyone else. Rising, she was startled when the knock sounded again, this time even harder.

Morian hurried to the door and pulled it open. A guard stood outside looking very grim. He bowed respectfully to Morian, but his eyes were searching behind her.

"My lord, we need you," the guard said urgently.

Creon stood up, frowning. "What is it?"

"It is the human female," the guard said grimly. "She escaped your chambers by knocking her guard out. We have recaptured her, but she is fighting us. I am afraid she might get hurt."

"Oh dear," Morian said, her hand going to her throat. She turned to Creon who was striding forward. "I will go with you."

Creon nodded, a tight expression on his face. "Take me to her."

~

Carmen ignored the throbbing in her ankle. She had hurt it when she kicked that last guy. These guys were harder to take by surprise. She was beginning to suspect the warriors on board the *V'ager* had been playing with her. She wouldn't be surprised if they had been coming to pick a fight with her just to relieve the boredom of being cooped up on a warship for long periods of time or that she was a novelty to them, because these guys were totally serious.

She had escaped by slamming a vase upside her guard's head. It had taken a fair bit of acting on her part just to get the guy to open the door to check on her. The loud scream and crash had finally done it. She had sent Harvey out for flowers for her. She had made up a story about how she would love to have some flowers to decorate the apartment with. After a few sniffles and a few flutters of her eyelashes, Harvey had reluctantly given in. She figured she had one chance to escape with Harvey and tall, dark, and confusing out of the way. Hell, she didn't even know his name!

Now, she was surrounded by seven—no, eight—very tall, very

grim-looking men. She was hurt too. Her ankle was throbbing bad enough that she knew it was at least sprained pretty badly. Hot, sharp pains were radiating up through her leg the moment she put pressure on it. Her left arm was throbbing as well. One of the men had slammed down on it when she had swung around to nail him as he grabbed at her. Despair swept through her. She hadn't been able to find her sister, Trisha, or Cara. She had no way off this planet. She had nothing left to live for. The one thing that kept her going the past three years was a single-minded need for revenge. Now, even that seemed like an impossible goal.

Depression hit her hard. As hard, if not harder than the first year after Scott's death and her losing their child. She felt totally useless. She swung around in a circle, favoring her injured foot. Her right hand went instinctively to the knife she carried. She felt as trapped now as she had that night on the tarmac. Her mind was beginning to splinter as she fought the panic of being trapped and helpless again.

Carmen pulled the knife out of its protective sheath and swung it in a wide arc, forcing the men to jump back. A wild look came into her eyes as she realized there would be no escaping, at least not alive. A low sob escaped her as the depression she had been fighting overwhelmed her with a feeling of total hopelessness. She tried to focus on the meditation techniques that Connie showed her, but she was beyond that. She'd tried to believe she could make it back home, but even that seemed beyond her reach.

"Get back," she growled out in a low voice. "Get away from me."

Harvey appeared outside the small circle. It pushed between two of the guards, ignoring their commands to stay back. The symbiot slowly moved closer to Carmen, as if it recognized that she was hanging onto her sanity by a thread.

"Go, Harvey," Carmen commanded in the same low voice. "Go on. I don't want you here. Go back to your master."

The symbiot shimmered in distress as it sank down to lie on the ground just a few feet from her. It watched her carefully, as if sensing she was frightened and fighting for control. A low humming sound escaped it as it flickered in varying shades of different colors.

"Not this time," Carmen whispered as her eyes flashed from one guard to another. "All I wanted was to find my sister and friends and go home," she said huskily to the golden figure watching her so intently.

"Carmen," a deep voice called out to her.

Carmen's eyes flew to the new figure moving toward her. It was her dark-haired warrior. Anger burst through her. It was his fault she was in this mess. He should have just sent her back home. It would have saved them all a lot of heartache.

"I want to find my sister and go home," Carmen hissed out, keeping the knife in front of her. "Just send me home."

Creon stared intently into the wild eyes of his mate. "I told you I cannot do that," he replied calmly as he motioned for the guards to leave them.

Carmen jerked sideways when she saw the guards behind her moving away. She stumbled a little as pain shot through her foot. She bit back a cry as the hot needles of pain shot up her leg.

Creon took a step toward her, but stopped when she swung the knife at him. "Let me help you," he said calmly. "You are hurt. Let me care for you."

"No!" Carmen responded tersely. "I don't want or need your help in anything but getting back home."

"I told you I cannot take you back," he said softly, taking another step closer.

Carmen took a painful step backward, away from him. "Then there is nothing left for me," she whispered, looking at him with pain-filled eyes. "I have no reason to keep fighting. No reason to continue…" Her voice faded as grief overwhelmed her.

A shiver of warning ran up Creon's spine at the softly spoken words. There was a conviction in it, an acceptance. He needed more time to understand how he could help her. He could feel he was losing her.

"Scott would not want you to end your life," Morian said quietly as she moved to stand next to Creon. "He would not want you to give up a chance to be happy."

Carmen swayed dangerously at Scott's name, her eyes reflecting her pain and sorrow. "You don't know what the pain is like, day in and day out. It is tearing me apart. I miss him so much," she choked out in a voice thick with tears. "It's my fault he is dead. If I had stayed back at the house he would still be alive. Our… our baby would have lived," Carmen whispered as a single tear broke loose and rolled down her cheek.

"Will killing the man who took this away from you bring either of them back?" Morian asked as she took a step closer to Carmen. "Would Scott have wanted you to go after the man, knowing how dangerous that would be for you? Do you think he would blame you the way you are blaming yourself?"

Carmen let her arm holding the knife drop back to her side. "No, it won't bring them back," she choked out. "But I made a promise to Scott, to our baby, and to myself that I would kill the man responsible," she forced out in a voice that was a little stronger, a little louder.

Morian took another step closer until she was standing within an arm's reach of Carmen. "Even if it kills you?" she asked gently.

Carmen looked into the warm gold eyes of the woman in front of her and nodded. "Yes," she answered in a barely audible whisper. "At least then the pain will be over."

"For you, but not for me or the rest of Creon's family. For if you die, so does my son. I am asking that you give this life a chance," Morian responded quietly. "The pain can fade if you give it a chance. Life can begin again. Just as with your phoenix. You have risen from the ashes, Carmen. It is time to begin your new life."

Carmen shook her head. Her eyes searched out the man standing quietly behind the woman. "How can my dying harm your son… Creon?" she asked, hesitating as she said the name of the warrior who refused to let her go.

"He is your true mate," Morian explained. "His life, the life of his dragon, and the life of his symbiot are in your hands. You have the power to decide if he lives or dies."

"But…" Carmen frowned at the woman before looking back at the man standing rigidly behind her, waiting to see what she would decide. "I don't understand," she murmured.

Morian smiled gently and held out her hand. "Come with us, my daughter. Give us a chance to explain."

Carmen looked down at the hand that was held out to her. Looking back up, she stared at the patient eyes, waiting for her to make her choice. Her eyes moved past the woman to stare into the dark, gold eyes of the man. Some instinct told her to give them at least the chance to explain.

Creon, she thought to herself. Now she knew his name.

Carmen slowly slid the knife back into its sheath and placed her trembling fingers in the woman's outstretched hand. Strong, slim fingers curled around hers and squeezed them in encouragement. A moment later a strong, muscular arm circled her waist, supporting her weight.

"Would you allow me to carry you?" Creon asked huskily.

Carmen blushed and nodded. "I hurt my ankle," she muttered.

Creon's face tightened in anger. "I will discipline the men for hurting you."

Carmen scowled as Creon picked her up. "They were following your orders, so if anyone needs to be disciplined, it's you!" she snapped back. "They were just doing what they were told."

Morian's chuckle prevented Creon from responding. "I think you have met your match, my son. She is as protective of the warriors as you are."

Creon groaned. "I was trying to impress her with my protectiveness!" he growled back.

Carmen looked at him skeptically. "I don't think telling the men to keep me a prisoner, then disciplining them when they do, is being protective. If you would have just let me go in the first place, none of this would have happened."

"I thought we were beyond that. How many times do I have to tell you that I will never let you go?" he snapped back, tired of her not listening to him.

"Well, for your information, listening goes both ways!" Carmen responded just as heatedly. "You aren't listening to what I am saying, so why should I listen to you?"

"You are the most confusing, aggravating, infuriating female I have ever met!" he bit out.

"Confusing? Me?" Carmen looked up at him in surprise. "You put me in your apartment, climb into the shower with me when I'm naked, and tell me I belong to you like it is some great privilege. I didn't even know your name until two minutes ago! I'm not the one who is being confusing. I told you exactly what I wanted!"

A chuckle startled both of them back to the realization that they were not alone. "Creon, why don't we get her healed, have some refreshments, explain to her where she is, why you are claiming her, and what that means to you both," Morian said in exasperation. "I am beginning to understand why she is so confused."

Creon grunted in response to his mother's cheerful observation. He climbed the white stone steps leading back to his living quarters. Harvey trotted by his side, waiting to get a chance to heal his mate. Creon half wondered if his symbiot could heal his little white-haired she-demon if he throttled her. He grunted when he felt a sharp tug on his hair.

"You said that out loud," Carmen muttered under her breath as she released her hold on his hair. "You are not allowed to throttle me if you are protecting me."

Creon's eyes glittered wickedly for a moment before he leaned over enough to whisper in her ear. "What about spankings? Do they count?"

Carmen jerked back, blushing furiously. "Yes," she hissed out. "They count!"

"But as what?" he murmured as he set her gently down on the couch in their living area.

CHAPTER EIGHT

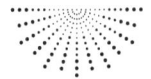

It had been over a week since she arrived on the planet and she was feeling just as confused now as she had when she first came. And just as frustrated. After her capture in the palace courtyard, Creon had carried her back to his living quarters. His mother, Morian, had patiently fixed them all something to eat while Creon had Harvey heal her leg and arm. Carmen had been skeptical at first, but within a few minutes all the pain was gone.

Afterward, Morian and Creon had given her a brief history of their world and their beliefs, namely the beliefs about true mates. Carmen had listened, but it was impossible for her to believe that her leaving could harm, much less kill, Creon. In a way, she could understand it if it had been like her and Scott, where they had known each other all their lives and been together the whole time—but at first sight? That was why she tried to escape again and again and again.

She had made it to the corridors one afternoon, but he had cornered her in one of the back rooms when she took a wrong turn. She ended up in a room with no other exit but the door she came through. Her face burned as she remembered the scorching kiss he had given her. She had felt truly cornered that day as he trapped her against the wall and kissed her so passionately she was gasping for breath afterward.

He had hauled her ass back to his living quarters, telling her there was nowhere that she could go that he wouldn't find her. She was more determined than ever to prove him wrong!

"This is ridiculous!" she muttered, looking out of the window again at all the activity down below. "I think they were just making it up so I wouldn't try to escape."

It hadn't stopped her. She tried to escape several more times over the past week. Now, the number of guards stationed outside of her living quarters looked like a miniature football team. She was running out of ways to try to trick them. One of the times she tried to escape, she had convinced two of the guards that she needed help with a stopped-up toilet, of all things. She had locked the guards in the bathroom. She made it to the end of the corridor before Harvey caught her and dragged her back. The next day she had four new guards outside the door.

The time after that, she had tried sneaking out dressed as one of the servants who came to clean. She had hog-tied the poor girl and stuffed her in the back bedroom. She made it halfway down the stairs before the alarm sounded, once again thanks to Harvey! The golden symbiot was beginning to get on her nerves. Creon had exploded in a rage when he saw her running hell-bent for the gates of the palace. He had caught her and hauled her ass back upstairs. She ended up with eight guards that evening. They were instructed to identify every individual who entered and exited their living quarters.

Carmen glared at Harvey. "He's still pissed that I'm not talking to him."

An image of the huge bed in Creon's room flashed through her mind. Carmen scowled down at the gold bracelets around her wrists. Harvey refused to remove them after the incident in the palace courtyard. She had tried to pry them off, but nothing she did would remove them.

"And all because I refuse to sleep with him!" she added, "If what they say is true, then sleeping with him and letting him claim me completely would be even worse for him. Maybe if he doesn't claim me like they say and I leave, he will be all right. He'll be able to find another girl to mate with," she reasoned, ignoring the stab of jealousy at the idea of Creon being with another girl.

She cursed under her breath again. The feelings inside her were getting harder to ignore. Fortunately for her, so far, Creon had been the perfect gentleman. He hadn't tried to push his whole "I claim you" thing on her.

He had made sure she had food, which she picked at while he grumbled. He only let out a few snorts and growls when she took the clothes that Morian had delivered to her into a smaller guest room instead of his bedroom. He had even given in somewhat gracefully about her refusing to attend the dinner. She figured it had something to do with the muttered words, "At least I won't have to kill another warrior if he tries to claim you, since I haven't yet."

Then two days ago, he'd disappeared, and she hadn't seen him since. She knew something was going on. The activity down in the courtyard had increased almost as dramatically as the number of guards outside her rooms. She had gotten so pissed yesterday that she had tried to just storm through them. They were learning it was easier to catch her if they worked as a team. She also suspected Creon promised to skin any of them alive if she got hurt again because they were really careful whenever they fought with her to make sure they did it as gently as possible. It was royally pissing her off!

She had been kept a virtual prisoner here. Morian had come to visit with her the day after the courtyard incident. Creon had left for a meeting shortly afterward. Morian tried to ask her questions about Scott, but Carmen refused to tell her anything else. She was afraid the more they knew, the more they would try to use the information to change her mind.

Morian had quietly shared how difficult it had been at first when her mate had died suddenly. She talked about the pain, grief, and loneliness that still affected her sometimes. When Carmen pointed out that she was still alive, Morian explained that while she had loved her mate deeply, he had not been her true mate.

"What is the difference?" Carmen had asked, even more confused.

"While Zlatan loved me as I loved him, his dragon and his symbiot never fully accepted me. They cared for and protected me, especially his symbiot, as I was a priestess. But it was not the same as if I had been his true mate. His dragon cared for me, but there was not the fire for me that a true mate would have had. But Zlatan the man..." Morian sighed as she took a sip of her tea. "Zlatan the man was very passionate and caring. He made up for what was missing."

"I still don't understand," Carmen said impatiently. "It is ridiculous to believe that just because you see someone, you will die if you don't claim them."

Morian studied Carmen carefully, seeing underneath the stubborn mask she wore to the frightened girl underneath. Carmen was afraid to let herself love again. She was terrified of opening herself to love. Her son would have to fight to overcome the walls this fragile young Earthling had built around her heart, for while she acted very tough, underneath she was balanced on a precipice that could lead to disaster for both her and Creon.

"A true mate is a very rare and special gift all warriors hope to be blessed with by the gods," Morian explained carefully. "Only a true mate is accepted by the three parts of the warrior. The man, his dragon, and his symbiot. All three make up the warrior and give him his strength. But, it is a lonely existence. Deep inside there is a hunger that only a true mate can sate. The need to feel complete eats at the warrior, growing as he ages. He may enjoy sex with a female, but it never sates that hunger. His dragon will become more difficult to handle as he grows older, wanting a mate of its own. This can only happen with the right female. Only then, will the dragon's fire burn. It becomes more difficult for the male to control once he discovers his true mate. The fire will burn hotter and hotter until he takes her."

"What if she doesn't want to be taken?" Carmen asked in a small voice, looking down at her clasped hands instead of at Morian. "What if she doesn't want to be claimed?"

"She has no choice, my daughter," Morian replied gently. "Once bitten, the dragon's fire will ignite inside her, transforming her, pulling her own dragon to the surface in answer to her mate's call. She will not be able to deny either the man or the dragon. Once she has been claimed, she can never leave her mate."

Carmen sat on the couch for hours afterward, thinking. She needed to get away before Creon bit her. That was why she had been trying to escape all week. She needed to put as much distance between them as possible before it was too late.

The sudden knocking at the door startled Carmen back to the present. She frowned. She hadn't been expecting anyone. Morian normally knocked once and came in. Whoever was at the door was pounding on it like it was a bass drum.

Carmen grabbed the small statue she had been using as a weapon to intimidate the guards and strode to the door. Flinging it open, her scowl turned to one of surprise as she looked her visitor over quickly. She glared at the guards who were watching her warily. Reaching out, she grabbed her older sister's arm and pulled her inside before slamming the door loudly.

"What did you do? Kill someone?" Ariel asked teasingly. "They have half a platoon guarding you."

Carmen rolled her eyes at the exaggeration before turning back toward the living area. "Aren't you stretching it a little bit? And no, I haven't killed anyone…yet," she added under her breath. "Where in the hell have you been? Do you know what is going on?"

Ariel moved toward the couch before replying. "Did you hear about Abby and Zoran?" she asked a question of her own as she sat down.

"Yeah, Morian told me. It seems shit happens even on alien worlds," Carmen said, moving to a cart and pouring a drink. She walked over and handed it to Ariel. "I thought you had dropped off the face of the planet. No one would tell me where you were, and I couldn't find you."

Ariel squirmed as Carmen looked at her intently. "I've been in the mountains," Ariel muttered before taking a sip of her drink. "With Mandra," she added quietly.

"Mandra, huh? Which one is he?" Carmen asked with a raised eyebrow.

Flushing, Ariel stared into her drink for a moment before raising troubled eyes to Carmen. "He was one of the guys in the transporter room, the one trying to catch me."

"Looks like he did more than try," Carmen replied drily, eyeing the mark on her sister's neck.

"Yes, he did," Ariel responded, biting her lip. "I like him, Carmen, a lot. I...I love him."

Carmen stared at her big sister with sad eyes. There wasn't much she could say. She had noticed the mark on Ariel's neck when she pulled her through the door and recognized that glow in her eyes. She'd had that same glow a long time ago when Scott was alive. She was happy for Ariel. It would be easier leaving her knowing she would be taken care of and wouldn't be alone. Everything would be all right. She knew in her heart now she could leave her big sister without feeling guilty.

"I'm happy for you, sis. If anyone deserves happiness, it's you," Carmen said quietly.

Ariel's head jerked up. "You're still going to try to get back home, aren't you?" she asked in resignation.

"Yes," Carmen responded.

"Then I'm going with you," Ariel said, reaching down to set her drink on the small table. "It would be best to go while most of the guys are gone."

Carmen shook her head sadly. "No, Ariel. You have a life here now. This isn't your battle, it's mine. There are some things that I have to do alone. This is one of them. I want...need to know you are safe and happy," Carmen said, hoping Ariel would understand and agree. "Please, I need to know you are safe and happy."

Carmen watched her big sister's eyes fill with tears. "We promised we would always be there for each other, no matter what. I am going with you, so just shut up and accept it," she muttered.

Carmen let out the breath she had been holding. "I've been trying to figure out a way of escaping. Do you have any ideas?" she asked, looking down at her sister.

"I'm not sure. I tried going out the window and almost killed myself," Ariel said with a twisted grin. "Miss Grace, I am not. The ledge was too narrow for me to hold onto. I was going to work my way over to another room and sneak out through that room."

Carmen thought for a minute before she grinned. "What about if instead of going along the ledge, we went down the side? We could rappel down to the balcony below us."

Ariel looked doubtful. "Do you have any rope?" she asked.

"No, but I have curtains. We can tie them together like we used to do when we were kids," Carmen said, suddenly excited.

"Ohh-kay," Ariel drew out. "What then?"

"I've been watching shuttles lifting off not far outside the city. We make our way there and steal one of them. You said you thought you could fly one, didn't you? Then, we program it to take us home," Carmen said, coming to kneel in front of Ariel and grasping her hand tightly.

Ariel looked into Carmen's eyes with worry. "What if we can't find our way back?"

"You can," Carmen said earnestly. "I know you can, Ariel. I have to get away before…"

Ariel squeezed Carmen's hands. "Before what?"

"Before he claims me," Carmen said, a look of pleading in her eyes for her sister's understanding. "If he bites me, it will kill him for sure when I leave. I don't want to hurt him. I need to leave before he does."

Ariel bit her lip in uncertainty. "Would it be such a bad thing, Carmen? You have a chance to let the past go, to start over. Can't you give it a chance? Scott…" Her voice faded as Carmen pulled away in anger.

"Forget it," Carmen said, standing up and turning away from Ariel. "I think it would be best if you left now."

Ariel stood up and gripped her little sister's arm, turning her so Carmen was forced to look at her. "No, I won't forget it. I will help you, but you have to listen to me first!" she said forcefully. "Scott would have never wanted you to do this. He would have wanted you to move on! He would not expect for you to take on some suicide mission to avenge him. Why can't you let go? Why can't you move on with your life?" Ariel demanded.

Carmen's face was frozen in an unemotional mask. "Because the bastard who murdered Scott also murdered our baby. I lost more than you can imagine that night. I won't ask you to give up the man you love, Ariel. I know what it feels like to be loved and to love someone else with every fiber of your being. What do you expect me to do? Forget about them? Act like they never existed? I don't want to ever fall in love again. I won't take a chance of opening myself up like that again."

Ariel's face softened as she saw the fear in Carmen's eyes. "You care about Creon, don't you?"

Carmen tried to pull away from Ariel's knowing look, but her sister refused to let her go. "He makes me feel confused," Carmen finally whispered. "When I look at him I feel things I never thought I would again. I try to annoy him, but he just looks at me like he can see inside me." Carmen looked at Ariel with a confused expression. "I'm scared, Ariel. I knew what to do back on Earth. I don't know what to do here."

"Do you think running away will solve the feelings you are having?" Ariel asked with an understanding smile.

"No," Carmen replied with a small smile of her own. "But, it can't hurt to at least try."

"You know we are probably going to get caught, don't you?" Ariel responded lightly. "And, when the guys find out, they are going to be more than a little bit pissed at us."

A slight flush rose on Carmen's face as she remembered Creon's threat to spank her ass. "Yes, but think of the fun we'll have before they do."

Ariel laughed in a low, husky voice. "Carmen, you are grabbing a dragon by his tail and pulling it."

"At least it isn't his teeth," Carmen said softly, turning toward Creon's bedroom where long curtains hung around the massive bed.

Ariel watched her little sister as she walked toward the bedroom. "I wouldn't count on that," Ariel muttered with a flare of hope.

A huge grin lit up her face. Her sister was making one last-ditch effort to escape in order to absolve the guilt she felt at not being able to fulfill the promise she made to herself. But deep down, Ariel could see the hope in her sister's eyes that she would fail.

CHAPTER NINE

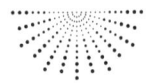

Creon rolled his shoulders to ease the tension in them. He had spent the last two days with his brothers, Ha'ven, and a small group of warriors in the mountainous regions north of the city. They had discovered where the Curizan traitor, Ben'qumain, had taken Abby, only to find she had escaped him by transforming. Zoran had gone in search of her.

Ha'ven had given Creon the final confirmation he needed that his father's older brother, Raffvin, was still alive and responsible for his father's murder. Ha'ven also related that his brother, Adalard, had almost been killed in an assassination attempt, and that Vox had been kidnapped.

"I'm ready to kill the bastard for almost killing my brother, but I have to appreciate that he was able to kidnap Vox," Ha'ven said with a grin. "It takes a lot to sneak up and capture that big kitty."

Creon fought back a laugh. "You know he is going to kick your ass if you keep calling him that," he responded as they moved back to the shuttles waiting to return Creon to the palace and Ha'ven to his warship.

"Like that big pussy would even have a chance," Ha'ven said. "You know we are going to have to go rescue his sorry ass. I am so looking forward to rubbing that in his face. I heard they sold him to a mining operation run by the Antrox. I hate dealing with those emotionless insects," he grumbled.

"I'm sure Vox is having the time of his life right now," Creon responded quietly, his mind already back to trying to figure out how to deal with his mate.

I tell you how to deal with her, his dragon growled out stubbornly. *I tell you over and over, but you no listen to me. Let me bite her. I take care of it. You too scared of her. I not scared. I teach her who in charge.*

I am not scared! Creon bit back in frustration. *I am trying to give her time to accept us!*

No. You scared, his dragon replied drily. *She not Aria. I never like Aria. Harvey never like Aria. We like Carmen. She is good mate. She is stubborn mate. She more stubborn than you. She make good perfect mate.*

I know she is not Aria! I just… Creon blew out a frustrated breath. "Dragon's balls!" he growled out under his breath.

Ha'ven looked at him with a raised eyebrow. "What has you so twisted? I could tell you and your dragon were arguing about something," he said with a motion of his hand to Creon's arms which were covered with black scales. "You don't often let anything upset you enough to lose control. What is it? Zoran and his mate will be fine, and you know Vox can handle anything the Antrox throw at him."

"I have a true mate," Creon said reluctantly. "She is from a species we have never encountered before."

Ha'ven stopped walking and looked intently at his friend. This was big news. Ha'ven knew Creon had refused to let another female close to him after Aria's betrayal. He also knew it was almost impossible for a Valdier to find his true mate. The fact that Creon had found his with an unknown species was, well, incredible.

"So, what is the problem? I thought a Valdier warrior was supposed to embrace finding his true mate and everything. You look more like you would prefer to change places with Vox in the mines. Is she ugly?" Ha'ven asked curiously.

Creon shot his best friend a disgusted look. "No, she is not ugly. In fact, she is very, very beautiful. It is just—" Creon grimaced before he muttered out the rest of his sentence. "It is just she won't have anything to do with me."

Ha'ven's bark of laughter echoed around them. "She doesn't—" Ha'ven laughed even harder. "She doesn't want anything to do with you?" he hooted out, trying to catch his breath. "You find your true mate, and she is the only female in ten star systems to not want anything to do with you! I have got to meet this species."

Creon punched Ha'ven in the jaw, knocking the huge Curizan prince on his ass. "It's not that funny!" he growled out.

Ha'ven sat up, rubbing his chin. "Maybe not for you, but for the rest of us, it is!" He chuckled, rolling to his feet just in time to miss being kicked by Creon. "Come on! How many females have you stolen when we stopped at the bars at the spaceports? The females get a whiff of a Valdier dragon prince, and the rest of us fade to the background."

"You are exaggerating. It happened one time, and the females had no idea you and Vox were princes as well, because you were acting like you were my servants. I won the toss. Vox had been the prince the time before, and they were all over him," Creon retorted. "And don't you dare say anything to my mate about that. I am having a hard enough time with her without you telling her tall tales."

"Maybe she would want you if she thought other females were vying for your attention," Ha'ven asked as he brushed the leaves and dirt off his ass. "It couldn't hurt, surely?"

"By the gods, I mean it, Ha'ven. I've been reading up on the information Kelan and Trelon downloaded about the women of Earth. They don't like it if their mates look at other women. I read one report that a woman actually cut a man's staff off for doing it. I would not put anything past my mate. She is a fierce fighter. She wouldn't stop at just cutting that off," Creon warned.

Ha'ven flinched and cupped himself protectively. "Maybe I don't want to meet this species after all," he muttered.

"Come on," Creon said tiredly. "I've left her alone too long as it is. She has tried to escape at least a dozen times this past week. I've had to triple the guards. She keeps attacking them, and I am afraid she will get hurt."

"Good luck, my friend. I will take care of the necessary arrangements to go after Vox and meet up with you tomorrow, unless you want to let him sit for a little while longer. Tell Mandra he is to meet up with Adalard. He is already expecting him. Once we have rescued the pussycat, we'll meet up with him and Adalard. By then we should know where your uncle is hiding," Ha'ven said with a sympathetic slap on Creon's shoulder.

Creon nodded as they broke through the clearing. "Be safe, my friend. Until we meet later."

Creon stepped toward the shuttle that would take him back to the palace while Ha'ven climbed into the one that would take him back to the warship they would use to go after Vox. Perhaps it was time to take Carmen somewhere she wouldn't be able to escape from. Once she was on the warship, there wasn't anywhere she could go that he couldn't find her.

∽

An hour later, Creon shook with a deep rage. Carmen had escaped again. This time with her sister. He listened in cold silence as the guards told him that both women had disappeared the day before. The guards did not realize anything was amiss until they became concerned when there was no answer to the servant bringing evening refreshments. They had not been found yet.

"Nothing! Where in the hell are they?" Mandra bit out savagely.

"We do not know, my lords. We have searched the palace extensively and have expanded the search further out. It does not appear they were taken, but left on their own," the guard said hesitantly.

"How did they get past you?" Creon snarled with a cold intensity that had the guard swallowing nervously.

The guard stood frozen as he saw Creon's eyes darken. He had heard the tales of the young lord, some that would chill the blood of any warrior. His eyes flickered to the long curved knife the youngest royal held clenched in his fist.

"They climbed over the balcony and scaled the wall down to a lower balcony using the curtains around the bed as a rope," the guard replied.

Creon snarled again and threw the knife in rage. Black scales rippled over his arms and up his neck. His face began to elongate as he let the change take over him. He would kill every single guard if anything happened to his mate. He had given them strict instructions to protect his mate and not let her escape. The group of guards froze as the knife quivered where it stuck in the wall. Creon pulled his dragon back under control, ignoring its displeasure when he felt Mandra's hand on his shoulder.

"We will find them," Mandra said in a deadly voice. "They cannot have gotten off the planet."

A knock at the door caused all the men to look around. A guard wearing the standard uniform of black leather pants, black vest, and black knee-high boots stood at the door. He waited until he was acknowledged before speaking.

"My lords, we have them," the man said, nervously looking at Creon.

"Where?" Mandra growled out menacingly.

"At the launch base, my lord," the man replied hurriedly. "They stole one of the shuttles, but we were able to override the controls."

Creon turned and headed for the door the moment he knew where his mate was. He would no longer give her time to accept their mating. He would claim her as soon as he had her alone, and then he would take her away from here until she understood he would never let her leave. He pushed out of the door, transforming into his dragon as soon as he was clear of it. He moved with a rapid burst of speed toward the launch base.

And, he promised silently, *I will give her the ass-whipping I threatened to give her before.*

Finally! his dragon muttered in agreement. *You finally grow some dragon's balls.*

Fuck you, Creon growled as he circled to land near the hanger holding his mate.

Not fuck me. Fuck our mate, his dragon growled back in triumph. *We finally claim our mate.*

Carmen held her arm gingerly against her chest. It was swollen and hurt bad enough it made her nauseated. She knew her wrist was broken. She felt the bones snap when the guard grabbed her. Her face stung, too. She knew it was swelling from the heat radiating out from her cheek. She wanted to touch it, but she was afraid to let go of her wrist long enough to feel it. She kept her chin tucked into her chest instead. She had used every move she had learned from Scott and from the warriors on board the *V'ager*, but the guards had been too strong. In reality, she hadn't planned to fight any of them. She had finally accepted she would never be able to return to Earth unless Creon took her.

Her eyes flickered to the largest guard. He was almost four times her and Ariel's size. He had grabbed Ariel roughly when she stumbled. He must have thought she was going to try to escape because when he grabbed her, he almost jerked her off her feet.

When her sister cried out in pain, Carmen went after him. No one hurt her big sister. Everything went to hell after that. When one of the guys backhanded Carmen, knocking her to the ground, Ariel jumped on his ass. It wasn't until Carmen screamed out in pain when her wrist broke that everyone froze. She had crumpled to the floor in agony while Ariel shielded her from the guards, refusing to let any of them touch her little sister.

Now, the big guard was looking with increased unease at the door. He refused to look at Carmen after they brought her and Ariel into the small office. Ariel had helped her into a seat. Almost immediately, two of the guards attached restraints to secure them in their chairs. Since they couldn't restrain her arms, they secured them to her slender ankles. Carmen bit her lip to keep from whimpering while silent tears of pain coursed down her cheeks.

A short time later, the loud roar of a dragon echoed through the hanger. The three guards standing in the room with them blanched at the sound. A moment later, Creon burst into the room. He had not fully transformed back into his two-legged form. His face was still slightly elongated, his eyes were two dark, golden flames of fury, and black scales still covered his arms, neck, and cheeks.

His eyes zoomed in on Carmen. The low, dangerous growl rumbling from him had the men in the room backing up until they were pressed rigidly against the wall. His eyes moved from one to the other before they settled back on Carmen's battered body.

"Who hurt her?" he asked in a quiet, deadly voice. When no one answered immediately, he looked at the guards again and roared out. *"Who hurt her?"* he repeated, taking a menacing step toward them.

"Creon," Carmen called out quietly. Creon's eyes jerked back to hers. "I..." Carmen began, before stopping to lick her suddenly dry lips. "I... need your help," she requested quietly. "Please... will you help me? I don't want to hurt anymore," she added softly as fresh tears filled her eyes and flowed down her pale cheeks. "Please," she whispered brokenly.

Creon stared into her huge, glittering brown eyes. He heard her unspoken words. She was finally ready to give them a chance. He wasn't sure what had changed, but he could hear the silent plea. She was afraid, but she was ready to take the first step toward healing, the first step toward accepting him and what was to be her new life. She was finally ready to rise from the ashes.

Carmen looked at him, silently begging him to understand what she couldn't say. She saw the moment he recognized her unspoken plea. Creon drew in a deep, shaky breath as he walked over to her. He heard Mandra enter the room and walk over to Ariel, who was sitting quietly next to her sister.

"Her wrist is broken," Ariel murmured softly to Creon. "She also took a hard blow to her face. Please take care of her. She was trying to protect me."

Creon looked at the battered face of his brother's mate. His eyes moved to the men standing to the side. He would be meeting with each one to show them what would happen if they ever laid another hand on his mate or any of his brothers' mates. All three men bowed their heads in acknowledgement, realizing they had used unnecessary force against the two small females.

"Creon," Carmen whispered, looking down at him as he snapped the restraints around her ankles. "Don't blame them or Ariel. It was my fault."

His head jerked up, and his jaw tightened in anger. "We will discuss this after I get you healed. Never again, Carmen. You will be by my side from now on until I know you will not try to leave me. I claim you. Once you are healed. I will finish my claim, and if the gods and goddesses bless us, you will be mine forever more," he said tightly, standing up.

Carmen gave a small nod to show that she understood there would be no more escaping. "I had to try one last time," she said in a voice so faint he almost missed it.

Creon bent down and gently lifted her into his arms, careful not to bump her injured arm. He turned and snarled out to Harvey to return to their living quarters and wait for them. The huge golden creature shook with anger, turning its massive head to stare intently at the three warriors who stood silently in the door. It emitted a low snarl before it transformed into a huge bird and took off for the palace.

He paused at the door, turning to look at each man. "If any of you ever touch my mate again, I will personally gut each and every one of you. I will take my time, and I will enjoy every moment of it," he said coldly. "This is not finished."

The largest warrior stepped forward and bowed. "Please accept my apology for harming your mate, my lord. She is a fierce fighter and very protective. She is a strong mate for you. I will be ready to answer for the harm I have done."

Carmen felt horrible for the big guy. He had only been doing his duty. It wasn't his fault that she was just a little more breakable than what he was used to. She turned her face into Creon's neck and nipped him lightly to get his attention.

The soft rumble of a purr startled both of them. "Don't be mad at him. He was doing his job," she whispered, looking wide-eyed at Creon.

Creon's eyes narrowed on his mate's pale, bruised cheek. He nodded to the warrior. He needed to get his mate back to the palace. He had left in such a hurry, he hadn't thought about transportation back once he found her. He saw Mandra helping Ariel into his symbiot which was in the shape of a small skimmer. He had sent his back to the palace already.

"Hang on," he said gruffly before he called forth his dragon.

Come, my friend. We need to get our mate home, he whispered.

Carmen gasped as the arms holding her transformed around her. They thickened and grew. Midnight black scales rippled and formed. Long, leathery wings unfolded and expanded even as she felt the world around her shifting so she was much higher than she had been moments before.

In a matter of seconds, she was staring with wide eyes at the sleek head of a dragon. She was cradled in its front claws. Unable to stop herself, she reached out with her good hand and tentatively touched the midnight black scales on the dragon's chest. The scales were hard and smooth to her touch. She felt a shiver run through the huge body as she let her fingers explore as far as she could reach. The elongated black head turned to her and puffed out a breath of hot air. Carmen reached out and gently touched the tip of his nose, running her fingers along one rounded nostril.

"You are so beautiful," she breathed out, forgetting her pain and fear in a moment of pure wonder. "You are magical."

Creon wanted to roar out as she touched him, but was afraid of scaring her. Instead, he moved onto his back legs, pumping his wings, and took off up into the skies. He let out a series of coughs at his mate's startled squeal and pulled her closer to his warm body.

He felt her relax back against him. A new sense of triumph flowed through him at her trust in him in his dragon form. Tonight a new dragon would be born. He had no doubt in his mind that his mate would survive the transformation. She had survived more than most warriors. She was his phoenix.

CHAPTER TEN

Creon touched down lightly on the balcony to his living quarters, gently balancing as he transformed. He hopped down, trying not to jostle Carmen any more than he had to. She was paler than she had been earlier, and he was worried that she had internal injuries.

He called out for Harvey. The gold symbiot was bouncing from one foot to the other. He was back in the shape of the strange creature that Carmen seemed to find so comforting. His long, golden ears bounced up and down and were so long it looked like he might trip over them in his excitement to get to Carmen.

Creon walked swiftly down the hallway to his bedroom. He carefully laid Carmen down on the soft covers. She was holding her arm and biting her lip. Tight lines of pain pinched the corners of her mouth, and a haze of pain clouded her beautiful brown eyes. She was drawing short little breaths through her mouth.

"Heal her," Creon said urgently to his symbiot.

He sat on the edge of the bed and ran his hand tenderly over her forehead. Harvey dissolved and flowed over Carmen, golden tentacles moving over her broken wrist first, then continuing until it had touched every inch of her bruised body. Creon watched as a mist of gold ran up his mate's neck and over her bruised cheek. Carmen jerked, then lay perfectly still as the symbiot moved over her skin.

"It feels so soft and warm," Carmen murmured, looking up at Creon with wide eyes filled with awe. "It tingles."

Creon smiled down at the breathless whisper of wonder. Since a Valdier warrior was united with his symbiot while he was still an infant, he never thought of how it felt when it healed him. It was as natural as breathing. Just as his dragon was. He could not imagine what it would feel like if he did not have either one.

"I have never thought about it before, but you are right. It does tingle when it heals," he replied, still running his hand over her forehead before letting his fingers flow through the silky strands of her hair.

"Why did you run again? Surely you knew you would never have made it off-planet. Even if you had, you would have been captured before you got far. It would have been suicide to think you could return to your world in a transport shuttle. You would have died before you got a fraction of the distance to your planet," he asked huskily.

Carmen turned her head into his palm. "I didn't want you to bite me. I thought if I could get away from you, you would find someone else. I mean, if you didn't claim me, then when I left, nothing would happen to you, not if you hadn't claimed me all the way," Carmen tried to explain.

She was having a hard time thinking straight. She wasn't hurting anymore, at least not from her now healed wounds. Her body was calling out to his. She could feel the pull. It was stronger than it had ever been before. It was as if there was something deep inside her that called to him.

She watched as his eyes darkened to an even darker gold. Twin flames burned with an intensity that sent a shiver of awareness through her until she felt like her blood was boiling. She turned her head when Harvey reformed next to her. The huge, gold basset hound ran a long, golden tongue up the side of her face.

"Oh," she giggled, startled. "Thank you," she said quietly, leaning up on one elbow so she could brush a kiss across Harvey's golden nose.

A gasp escaped her as she was suddenly lifted into a pair of very strong, very possessive arms. "There can never be another for me. You are my mate, forever," Creon muttered before his lips crushed down on hers.

Carmen's whimper turned into a soft moan as she timidly wrapped her arms around his neck. Creon pressed down until he felt the soft full lips of his mate open hesitantly. He took advantage of her startled gasp to deepen the kiss, tangling his fingers in her hair and tilting her head to one side.

When he pulled back, her eyes had turned to such a dark, rich brown it was almost impossible to see her pupils. She was drawing in short, deep breaths. He moaned as he felt her chest expand, rubbing her taut nipples against his chest as she tried to steady her breathing. He buried his face in her neck and drew in a deep breath of his own. The moment his lips touched her heated skin, he felt his teeth elongate.

I claim my mate now, his dragon growled out.

Creon was startled as his dragon gained control suddenly, striking out with a single-minded determination to claim his mate. He groaned loudly as Carmen's sweet blood poured into his mouth. His dragon roared inside him as it felt his mate's responsiveness to him and the taste of her blood.

The dragon's fire burned in his throat as it built and poured from him into Carmen. A sharp cry echoed in the room as Carmen's body arched into his at the intensity of the heat pouring through her. She felt like she was catching fire from the inside out. Heat gathered and pooled between her legs. She moved restlessly, trying to get away from the scorching fire.

A low growl warned her not to fight. Creon continued breathing the fire his dragon had started, determined to not let his mate escape him again. A primitive need to mate, to claim, to possess held him tightly in its claws.

He pressed the slender body under him further down into the soft covers of his bed, crawling over her until he had her caged. His legs ran along the outside of hers, and he ground his heavy cock into her to let her know the effect she had on him. He kept his upper body raised just enough so he didn't crush her. His fingers were still locked tightly in her silky locks, holding her head still as he continued to breathe the life-changing fire into her.

He could hear her harsh gasps in his ear as she fought for breath as the dragon's fire burst through her. Her hands clawed at his back and shoulders, alternating between trying to push him away and gripping him tightly to her.

"Creon, the fire…." she whimpered.

All he could do was groan as the fire poured in never-ending waves, crashing against the walls of her resistance, breaking down the fear and replacing it with need. His dragon fought fiercely to overcome the last of her resistance. It was as if he understood that, like that of the mystical phoenix, only when Carmen's resistance was finally burned to the finest ash could she rise to be reborn, free from the pain and grief of her old life.

Creon groaned louder as the fire inside him grew to a point where he wondered if he would burn with her. Carmen's scream pierced the room as the wave of fire flared, engulfing her. Unable to stand the cry of anguish coming from his mate, Creon ripped his mouth away from her delicate skin and swiped the mark with his tongue to ease the pain and seal his mark. The symbol of a pure black dragon, wings spread wide with one of its front legs raised in challenge showed clearly on the curve between her neck and shoulder. Never had he seen a clearer mark on a mate or a more beautiful one.

She is mine, his dragon snarled. *I claim her.*

Gods, what have we done? Creon muttered to his dragon. *You should not have breathed so much into her. She is too fragile to handle so much dragon's fire at one time.*

My mate, his dragon snapped out fiercely.

Creon looked down at the peaceful face of his mate as she lay against the pillows. Her face was flushed, her cheeks a rosy red. Her lashes lay like crescents against her cheeks, and a light dew covered her forehead, strands of white-blonde hair darkened from the moisture lying against it. He pulled back and breathed a sigh of relief when he saw the slight rise and fall of her chest. She had fainted as the last burst of dragon's fire seared through her.

He frowned as he saw the light smear of dirt on her cheek where she had fallen when she had been hit. He pulled back and quickly removed his clothes before he began undressing her. He would bathe her and prepare her.

When she woke, the dragon's fire would burn through her with an intensity that would frighten him. Normally, from what he had read from the archives, a warrior would bite his mate several times during the mating process. Each time, the dragon's fire would increase in intensity, changing his mate on the inside, reshaping her blood, organs, her very essence as a new dragon was born.

His dragon had poured everything he had into that one bite. A soft moan escaped Carmen, and she moved restlessly on the bed as the fire began to build. Creon cursed his dragon's impatience and his inability to control him at times. He quickly scooped Carmen into his arms and moved to the bathing room. He crossed to the huge bath, stepping down the steps and sinking down into the heated water.

His breath caught when Carmen's eyes suddenly opened to stare up at him silently. Gold flakes mixed with the dark brown now, glowing in the dim light of the bathing room. Her lips parted as if to say something, but nothing came out. Her eyes widened, turning a darker gold. She drew in a sharp breath before leaning forward to lock her mouth with his in a kiss that was as possessive of him as his had been earlier for her.

Creon shuddered and ran his hands around her waist, moving them up to draw her closer. He paused when he felt movement along her back under her skin. He broke the kiss to look down in shock and concern as he saw the ripple of white, red, pink, and purple scales sliding over her skin. Her fingers dug into his shoulders, her nails drawing blood as a wave of fire burst inside her, forcing a low keening cry of need from her throat.

"Please," she cried out hoarsely. "The fire is burning me."

"Do not fight it, my beautiful phoenix," he whispered in awe as he watched the changes in her. "Give yourself to me and I will care for you."

Carmen started to shake her head, fear clenching her jaw. "What if you leave me?" she asked, bright tears burning but never falling.

"Never," he promised. "You will never be alone again. I swear."

Carmen fought against the fire burning in her. She wanted to scream from the force of it. A power she didn't understand was taking her over, changing her, making her into something new, something different. She looked into the eyes of the man who had taken her by surprise. He had fought to break through all the barriers she had erected. He refused to let her give up. Her old life was coming to an end. Her nest was built, ready for her to burn to ash so she could rise and live again.

"Take me," she finally whispered, falling forward until she was wrapped tightly against his body. "Take me, hold me… Love me and never let me go," she said as the tears she had held in for so long finally fell, washing away the pain and grief.

Creon's heart swelled with love for the strength, beauty, and courage held in the slender body wrapped tightly in his arms. He turned her gently until she straddled him. Capturing her lips with his, he gripped her thighs, guiding her until she was aligned with his swollen cock and pulled her down as he tilted his hips, impaling her on his long length. He felt Carmen's fingers sliding along his scalp as she twisted her fingers in his hair to draw him closer and began rocking back and forth. Her salty tears mixed with their kiss, sealing them together.

"I love you, *mi elila*," Creon whispered against her lips. "You are my life. I claim you as my true mate. No other may have you. I will live to protect you. You are mine, my beautiful phoenix."

Carmen refused to look away from the golden eyes of the man who had given her a reason to want to live again. Her eyelids drooped as the flames inside her burned brighter, pulling a deep groan from her as intense pleasure built. She could feel his long, thick cock stroking her deep. The erotic feel of the warm water swirling around them combined with the hard, sharp thrust as he moved deep inside her was too much.

"Yes," she panted as her climax built. "*Yes!*" she gasped out as her body exploded around his.

A low growl escaped Creon as he felt her body tighten down on his, fisting his cock as she pulsed around his. She was so beautiful as she came. Her eyes were closed, and her head was thrown back slightly, exposing the slender column of her throat to him. A look of bliss curved her lips. Unable to resist, he rocked into her harder, faster, enjoying her gasp as her eyes popped open in shock as her body tightened again.

"Creon," she breathed out hoarsely. "Oh…" she cried out, gripping his shoulders as her body stiffened again.

"You are mine," he roared out as his own body answered hers.

Creon's eyes closed as he felt his seed pulsing deep inside her. He could feel her vaginal walls stroking him, pulling more out of him. Inside, his dragon roared out, wanting to see it mate being born. Dragon fire burned his throat again. He didn't think it possible for there to be any more left inside him, but his dragon refused to be sated until it knew its mate was transformed. His eyes popped open, focused on the pale, slender column in front of him.

Bite! His dragon roared out determinedly.

It seized control once again with a force Creon had never experienced before. Midnight scales rippled and his teeth lengthened. His eyes lowered to Carmen's small, firm breast. Lowering his head, he sank his teeth into the rounded globe. His hands prevented her from jerking away and injuring herself as he once again placed his mark upon her.

"Creon?" Carmen asked in a confused voice.

Her head jerked down when she felt the sharp pinch, followed by the tug on her left breast. Her eyes widened as she watched Creon suck on it. A small trace of blood ran down one side, slipping down until it dropped into the warm water of the bath. A whimper escaped her as she felt warmth flood it, causing her nipple to swell in response. Soon, the throbbing between her legs matched the sucking motion of his mouth as he continued to move back and forth, running his tongue over her taut nipple until it became ultra sensitive.

"You are going to kill me," she moaned in a husky voice as the waves of desire and need built again.

A low rumble was the only response to her moaned words. Need fed and grew to an explosive level inside her. She erupted as it crested, grinding her hips down against his, seeking relief. She felt a slight tug as he released her breast followed by a hot tongue over the hypersensitive nipple. Pleasure/pain exploded through her at the sudden release.

Her head fell forward to lay against his shoulder, as shaken sobs ripped from her throat. The world tilted as one strong arm slid down to support her ass as he stood. Water poured down their bodies that were still connected. His other arm supported her around her waist, keeping her pressed against his broad chest.

She knew he was walking back into the bedroom, but she didn't care. She was a mass of oversensitive nerves right now, unable to function or support her own body. She bit her lip as he pulled out of her, trying unsuccessfully to keep the cry of denial from escaping her swollen lips.

"Hush, it has only just begun," his deep voice whispered quietly against her ear as he laid her down gently on his bed.

Carmen forced her eyes open to stare up in disbelief. "What do you mean, it has only just begun?" she asked in shock.

"The dragon's fire," Creon replied, pressing a kiss to her shoulder, then her breast, before moving down to her stomach.

"What is the dragon's fire?" she asked in a strangled voice, staring up at the top of the bed as he continued moving down, pulling one of her legs over his shoulder.

"If the gods and goddesses bless us, we will be one when the transformation is done," his muffled voice said before he latched onto the small, swollen nub between her legs and began feasting.

Carmen arched into his mouth, still staring up. The images reflected in the mirrored surface above her showed her everything he was doing to her body. The sight and sound was so erotic she couldn't close her eyes to block them.

She saw the image of herself opening for him like a bloom seeking the sun. She spread her legs wider. Her fingers curled tightly in the covers of the bed. She could see the mark on her left breast. It throbbed, as if his mouth still held it captive.

A cry ripped from her throat as her body shattered suddenly. She could feel the force of her orgasm as it exploded out of her. The tugging increased instead of decreasing. Unable to stand it any longer, her fingers released the bedspread and wound in his long hair.

"Stop," she cried out even as she wrapped her legs around his head, trapping him to her. "Oh God!" she muttered over and over as pleasure washed through her.

Creon pulled back with a soft, rumbling growl. He gripped her thighs, pulling them from around his head and slid his hands up to her waist where he roughly flipped her until she lay on her stomach. Pulling her up onto her knees, he held her around her waist and slid his throbbing cock between the slick, swollen folds until he was buried as far as he could go.

He held her tightly, even as she fought against the intrusion against her sensitive core. He bit back a curse as the waves of the dragon fire ensnared both of them in its greedy grasp. His hips rocked back and forth faster and faster as it burned hotter. Scales rippled over both of them in response, his black scales against her white, red, pink, and purple ones.

Creon's eyes focused on the spider web of veins spreading out over her back. The image of the phoenix on her back gave the illusion of movement. Its wings spreading, opening, taking flight, the reds turning to flames while the pink and purple twisted, turning and reshaping into a dragon. His throat closed with emotion at the beauty of her transformation.

His body exploded in a kaleidoscope of sparks, bursting in an explosion that left him shaking and gasping for breath. He bent over her body, straining to pour every ounce of his essence, of his love into her.

"Never," he choked out through a throat thick with emotion. "Never will I leave you."

CHAPTER ELEVEN

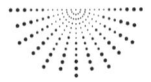

Creon lay on his side looking at his mate's relaxed face. He marveled at her beauty, her strength, and her determination. A smile curved his lips when he noticed there was a slight tremble to his hand.

He was in awe of her. She had not shied away from his or his dragon's claim. She had matched him touch for touch, taste for taste, fire with fire throughout the night only to fall into a deep sleep as the moons set and the sun teased the horizon. The smile faded slowly. He would never be able to let her return to her world alone.

During the night, she had haltingly told him about her life before. She talked of her husband, holding nothing back. He was surprised at first at the lack of jealousy he had for the other male.

Perhaps it was the sad, but peaceful way in which she told him of her life before. The more he learned, the more he was thankful the other male had been there for her. He held her tightly when she told him of how he was murdered and about the man who she had sought vengeance on. And he comforted her as she tearfully told him of losing the child she and her first mate had conceived due to the injuries she had suffered.

He had sworn then and there he would do three things. He would plant his seed inside her, not to replace the child she lost, but to fill the emptiness in her heart and arms. He would protect her with every fiber of his, his dragon's, and his symbiot's being. And last, they would return to her world, and he would personally kill the man who had taken so much from her.

His hand moved down to gently touch her flat stomach. The smile slowly grew again as he thought about the fact he had accomplished his first task. Just before the moons set, he had planted his seed deeply inside her. He felt her dragon stirring in confusion and wonder as the twin tiny lights sparked to life, anchoring deep inside her womb. Her dragon gave a contented purr before wrapping protectively around them.

My mate, his dragon purred in delight. *I tell you I claim her.*

Yes, you did, Creon replied dryly before reluctantly rolling out of bed. *You really need to learn a little about control.*

Control for wimps, his dragon replied with a roll of his eyes. *You needed my dragon balls to lose control.*

Fuck you, Creon growled back playfully.

No, fuck my mate, his dragon answered back with a huge yawn. *After nap.*

Creon shook his head. He would probably need a nap later, he thought, as he stumbled toward the bathing room. He needed to finalize things with his brothers before he left. He also needed to talk to his mother. He wanted to thank her for her help. She had told him he needed to look beneath the mask to the wounded creature beneath. He now understood the depth of pain and grief his mate had suffered, and he would do everything he could to make her life a happy and fulfilling one. Today was the first day of her new life, and he was determined it would be one she never, ever regretted.

∽

Several hours later, Carmen was walking next to Cara, Ariel, and Trisha toward Abby's living quarters, along with over a dozen guards who kept a marginal distance behind her. Carmen had been surprised at the knocking at the door and out of habit had picked up the vase she kept near before realizing she probably didn't need it anymore. She opened the door to find Cara bouncing like a energize ball. Behind her were Trisha and Ariel and a cart laden with pots of…

"Coffee?" Carmen asked hopefully, looking at the cart with a look that had the guards backing up even further. "You have coffee?"

Cara's light laughter filled the corridor. "Pots and pots and pots of it. All the good stuff! I've been reprogramming the replicators to make it. It took a while, but I think I have it figured out. I also made a bunch of other stuff. It is so cool. Did you know if you…"

Carmen had lost track of what Cara was rattling off about. Something to do if you cross this wire with that and add something else you end up with something new. All her brain could process was that it smelled coffee. She would have followed the women anywhere if it meant getting a cup or a hundred.

"We're headed to see Abby. She had the most amazing adventure!" Cara said excitedly. "I heard Mandra, who told Kelan, who told Trelon that she burned up this guy who kidnapped her! I want to learn how to do that."

Carmen shook her head and put her hand on Cara's shoulder to stop her energetic movements. "The only question I have is do I get a cup of coffee if I follow you?"

"Yes!" the answer came from three giggling voices.

Carmen looked at the guards who moved back another step. She frowned in confusion at them. Before, at least two or three of them would have been on her ass by now.

She took a step toward them, and they almost stumbled trying to move backward away from her. She shook her head in confusion before closing the door and following the other women down the corridor. Every once in a while she would glance over her shoulder to see if the guards were still there.

They were, but they were like a school of barracuda. They kept the same distance from her. If she moved toward them, they moved back. If she moved forward, they took a step closer. It was downright weird.

"So what's with all the guards?" Cara asked as she bounced down the corridor. "I would have thought we had enough protection with all our gold BFFs."

Carmen wouldn't have been surprised if Cara didn't start dancing on the ceiling with the amount of energy she was putting out. If they could harness it, they could power the entire planet for at least a month or two. Instead, she scowled when she listened to her sister's response.

"Oh, they are guarding us. They are here to prevent Carmen and me from trying to escape again," Ariel was saying.

Cara turned around, walking backward, practically shaking with excitement. "Do you need help? I bet I could rewire the *V'ager*! We could go exploring. Maybe we could try…" Loud groans from the guards drew laughter from the women.

Even Carmen couldn't quite hide the smile that curved her lips. Cara was addictive and exhausting all in the same sentence. It was obvious she was in rare form today.

She wondered how Creon's brother was holding up. Tired, exhausted, worn-out were a few adjectives that came to mind. Carmen had visited Trisha and Ariel enough over the last three years to know what their little friend could be like. Outrageous on a good day and destructive on an even better one. She had never seen Cara have a bad day, so she figured the world would be safe until that day arrived.

She gave a silent thank-you when they arrived at Abby's door. She was about ready to go feral if she didn't get a cup of coffee soon. The smell was heaven, and she was ready for more than a whiff of it. She bowed her head to hide the blush that rose on her cheeks as she remembered why she was in such a desperate need for a cup. She was working on about three hours of sleep. Creon had been insatiable last night. It had been a long time since she'd had a workout like that. Not since she and Scott spent that long weekend in Rio de Janeiro.

A soft, warm glow filled her. She could now think of her memories with him with a measure of happiness instead of just pain and grief. They had lived, loved, and laughed life to the fullest. Now, it was time to let go and live again.

Tears burned her eyes. Not from sadness this time, but with a gratitude that she had been given a chance to be loved like that not once but twice in her lifetime. Her fingers fell to her side. She felt a warmth spread through the tips of her fingers up her arm as Harvey brushed against her. Long tentacles of gold spun out from his coat, wrapping around her arms and moving under her shirt to encase her neck.

"Thank you, my friend," she murmured quietly.

He let out a small snort before trotting through the open door into Abby's living quarters where he promptly turned around in a circle several times before lying down in the first sunny spot he could find near the windows. Carmen listened to the other women chatting excitedly about everything that happened.

She quietly poured herself a cup of coffee and walked over to the chair nearer to where Harvey lay. Curling her legs up under her, she followed along with Abby's tale of everything that happened to her. She leaned forward when Abby dropped her little bombshell.

"I can change into a dragon," Abby was saying with a nervous giggle.

The words echoed through Carmen as Abby described to Cara how she did it. Carmen looked down at the soft, peach-colored skin of her arms, but she was remembering last night. She had watched as ripples of color had run up and down them.

Just like when Creon transformed at the hanger, she thought, stunned. *That was what he meant about the transformation. That was what the burning fire was inside me. He was changing me... like*—her mind froze for a moment—*like the phoenix. I was reborn last night.*

A small nervous chuckle escaped her as more memories came. How she had felt like something was moving under her skin. How her back had burned and itched as if something was trying to burst from it. How his eyes had lit with passion, desire, and delight as he stared down at her. How something deep inside her was reaching out to touch...

My mate, the husky voice inside her whispered. *I want my mate.*

Carmen remained motionless, listening to the voice inside of her instead of to the giggles coming from Cara and Abby. She lowered her head so the others couldn't see the confusion in her eyes or notice when she closed them as she focused inward. She reached out again to see if what she had heard was imaginary or real.

I real, the voice purred. *Just like our babies.*

Carmen's eyes flew open, and her pulse sped up until she felt like she was about to hyperventilate. *Our what?* she choked out silently.

Our babies, the voice said with a satisfied sigh. *See, you look. You see me and our babies our mate gave us.*

Carmen let out a trembling breath and closed her eyes again. She focused deep inside her, unsure of what she was looking for or what to do. It was as if some invisible thread suddenly began to glow inside her mind. Images swirled, mixing and forming into a solid shape, becoming clearer the longer she focused.

The image of a beautiful, slender dragon in the colors of the phoenix on her back appeared. Shades of white blended with reds, pinks, and purples from the tip of her long, narrow snout down to her tail. Her wings were folded in close to her body.

Look closer, the husky voice said. *Look at our mate's gift to us.*

Carmen watched as one delicate wing lifted to reveal two tiny sparks of light. They were so small and fragile, but glowed with a strength that belied their size. They moved closer to each other and to the dragon curled protectively around them. Carmen could feel the tightness in her chest as she fought with a collage of emotions. She reached out with her mind to gently stroke the tiny sparks.

Will I be able to transform into a dragon like Abby? she asked her dragon with a trembling thought.

Silly, how else do I touch my mate if you no change! Her dragon said as she wrapped her wing around the two sparks again. *My mate as horny as yours. He not want to wait for long. You watch. He call to me.*

Carmen couldn't stop the nervous giggle that burst from her. She opened her eyes and stared at Abby again. Once she started she couldn't stop. The air filled with her giggles as happiness unlike anything she ever thought possible again filled her. All eyes whipped around to stare at her, unable to believe where the giggling was coming from.

Carmen wiped her eyes, trying to stop from laughing. "Oh, Abby, please teach us. I would love to be able to give someone else hell, and I'm sure I could think of a hundred different ways to do it in the form of a dragon," she said as images of Creon in his dragon form trying to catch up with her formed in her mind.

Soon, they were giggling and making up ways they could drive the men insane by switching between human and dragon and using the symbiots. Cara was the most creative, but Carmen came up with the most devious.

She could escape out the windows and fly down different levels or soar out over the ocean she had seen in the distance, or when he got bossy she could wrap her tail around him and hang him upside down over the balcony until he gave in. The list went on and on, each getting more ridiculous than the one before. When Zoran walked into the room a couple of hours later and found all five women in hysterics, he groaned loudly. Carmen looked at his face and burst out laughing even harder.

CHAPTER TWELVE

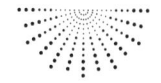

Creon ran an exhausted hand through his hair. They would be leaving in the morning. Mandra was taking Ariel with him to meet Adalard. Creon paused outside the door to his living quarters and looked at the group of men standing outside it. All of them were looking warily at him. It appeared his threat to personally gut any man who touched his mate had spread. Each one of them looked like they expected him to start carving away on them at any moment.

"Did she try to escape today?" he asked the first guard brave enough to look at him.

"No, my lord," the guard replied hesitantly. "She spent most of the day with the other females. She did not try to attack any of us."

He would have released a sigh of relief if it hadn't been for the hesitant pause in the guard's voice. Something had happened. A feeling of dread ran through him. There was no way she could know about him giving her— He looked at the door as a feeling of trepidation ran through him.

"What aren't you telling me?" he asked as his jaw tightened in determination.

The guard looked at a couple of the men standing near him, but they just looked up at the ceiling and put their hands behind their backs. He scowled at the cowards. They were leaving him to face the wrath of the young royal known to show no mercy when dealing with those who displeased him.

"It sounded like she was moving things around inside. We could not go in to make sure she was well. Every time we tried, she threatened to make sushi out of us," the guard said. "We were not sure what sushi was, but it sounded very dangerous. She said if she needed us she would ask for our help when hell froze over," the guard added. "We were not sure what that meant either, but decided she was well if she was yelling and threatening us."

Creon rubbed the back of his neck with a tired hand. She was not happy about something. He hoped she didn't find out about her friend, Trisha. He tried to think if there was any way she could have. Her friend had knocked out one of the guards with her and disappeared. His brother, Kelan, was beside himself. Something had been said or something happened when they were with their friend Abby. He should never have let her go! Everything was too new and strange for her.

Straightening his shoulders, he nodded to the guards, dismissing them. He would handle whatever was wrong. The last thing he wanted, though, was the warriors hearing him battling it out with his mate.

"You may all leave. I will handle this," he said gruffly, waiting until they had all left before he turned toward the doors of his living quarters.

Might as well get it over with, he thought in despair.

I can bite again, his dragon said hopefully.

NO! No, I think you've done enough. Let me handle it this time, Creon replied sternly.

You need bigger dragon's balls, his dragon muttered.

Fuck.

I know. Fuck me. I no want you, I want my mate. She more my type, his dragon drawled sarcastically.

Creon closed his eyes and counted to ten before he opened them and the door with determination. Ready or not, he was going to face his mate. He stepped into the darkened room and shut the door.

He hadn't taken more than three steps into the room when he felt something wrap around his ankles, lifting him up so rapidly he didn't have time to react. Before he knew it, he was hanging upside down, staring into a pair of glittering dark brown and gold eyes. A pair of very proud and very determined brown and gold eyes attached to an equally proud and determined female dragon who had white scales edged with reds, pinks, and purples. She twisted her neck and tilted her head until she was looking at him while he hung suspended in the air from her tail.

"You discovered your dragon," Creon said, fighting the grin, trying to break free as his mate looked at him as if wondering if she wanted to drop him on his head or gobble him up.

A puff of heated breath answered his observation. "I suspect you discovered more than your dragon," he murmured as she lifted him up higher so she could look him in the eye easier.

A low growl followed by a snort answered that observation as well. He eyed her warily as she turned her head to look around the room. His eyes followed hers. He saw that all the furniture had been pushed to one side, giving her more room to maneuver in her dragon form. He started getting a little nervous when she began swinging him back and forth.

"Carmen, I can explain," he started to say just before he felt himself going airborne.

He landed on his back on the plush couch with a soft thud. He stared up at the ceiling for a moment, trying to still both his heart and his head. Sitting up, he opened his mouth to try to calm his mate when she went rushing by him. Before he could say a word, she was gripping the balcony and pushing herself off. A roar of rage burst from him as his dragon responded to his mate's escape. He rolled off the couch, landing on all fours, shifting. With the skill of centuries behind him, he rushed through the large, open doors, jumping up onto the balcony and soaring after his mate.

∽

Exhilaration flowed through Carmen as she soared through the warm, night air. She breathed in deeply, picking up the scent of the ocean. She felt free, alive, and happy. She never thought she would ever feel this way again. She had spent the afternoon when she came back from visiting with Abby and the other girls trying to transform. She was too restless to rest even though she knew she should be exhausted from not enough sleep.

Instead, she had been more energized than she had been in the past three years. She had moved all the furniture to one side wanting to give herself enough room to change. The guards had driven her nuts with their constant knocking, wanting to know if she was okay, did she need anything, and wanting to know what was going behind the closed door. She had a sneaking suspicion that Creon had talked with them, or more like threatened them with bodily harm, if they so much as touched or upset her in any way.

It had taken a couple of tries, but before long she was able to transform. She had started out with just letting the scales run up and down her arms. It felt weird, but her dragon assured her it wouldn't hurt. After she finally gave in to her dragon, it was amazingly simple. Her body tingled and a warm rush flooded her. The next thing she knew, everything looked clearer, sharper, and smaller! It was a good thing she had moved the furniture, otherwise it would have gone flying when she tried to get a good look at her new body.

Her dragon had burst into low, husky coughs of laughter as she tried to grab her tail in her front claws. She ended up flipping herself until she was rolling on her back on the floor. Her wings were another source of amusement to her dragon as she kept holding them up so she could stare at them. She was beautiful!

She had practiced transforming back and forth until she felt comfortable. Then, she had started planning. She wasn't angry with Creon for not telling her what was happening to her.

Truthfully, it would have been the last thing on her mind and the least important. She would have agreed to anything once he touched her. A shaft of pleasure so intense it felt almost like pain moved through her as she remembered the incredible things he did to her.

No, she had no regrets. She had finally learned life was too short to have them, much less dwell on them. She had been doing that for the past three years, and all it had brought her was more heartache.

Instead, she decided to focus on today. She opened her wings wide enjoying the feeling of freedom and the warm air circulating around her body. She was about to bank to the left when a shadow appeared out of the corner of her eye coming straight for her. She rolled, trying to see more, but it was too fast. Suddenly, something wrapped around her tail, twirling her upside down, and holding her suspended so that it could grip her upper and lower legs.

Now it is my turn to hold you, Creon said in a dark, husky voice.

Only if you promise to never let me go, Carmen replied in a trembling voice.

I not only promise, I swear on my life, he vowed as he pulled her even closer to his larger body.

Carmen relaxed against him, letting her wings hang down like veils under her. She lifted her head until she could rub it against his long, muscular neck. Both she and her dragon responded to the smooth texture and scent of their mate.

Her dragon moved closer, rubbing her belly against the larger male. Unable to resist, Carmen turned her head and ran a long, narrow tongue up Creon's throat and under his jaw. A low, deep rumbling sent waves of need through her.

I...love you, Creon, she said quietly. *I need you.*

Hold on to me, he said in a strained voice.

Carmen gripped his massive forearms with her smaller claws. She gasped as he swooped down. She couldn't see where he was taking them. She could only blindly trust that he would take care of her. His powerful wings moved with strong downward strokes as he neared a clearing on the high cliffs along the coast. He released her back legs, but kept her tail securely tethered to him with his longer one. He landed gently on a small grassy ledge, balancing on his back legs as he carefully laid Carmen's smaller body down under him.

Once she was lying quietly under his larger frame he released her front legs. He stood over her, looking down at her exposed belly. He could feel his dragon growing hard at the image of its mate's submissive pose.

The folds that covered his lower region parted, revealing his desire for his mate. His eyes blazed as he looked carefully around, scenting the air to make sure they were safe before he took her. He was a male in his prime and at his most dangerous now. Nothing would survive his fury if he or his mate were threatened.

He raised his head and let out a long, loud roar, warning any within hearing distance to stay away from the area. His eyes scanned the horizon, and he listened carefully before lowering his head to his mate. The blazing fires held in his eyes warned her it would be a long, hard coupling. The huge male's lips pulled back to reveal his long sharp teeth. A low, snarl was the only warning the smaller female got before those teeth clamped down on her slender neck, piercing the smooth scales and holding her in place as he lowered his body down over hers.

A series of husky coughs escaped the smaller female as the huge male above her slowly impaled her with his thick, long shaft. Her head tossed, trying to break the hold the male had on her as her body struggled to accept his hard shaft. The male, sensing his mate's attempt to break his hold and flee, surged forward with a low growl, biting down harder. Warm, fragrant blood spilled into his mouth, flowing over his tongue and down his throat. The taste was so rich and sweet Creon lost the little control he had over his dragon. The primitive need to mate and claim overcoming his deteriorating hold of civility. He was pure male at its most animalistic.

Carmen's smaller form writhed under the huge male. She stretched her neck, giving him better access to her slender column. Fire burned through her and into him as he held her down, drinking from her as he rocked harder, deeper, and faster.

He stretched his wings out, the claws in the center and at the ends, locking with hers until she was spread out underneath his massive body unable to resist. He pulled his tail upward forcing her lower body to rise up. The position drove him even deeper, pulling a long, low cry from her as he continued to drive into her over and over. Even as he swelled, locking their bodies together, he continued moving.

Creon! Carmen cried out as she felt the power of her dragon's climax all the way to her soul.

Creon's groan was the only sound he could get out as his own body, trapped deep inside his dragon responded to the male's taking of his mate. His mind shattered as the powerful release wrapped itself around him, pulling at his own essence buried deep inside the male.

The large male released his mate's neck as his body tightened until pleasure and pain became one. He jerked once more before his hot seed filled the smaller female locked to him. His head swung up until he looked at the stars glittering overhead, and he roared out his claim as his massive body shook over and over as he released his scent, his essence, his very soul into the delicate dragon trapped beneath him.

His body strained, muscles tight and bulging as the last of his seed poured out of him leaving him truly sated for the first time in his long, lonely life. Only then did he lower his head to gently lick at the wounds he had inflicted. He released her wings, letting her draw them close against her shivering body even as he tenderly wrapped his own wings around her.

He held his weight off her smaller form, waiting for the swelling in his cock to subside enough that he could pull out of her without harming her. His tail flickered back and forth, rubbing hers for comfort. Soft coughs escaped her as she came down from her orgasm.

You are so beautiful, Creon repeated over and over as his dragon caressed her neck with his tongue. *I love you so much, mi elila. You are the air I breathe, the light to my darkness. Now you know the fears I have. There are times when I cannot control my dragon. It is a constant battle. Can you forgive me? Can you forgive us?* he pleaded over and over.

The delicately shaped head of Carmen's dragon turned to stare up at her mate. She tenderly ran her long, silky tongue over his cheek and along his lips. Nuzzling him with her snout, she showed him through her touch that there was nothing to forgive.

I wouldn't want you any other way, Carmen said sleepily. *Hold me,* she whispered even as she fell into a light sleep.

CHAPTER THIRTEEN

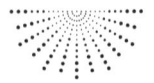

*C*armen nervously smoothed her hand down over her thighs again. She was more of an "on the ground" type of girl. Give her a motorcycle and she could run circles around anyone. She wasn't like her big sister who loved the idea of going up high or even into outer space. No, she liked it where the ground was close and the air around her was breathable.

She forced a shaky smile to her lips to show Creon she was fine. He must have known it was just an act. He carefully threaded his fingers through her tightly fisted hand, rubbing his thumb over the back as he continued talking to several men on board the shuttle with them. Carmen closed her eyes and focused on the meditation exercises that Connie had taught her. Breathe in, hold it for four, breathe out for four, do it four times. Carmen decided she was going to do it at least forty times instead. Hopefully by then they would be on board the *Horizon*. It was the Curizan warship disguised as a long-haul freighter using some type of cloaking device that made the outside of the ship look different than it was.

Creon had explained the Curizans were renowned for their technology and ingenuity. All she cared about was the damn thing didn't spring a leak in the middle of nowhere. She left the gadgets and stuff like that to Cara and the space travel and fast flying to Trisha and Ariel. All she wanted was wide open spaces and a fast bike under her ass. If she was feeling really adventurous, she would do it sans helmet. That was her idea of living dangerously.

"How much longer?" she choked out over the lump in her throat as a full-blown panic attack simmered inside her. "Maybe it would be better if I stayed behind. I could do some exploring and get more familiar with your world," she said hoarsely.

Creon turned with a dark scowl that dissipated when he saw the slight film of sweat beading her forehead, the pinch of her lips, and her almost translucent complexion. The shuttle bumped roughly as it exited the atmosphere of the planet. He would swear she turned even paler, if that were possible.

He tried to pull his hand free of hers so he could touch her. She held it in a grip so tight he could feel it going numb from the blood restriction. When she wouldn't release it, he used his other hand to tilt her chin so that she was forced to look into his eyes. He held her gaze until he could feel her beginning to relax slightly.

"Breathe," he murmured quietly.

"I am," she muttered on the verge of tears. "It's not working! I really think I should stay here. I don't want to go into outer space," she forced out, frustrated.

"We will be gone for many months. I cannot be away from you that long," Creon said, still maintaining eye contact with her. "Were you this frightened before? When you were aboard the *V'ager*?"

Carmen quickly shook her head. "I was pretty much dead when they brought me aboard," she whispered. "I really didn't think about it after that because it was like being on a big ship on the ocean, only with no windows for me to look out of, not to mention we were surrounded by aliens."

Creon's eyes narrowed at her mention of how close she had come to dying before he ever met her. He would have to remember to thank his brothers for their intervention. He could not imagine a life without her now. She was his world, and it distressed him that she was suffering so much because of him.

"I should have beamed us aboard," he cursed out under his breath.

"I wouldn't let you, remember?" Carmen said, squeezing his hand tighter. "I was afraid it would hurt the babies even though you said it wouldn't. I won't take a chance of losing them," she said, pulling in a steady breath. "I'll be okay. I'm just more of an on-the-ground type of girl, that's all."

"We will be on board the *Horizon* shortly," he reassured her. "The worst is behind us. It will be smooth now that we have broken through the atmosphere. Once on board, I will make sure I take you to our rooms so you may lie down for a little while. You have had a lot to deal with and little rest. You are also still too thin," he added with a stubborn thrust of his jaw.

She groaned and pressed a hand to her stomach. He had been trying to feed her continuously from the first day she arrived. A cart with food was always available in their living quarters, and he tried to check up on how much she ate throughout the day. He had grown even more persistent the last two days.

"Creon," she said, swaying in her seat. "I really, really don't think it would be a good idea to try to make me eat right now. Not unless you want to be wearing it."

He bit back a chuckle. If he had known taking her up into space would weaken her to the point she was a defenseless kitten he would have done it sooner. He focused on the gold symbiots wrapped around his wrists. He asked it to help his mate's motion sickness. A split second later, the gold around his wrists joined with hers and began moving. Tiny dots of gold appeared at her ears and around her neck, forming into a long chain that disappeared into the neckline of the silky black top she was wearing. He bit back a groan as the gold settled on the swell of her breasts, teasing him when she moved in her seat.

"Oh, *mi elila*," he groaned out huskily. "I hope you feel better later."

∼

A short time later, Creon glanced at Carmen to make sure she was doing better. He breathed a sigh of relief as she slowly relaxed back into him. The color in her face had returned once the vibrations of breaking through the atmosphere had quit. He had also included her in the discussions he was having with two of the warriors traveling with them in an effort to distract her. It appeared to be working as she listened carefully to the discussion, sometimes asking a clarifying question or two.

The two brothers were part of an elite team he had put together during the Great War. He knew he could depend on them to protect his mate with their lives. He also wanted her to get to know them and trust them as their responsibility was to make sure she was safe at all times. They would protect her when he could not be by her side. He refused to take a chance of anything happening to her or their younglings now that he had found her.

He had specifically picked the brothers for their deadly skills and loyalty. They were fast, fierce, and worked as if they were a single deadly fighting force. He had fought with them many times and valued their exceptional fighting skills. It was almost impossible to tell them apart. He had learned a long time ago to not even try. It had cost him more than one drink when he had been challenged to distinguish the brothers apart.

"So my lady, you do not care for space travel?" Cree asked with a polite smile. "Few females do."

Carmen raised her eyebrow at the slightly condescending tone. "It's not my thing. I prefer the power of a bike beneath me and wide open spaces. My sister and best friend love space travel, though. They were in the military back home and wanted to be a part of the space program there," she replied, studying each man carefully.

"Females in the military? You are joking, yes?" Calo asked using the same tone. "All warriors know that women are not made for fighting. They are made for pleasure."

Creon fought back a groan when he saw his mate's mouth thin and her eyes narrow at the unknown challenge. He had learned over the last few weeks that when she wore an expression like that, someone was bound to get hurt. He debated on whether he should correct the brothers, but decided that if they were going to help him protect his mate, then they needed to know what she was capable of doing. He almost changed his mind when Carmen ran one hand casually up along the front of her top until her fingers caressed her pale throat where the dragon's mark was clearly displayed.

A soft, sexy chuckle escaped her as she tilted her head to the side. "Would you be willing to put that to a test?" she asked innocently.

"Carmen," Creon growled out, suddenly having third, fourth, and fifth thoughts. "No, I forbid it."

She shrugged her shoulders and leaned back in her seat. "Okay. I wouldn't want to hurt them anyway," she said, smiling brightly at the two men across from her. "I know how 'fragile' Valdier warriors can be."

Calo laughed in amusement while Cree scowled. *"You* hurt *us?"* Cree muttered under his breath. "I'd like to see that!"

Calo chuckled again. "His mate has a good sense of humor. Who knows, we might need her to protect us on this trip, brother."

Creon's curse filled the shuttle. "I would not antagonize her if I were you!" he warned as he reached for her hand.

Carmen just sat quietly, listening and watching the brothers for the rest of the trip. She had been trained to look for the tiniest things that could be used against an opponent during the years she and Scott worked in security. She immediately discovered the difference between the brothers. Both had the same dark hair of the Valdier and gold-colored eyes. They both had the strong jaw line and proud features of the warriors, as well, not to mention the muscular build. One difference was the birthmark near the corners of their right eyes.

Cree's birthmark ran in a semi-circle ending at the corner. Calo's birthmark ended just before it. It was just a small difference, and most people would miss it, but it was there. Cree also used his left hand more than his right, was the quieter brother, the more thoughtful of the two, and had a habit of touching the knife at his side every few minutes.

Calo, on the other hand, used his right hand a little more, was more open, and his eyes constantly moved around as if checking to make sure nothing had changed. She knew exactly what she was going to do the minute they disembarked, and it wasn't going to be taking a nap.

Creon breathed a sigh of relief when the shuttle began its final approach for docking with the warship. He would whisk Carmen out of the shuttle and to their living quarters before anything happened. He had caught the calculating gleam in her eye and knew she would not forget or forgive what the two warriors across from them had said. The voice of the pilot came over their comlinks telling them docking was complete and they could remove their seat restraints. He reached over and undid Carmen's first.

"Don't," he whispered into her ear as he leaned across her. "They will learn."

"You're damn right they will," she whispered back fiercely before throwing an innocent smile at the two men.

"Dragon's balls!" he hissed out, knowing she was about to set two of his best warriors in their place.

∼

Carmen breathed a sigh of relief as they disembarked the shuttle. She could fully appreciate why some sailors of old would get down on their hands and knees and kiss the ground when they got off their ships. Granted, it was only a shuttle and she was now on an even bigger ship in space, but if her mind wanted to be in denial of that fact, she could handle that. She just didn't relish getting back inside something the size of a tin can and traveling into the great unknown and unbreathable!

The landing bay was filled with activity as supplies were unloaded and the shuttles moved and stored in preparation for the trip to the mining asteroids where they believed Vox was being held. According to the information she had listened to on the way up from the planet, there were three possible places he could have been taken, and they would need to check each one.

It sounded like the guy could handle himself if some of the stories the guys were telling was anything to go by. Anyway, they didn't really seem too worried about him. One mining area was on the outer edges of the Cardovus star system, which was the closest.

They would check that one first. If he was not there, they were going to stop at two different Spaceports before heading to the next one. Their biggest concern was whether an assassin had been sent to take care of him. If Vox was killed and rumors spread that the Curizan and Valdier had teamed up to do it, there would be another war. From the sound of it, that would have a devastating effect on both star systems, especially the Valdier.

Carmen moved closer to Creon as a very large male approached them. He looked like he could be a mean son of a bitch if he wanted to be. He was as tall as Creon and had that same dark edge to him—like he had seen and done things he had no regrets about doing. She stared back into his dark purple eyes, refusing to back down. A low growl escaped him at her challenge. Carmen smirked and raised her eyebrow.

"I thought you had a mate, Creon," the tall male said, looking Carmen up and down. "She looks little bigger than a child."

"Knock it off, Ha'ven," Creon growled out softly. "I know you are just trying to rile her to see what she will do, but I will not let you insult her to do so."

Ha'ven threw Creon a pained look. "I was hoping to see if your mate had the fire in her that you mentioned. She looks more like a kitten for Vox to play with."

Cree and Calo chuckled. Carmen let the smile stay on her face. If they wanted to see her as a kitten, then so be it. She was about to show them that this kitten had very sharp claws and a wicked tail.

Moving rapidly, she swung around, snatching Cree's knife out of its sheath while throwing a kick to Calo's jaw before swiveling in a graceful arch and knocking Cree's feet out from under him. She wasn't through with them either. In seconds, she had Ha'ven hanging upside down by his feet from her tail. She flashed a toothy grin at Ha'ven before she swung him into the two brothers who were climbing to their feet, their mouths hanging open for the briefest moment before they caught the full body of the large warrior across their chests.

Before they could get up, Carmen sat her white, red, pink, and purple self down on top of them. Maybe she wasn't a kitten after all but a big dog, because she was definitely the queen of this dog pile! None of the men could get up unless she did. She gripped the razor-sharp knife in her front claw. Bending down so she was staring down at all three faces with a grin, she sliced a small strand of hair from each of the men's heads before puffing out a small ring of smoke around them.

"I think you have proven your point, Carmen," Creon said, standing back with his arms folded across his chest, chuckling. "I am not so sure Calo can breathe. He looks like he is turning a funny shade of blue."

Carmen turned her head briefly to look at her mate. She snorted before slowly rising, making sure she "knocked" into a few delicate body parts as she did. Seconds later, a pair of strong arms surrounded her two-legged form. She held Cree's knife in one slender hand and three different lengths of hair in the other. They were her prizes, and she wasn't giving them back.

"Meow," Carmen said, her eyes glittering with humor and challenge as she looked at the three men now standing warily in front of her.

Ha'ven rubbed his crotch with his hand. She had kneed him as she was getting up, and it was throbbing painfully. He studied the female again with a new appreciation. She was fast, resourceful, and had a wicked sense of humor. He decided then and there he wanted one of his own.

"What species did you say she is?" he asked curiously, enjoying the soft brown of her eyes, her pale, delicate skin, sun-ripe hair, and full lips, not to mention the rest of her body.

In a flash, Carmen was pushed behind Creon's massive body, and he was snarling. Black scales rippled over his body and he partially shifted. He moved forward until he was mere inches from the other man's face.

"She is mine!" he snarled out. "Remember that or I will remind you."

Ha'ven's eyes narrowed as he studied the infuriated male in front of him. "I would protect your mate with my life, my friend. I have no desire to take what is yours. You have deserved this blessing for too long," he said quietly. "But I wouldn't mind finding one for myself," he added with a small, mischievous grin.

Creon stared intently into his friend's eyes. All he could see was the truthfulness behind his statement. With a quiet word to his dragon, he stepped back and took several deep breaths to calm both his dragon and himself. Gradually, he relaxed enough to nod his understanding.

"We are still very protective of her," he muttered to his friend.

Cree and Calo came up to stand next to them. The other warriors who had paused to watch the little show Carmen put on and Creon's reaction to it slowly went back to work. Calo put his arm around his brother's shoulder and laughed.

"From the looks of it, she is the one who could do the protecting!" he said with an amused laugh. "Can I have my knife back now, little kitten?"

Carmen raised her eyebrow and smirked as she stepped forward to stand next to her mate. "It's not yours, Calo. It belonged to Cree. Now, it belongs to me," she said before turning to Cree. "I can use it when I have to protect both of your asses."

Ha'ven's laugh echoed through the docking bay. Cree and Calo stood with their mouths hanging open again and looking on in astonishment as Creon put a possessive hand on his mate's lower back and guided her toward one of the exits. Both brothers stood frozen until they realized they were being left behind.

"I want to find one for us too," Cree muttered under his breath to his twin as he strode after the sexy, swaying ass of the female they had been assigned to protect.

"Do you think her species could handle two of us together?" Calo asked in wonder.

Cree's eyes suddenly lit up with fire. "I think the question is going to be if the two of us can handle the one female!"

CHAPTER FOURTEEN

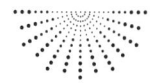

Carmen placed her hands on Creon's cheeks and pulled his head down to hers. She pressed her lips against his, kissing him deeply before pulling back, out of breath. His eyes were blazing with desire as he stared down at her.

"I heard you the first, second, third, fourth—" She couldn't go on because he was kissing her again.

It had been two weeks since they left Valdier, and they were no closer to finding Vox than they had been before. The mining area they visited first was abandoned by the Antrox, but they had not taken everything when they moved on.

The Antrox had left an old man and one young boy behind when they left. Carmen's heart went out to them. They were human. They had been taken over four years before from Earth.

According to the account Creon gave her, the man was no longer considered viable as he could not produce enough work each day to justify his food. They had been left with only a few supplies and one young pactor too lame to work. The old human said the boy was his grandson. The boy had escaped, hiding in the tunnels so he couldn't be separated from his grandfather. From what the old man told Ha'ven and Creon, the boy had been responsible for taking care of the pactors.

Creon reluctantly broke the kiss and leaned his forehead against hers. "Perhaps you can speak with the old man and the boy today. It might make life more comfortable for everyone. The boy wouldn't leave the pactor in the mines. He refused to come out of the tunnels until we promised he could bring it with them. Why he has grown attached to the ugly beast, I'll never understand. He has a way with the creature, though. It follows him everywhere.

The old man and boy have refused to interact with anyone either. The old man has a foul mouth on him. He won't let anyone near the boy, saying he is mentally unable to understand what is being said. He also said the boy was a mute. At least, that was the reason he gave for keeping the boy away from everyone.

He refused medical assistance for the both of them. Tandor didn't push it as they both seemed fine, and the initial scans when they were brought aboard didn't flag any disease or illness. Still, they are being very uncooperative," Creon said huskily. "Perhaps they would be more receptive to our assistance if you were to talk with them."

"I can try," Carmen replied, pulling away so she could pull on her clothes. "You can hardly blame them. Look at what they have had to endure for the past four years. They've been ripped away from everything and everyone they have ever known and used as slaves. This goes against everything we believe in."

"It has been over a week since we brought them aboard. We have tried to assure them that things will be better. Ha'ven finally ended up sectioning off one of the repair bays. The old man, boy, and pactor are using it as their living quarters," he said, distractedly watching as she reached for her clothes lying on the floor where he had tossed them earlier. "I like you better the way you are," he added huskily, his eyes glued to her rounded ass.

Carmen threw an amused look over her shoulder as she bent over to pick up her pants that he had taken off her. She bit back a chuckle when she heard him groan loudly. It was becoming a bad habit of his to try to keep her naked. She was learning that if she wanted to leave their living quarters on board the *Horizon*, she'd better do it before he got out of the cleansing unit or she wouldn't make it out until much later.

"What level are they on?" Carmen asked as she slipped the pants on.

"First...come here," Creon demanded huskily.

Carmen laughed as she picked up his shirt and threw it in his face. "No, if I do neither one of us will be leaving. I thought you had a meeting with Ha'ven and were going to talk with your brothers."

A heavy sigh was the answer to her reminder. "Shit! I forgot. You are too much of a distraction for me, *mi elila*," he replied at the same time as his comlink sounded.

"Creon?" Ha'ven growled out in annoyance. "Where in the dragon's balls are you? There has been a situation on Valdier. *Tilkmos* and that damn kid are causing problems again. He went after a couple of warriors with a shovel when they entered the repair bay to get some parts. We should have just left all three of their asses at the mine! The old man is just as bad."

"You go see what happened," Carmen said as she brushed a kiss over her mate's lips. "I'll go take care of the old man and the boy."

Creon reached out and gripped her hand tightly for a moment, looking at her intently. "Cree or Calo will go with you. I will not take a chance of them attacking you."

She paused for a second, about to argue before seeing he was genuinely worried. "Okay. Tell them to meet me outside the repair bay."

"Thank you," he said, brushing his fingers down along her cheek. "I love you, *mi elila*, so very much."

Carmen's eyes darkened with emotion. She cupped his hand and held it tightly against her skin. Tears burned her eyes at the intense emotion glittering in his. She could understand it. Those same feelings were coursing through her. She never thought she would have a second chance, and she was afraid something would take it away from her.

"I love you, too," she whispered, staring up into his beautiful golden eyes with a haunted look. "Sometimes I get so afraid this is a dream and I'll wake up."

He pulled her against him, wrapping his arms around her and

holding her tightly. "Then, I am having the same dream. One I never want to awaken from," he replied gruffly.

~

Creon eye's burned with rage as he listened to Zoran. Their mates had been attacked. They were able to rescue Abby before she was taken, but both Cara and Trisha had not fared so well. On top of that, the devastating news that his uncle now had a weapon powerful enough to destroy a symbiot was horrifying. Zoran coldly related the deaths of the guards and their symbiots.

He explained their findings, but as yet they were not sure what was powerful enough to destroy something made of pure energy. Trelon and Kelan were leading the attack on a Curizan warship that Trelon's symbiot was following. He would keep them informed when they retrieved Cara and Trisha. Zoran refused to believe that the two women would not be returned safely.

"Who took them?" Creon asked harshly, staring out the viewport in the conference room.

"N'tasha was behind it," Zoran answered in a deadly cold voice. "If Kelan or Trelon do not kill her, I will. She has committed a hideous crime against her people. I want to know every traitor who is in league with Raffvin."

"We are headed to Kardosa Spaceport," Creon said. "Vox was not at the first mining operation. It had been abandoned. Ha'ven and I have some contacts on Kardosa who may know which one he has been taken to. I worry Raffvin may send word to go ahead and assassinate him."

"Watch yourself," Zoran warned. "He is getting desperate, and if he now has a weapon capable of such atrocities as killing our symbiots, he is even more dangerous than we originally thought."

"Have you heard from Mandra and Adalard?" Ha'ven asked from where he was seated at the long conference table. "They should have met up by now."

"Yes," Zoran replied. "They met up with him earlier today. Adalard has an informant who knows where Raffvin's main base is hidden.

They are traveling to meet up with him. If they have a way to stop Raffvin, they will proceed with their attack. If Raffvin suspects anything, he will order Vox's execution immediately to inflame his brothers and the warriors of Sarafin. We could well have a war on our hands."

"Did you warn Mandra of the weapon Raffvin has?" Creon asked in concern. "It is too dangerous for him and Adalard to go after him alone."

"Mandra is aware of what happened and will use his best judgment. It may be the only time we have a chance against Raffvin. He will not proceed unless he is sure he can defeat him. He would not risk his life or that of his mate," Zoran assured his youngest brother.

"Remember also he is not alone. Adalard can be deadly," Ha'ven said with pride of his younger sibling. "He already has a reason to want Raffvin's head mounted on his wall. He will stand by your brother."

"Then, we continue on our course to Kardosa unless things change," Creon replied heavily. "Inform me as soon as the women have been rescued. I will contact Mandra and discuss backing him up should they find Raffvin."

"Stay strong and fight well, brother," Zoran said, quoting their farewell during times of battle.

"You too, brother," Creon said before signing off. He turned to stare at Ha'ven. "We need to find Vox as soon as possible and back Mandra up. I have a bad feeling Raffvin is going to do everything he can to kill him once he finds out we have joined forces instead of declaring war."

The grim expression on Ha'ven's face showed he agreed. "We will split up on Kardosa and see what we can learn. I worry about your brothers' mates. If he is successful in killing one or both of them…" his voice faded away as both of them realized the grim possibility that Creon and Valdier could lose two of their most valuable warriors.

Creon's jaw tightened. "It will not happen. Let's go over what we do know. It will help narrow our search."

Carmen looked at Cree and rolled her eyes. He tried to insist he was Calo at first, but finally gave up when she shook her head in disgust. It was actually fun watching him try to figure out how she could tell them apart. She refused to tell him which just made him even more aggravated. As it was, he refused to let her enter the repair bay first.

"You are under my protection," he insisted, trying to hold his temper when she just looked at him with a raised eyebrow. "Creon said as much," he added defensively, not knowing what else to say.

"Whatever," Carmen replied and pressed the control panel. "If it makes your big-boy britches feel better, be my guest. I can always drag your ass out if you get hurt."

"I would like to show you my…" he started before biting back a curse. "What I mean is…"

Carmen almost felt sorry for him… almost. "Go on. I know exactly what you were going to say," she chuckled out, enjoying how his cheeks turned a darker red.

She watched as he moved cautiously into the repair bay. He called out to the old man that he had brought a visitor. It was only when Cree saw the old man nod to him as he was coming out of the side room set up for their use that he stepped to one side to allow Carmen to enter.

"I don't see the boy," he muttered as she passed him. "Keep your eyes out. They say he isn't right in the head."

"I'll make sure I squeal like a girl if I see him. I'm sure that will make him feel better too," she responded.

"Smart ass. He is mute. He wouldn't hear you if you did," Cree bit out arrogantly.

Carmen shook her head. She wasn't going to correct Cree's misunderstanding. Mute meant the boy couldn't talk, not that he couldn't hear. She looked at the old man who was staring at her in concern. He moved forward, grabbing the shovel as he did.

Cree reached out to grab Carmen's arm and pull her behind him, but she ducked and twisted before he could, stepping away from him. She gave a warm smile to the man walking toward her. He looked to be in his mid-to-late sixties, though it was hard to tell from the wrinkles lining his face. His eyes were sharp, and he kept his gaze not on her but on Cree.

"He's really a gentle pansy," she said as she stretched her hand out in greeting. "My name is Carmen Walker. I'm originally from Wyoming."

The man stopped in front of her. He kept a firm hold on the shovel, but had lowered it so it rested against his right side. He wiped his left hand down along his tattered pant leg before he slowly reached out and grasped her hand in a firm but gentle hold.

"Cal Turner," he replied. "Me and the boy are from outside Clayton, Georgia."

Carmen let him hold her hand a little longer than was normal. It was almost as if he was afraid if he let go she would disappear. She squeezed his hand to let him know she understood.

"Would you mind if we sat for a spell?" she asked quietly. "Cree will be a good boy and stay by the door if it makes you more comfortable."

She chuckled when she heard Cree growl softly under his breath. "I'd like to show you—" He broke off with another curse and just glared at her back.

"He's huffing and puffing, isn't he?" she asked in an exaggerated whisper and winked at Cal. "They do that a lot, but they really are like overgrown puppy dogs."

Cree snarled again and folded his arms across his massive chest. The door opened beside him, and Creon's symbiot came through the door in the shape of an overgrown basset hound. This time its ears were exaggerated to the point they really did drag on the ground, and it tripped over one of them.

A soft giggle broke the sound of the repair bay. Carmen, Cal, Harvey, and Cree all turned toward it, startled. Harvey shook, causing his big ears to fly up into the air around him before he bounded over to the slender shape of the boy half hidden behind a strange creature about the size of a Shetland pony.

The figure quickly disappeared again before Carmen had a chance to get a good look at him. She turned, startled, when she heard a deep rumbling coming from Cree. Turning, she was shocked to see his eyes glued in the direction of the boy. His dark gold eyes had flames in them, and he looked like he was having problems with his dragon.

Carmen turned to see what he was looking at. He seemed to be focused on the young pactor. Perhaps his dragon thought it was lunch. Whatever was going on, it was making it difficult to convince the man standing in front of her he meant no harm as long as he was letting out a low, rumbling growl.

"Cree," Carmen called out sternly. "Could you please wait for me outside? I promise if I need you, I'll call. I have Harvey with me so I feel perfectly safe."

Cree's eyes were still glued to the pactor. He was panting and sweating profusely now. She had to call him several times before he reluctantly turned his eyes to look at her. With a pained look twisting his features, he gave a sharp nod of agreement and left, surprising her.

"Well, I guess his dragon likes pactors," she muttered. Turning back around, she shook her head in confusion. "Men! I don't care what planet they are from, I don't think I'll ever understand them."

Cal chuckled, lowering his shovel again. "I don't know about you, but I could use a hot cup of coffee. I couldn't believe it when they showed it to me. I thought I had died and gone to heaven."

Carmen laughed. "You and me both. Actually, they didn't have it until my friend, Cara, replicated it. She is bouncy enough normally, but by the time she had perfected it, I thought they could have powered a dozen warships with her energy."

Cal turned and looked at Carmen carefully. "They aren't abusing you and your friend, are they? You can stay with me and Mel if you want. We'll protect you."

Carmen laid her hand on Cal's forearm and squeezed it. "No, they have never abused any of us. In fact, I would be dead now if not for them. If you would share your coffee with me, I'll tell you the story of me, my sister, and our friends. It has turned out to be a really incredible one," she promised, waiting for him to decide if she was telling the truth or not.

CHAPTER FIFTEEN

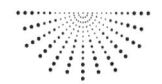

*L*ater that evening, Carmen sat on the edge of the bed waiting for Creon to tell her what was bothering him. He had come back later than usual and was very quiet. She watched him carefully as he came toward her. Dark lines of worry were etched around his mouth and his eyes held the distracted look in them she had seen in Scott's before a difficult mission.

"Tell me," she said quietly, running her hands over his smooth shoulders. "What happened?"

Creon looked away. Carmen knew he was weighing whether to tell her part of the truth or nothing at all. She pushed him back until he was lying down and nudged him to let him know she wanted him to roll over. He grunted, but did as she wanted.

Once he was lying flat on his stomach, she climbed on top of him, straddling his waist. Starting out slowly, she began massaging his massive shoulders, working on the tight knots of tension in them. A low, rumbling vibration, similar to a cat's purring, began as she used her strong fingers to relax him.

Bending over so she could whisper in his ear, she asked him again, "Please tell me. I need to know the truth about what is going on."

Creon rested his head on his bent arm. Her fingers working into his muscles could be described as nothing short of bliss. He appreciated that she didn't try to pressure him with tears and tantrums. She waited calmly, as if she knew he just needed a few minutes to get his thoughts in order.

"Cara and Trisha have been taken. N'tasha, one of the women at the palace, was behind the attack. She was one of Trelon's lovers before he met his mate. They tried to take Abby, but one of the guards was able to intercept the man holding her before they could transport off the planet," he began quietly.

"Do your brothers know where they might have been taken?" she asked, keeping her voice calm even as her heart beat with fear for her two friends.

"Cara had a piece of Trelon's symbiot on her. It was sending signals to the symbiot left behind. They are pursuing them and should intercept them at any time," he replied huskily.

"But…" she prompted.

Creon tiredly rubbed his forehead against his arm. "Raffvin has a weapon unlike anything we have ever known before. It is powerful enough to kill a symbiot, something we thought impossible to do."

Carmen froze for a moment before forcing herself to continue. "Did he use it against your brothers' symbiots?" she asked tightly thinking of how horrible it would be if something bad were to happen to Harvey.

He let out a deep sigh. "Yes and no. Two of the guards protecting Trisha and their symbiots were killed. Trisha was wearing a small amount of Kelan's symbiot. What was left of it was found in their bed where she had been resting," he told her heavily.

"Do…" she began before her throat tightened in fear for Trisha. "Do they think she was killed as well?" she asked hoarsely as her hands clenched against the hot skin of his back, waiting.

He rolled over so swiftly she found herself sitting on his stomach instead of his back. He gripped both of her clenched fists tightly in his hands. "No!" he said firmly. "She is not dead. Kelan would know immediately if she had been killed. He would feel it all the way down to his soul. There was no blood. They believe she was taken alive. They will find her. Kelan will never give up looking for her," he stressed, forcing her to look into his eyes so she could see that he was telling her the truth.

"She doesn't deserve this," Carmen whispered. "She has been through so much already. Why would they take her? What could they possibly want with her?"

"Raffvin knows that to kill our mates is a death sentence for us," he replied hoarsely, looking into her beautiful brown eyes. "You are our greatest strength and our greatest weakness. We cannot survive for long if you are taken from us. Our dragons would mourn, our symbiots would lose the essence they need to survive away from the hive, and I…" He paused and took a deep breath. "I could not live with the emptiness of a life without you."

Carmen nodded as she looked down into his tortured face. "I know what you are talking about. I know what it feels like to lose something so precious that the emptiness eats away at your will to live," she whispered brokenly.

A low groan was pulled from him at the pain and grief in his mate's eyes and voice as she remembered her past life and losses. It tore at him that she should ever have to remember such overwhelming grief. He pulled her down to him, crushing his lips against hers in a desperate kiss of need and fear.

"I would take your pain away if I could," he said with a shudder. "I would give you only happy thoughts and feelings forever."

Carmen pulled back to look down at him. "You have. You have taken the pain and emptiness and filled it with light, love, and hope. You promised me forever, Creon. I want every second of that time," she said, tenderly brushing her hand down over his hair and laying it against his cheek.

He turned his head enough so he could press a kiss into her palm. "I would give you nothing less," he replied before pulling her back down and making slow, tender love to her.

Creon looked down at Carmen again as he pulled her closer to him. He was torn between locking her in their living quarters on board the *Horizon* or tying her to his side where he could see her at all times. Instead, he was doing neither. His gaze moved to Cree and Calo where they stood in the corner of the large lift with their symbiots. He had given them strict instructions that they were to stay at his mate's side as if they were a part of her. Harvey was going to be with them as well.

"You will listen to Calo and Cree," he murmured as the lift started.

They had arrived on Kardosa a couple of hours ago. He and Ha'ven were going to split up and meet with several different informants they had on the spaceport. Carmen was too unusual not to draw unwanted attention to them. Her fair complexion and unusual looks had already caught the attention of all the crew members aboard the *Horizon*. Luckily, the warriors aboard knew better than to mess with the mate of a Valdier dragon, much less the mate of one of the princes.

"I will," she responded calmly, trying not to let her excitement show. "I am to stay in their sight at all times, not wander off, and if they tell me to do anything, then I am to do it immediately," she said, reciting his instructions verbatim.

He tilted her head so he could look into her eyes. "Promise?"

"Of course… I'll try," she said mischievously. "Who knows, I may have to save their asses! Besides, I won't be alone. Mel and Cal are meeting up with us. They both need some supplies, and it will give me a chance to spend some time with them. Mel still won't come near me. He seems to be curious about me, though. Cal wants to see a real spaceport. They have been locked up for the past four years, then on the *Horizon*. I think it will be good for the both of them to get out. It might help Mel, too."

"He better not attack anyone, or I'll leave his ass here. He started throwing things at Yar yesterday when he went to get some parts for one of the engines," Creon scowled fiercely. "I won't have that youngling hurting you."

"He won't. He's always kept his distance when I visit with Cal. I know he understands what is going on as he listens in to our conversations. I think he is just young and scared," she reassured him. "Don't worry. I'll have Harvey and the Bobbsey Twins with me."

"One of these days," Cree muttered under his breath from behind her at her teasing taunt.

"Yes, I know. 'One of these days, Carmen! *POW!* Right in the kisser,'" she said, changing her voice to sound like Jackie Gleason before she broke down in giggles, feeling young and free and wild again.

Creon's eyes widened at the excitement burning in his mate's eyes. She was having fun! This was the first time he had seen her eyes completely clear of shadows. She was…glowing. His throat tightened at how truly, breathtakingly beautiful she was when she was smiling and happy. He was unable to resist pulling her against him and running his hand down over her flat stomach. Soon, it would start to swell with their younglings.

Closing his eyes briefly, he reached out from the symbiot wrapped around his wrists to the ones on her to connect. He searched deep inside her until he found her dragon curled tightly around the tiny sparks of life inside her. Her dragon opened her wing as soon as she sensed her mate's search. Warmth flooded him as he focused on the twin beacons. He felt their response to his light touch.

He withdrew as he felt the lift slowing to a halt. Opening his eyes, he glared down at her with a combination of pride and possession. He watched as her eyes crinkled and her lips curved in a knowing smile as she acknowledged she belonged to him.

"Forever," she whispered before the doors opened and the crowded streets of Kardosa forced them to separate.

∼

Creon watched Carmen head off eagerly into the crowd, Harvey in the shape of the droopy-eared creature trotting next to her while Cree and Calo, and their symbiots in the shape of twin Werecats, followed closely behind. His jaw hurt from clenching it so tightly in an effort to hold back his demand that she return to his side. A dark frown twisted his features when he lost sight of her.

"She is in good hands, my friend," Ha'ven said quietly. "Let us find the information that we came for so you can be reunited with her."

"I swear on my life, Ha'ven," Creon muttered darkly. "When I find my uncle, I am going to gut him. He has caused too much grief to be given even the privilege of a warrior's death."

"I agree. But first, we must find Vox," Ha'ven gently reminded his friend. "You have to admit it will be a lot of fun watching Vox's face when we rescue his sorry ass."

Creon grunted, fighting the urge to charge through the crowd after his mate. "Let us finish this. I want to take my mate somewhere I know she will be safe."

Creon turned and strode off, blending into the crowded streets. He would find Devnar first. He was a Toluskin, a thick-hided beast with two legs and four arms. Devnar owned a parts and recovery business dealing in legal and illegal equipment. Anyone who needed a part for their transport went through him.

He dealt with a few honest freighter captains, a couple of honest military personnel, and a lot of dishonest ones, not to mention the wide assortment of space pirates who visited the Spaceport. He also never forgot a conversation or a face, which made him better than any holovid feed.

He moved through the crowded streets easily as most patrons took one look at him and gave him plenty of room. He kept one hand on the short sword on his hip and the other on the laser pistol gripped tightly in his hand. His long black hair was tied back at his nape. He wore the typical uniform of black leather pants and vest with a black undershirt. He had several knives hidden around his body, including two in each low-cut boot. This was a world he was very familiar with, and he knew better than to let his guard down.

Turning down a narrow alley, he glanced at a couple of Marastin Dow, a slim, purple species that were known space pirates. They followed no star system's rules. Their own world was a deadly maze of murderers, thieves, and cutthroats. Their young were taught early that life was either kill or be killed. In fact, the males and females were given the same training in the art of piracy. He had been to their world several times and had no desire to ever go again.

Creon ignored them, knowing they were primarily scavengers and would never attack a full-grown Valdier dragon warrior unless they were in a large group. They preferred sneaking up on their opponents and slitting their throats. He turned down several more alleys before he came back out onto a larger thoroughfare near the lesser-kept docking berths.

He paused to look around carefully. He knew he was being followed. He could feel it and so could his dragon. It was pacing back and forth in agitation.

I feel it too, my friend, he said silently. *Patience—they will show themselves soon enough.*

I kill, his dragon snarled angrily.

Only after we get the information we want, Creon assured his more temperamental self.

He pushed through the partially opened door, listening as a chime sounded to let Devnar know he had company. The huge round body of the Toluskin had to turn sideways to get through the back door of the small shop. The shop was dimly lit, but that was not a problem for Creon as he called his dragon to the surface. His eyes narrowed into long slits and glowed a dark, rich gold.

"You know, I could get good credits for those eyes of yours," Devnar snorted out.

"Credits are of no use to a dead man, Devnar," Creon replied as a return greeting.

Devnar's deep laugh caused his whole body to move. The leathery, dark orange and gray skin rippled as he crept closer to the narrow counter separating the front from the back. He leaned two of his arms on the counter while keeping the other two hidden below the scarred surface of it.

"What can old Devnar do for a Valdier dragon prince?" Devnar snorted out in a thick-accented voice. "You ever want to join the fight rings, I can get you some good opponents. I could do sixty/forty with you. Best offer I've ever made to anyone."

"The first thing you can do is raise your other two arms up above the counter before I remove the ones resting on it. I have no desire to harm you, my old friend, but I have little patience right now," Creon said, pulling his short sword out of its sheath partway.

Devnar snorted several times, but slowly raised his other two arms, resting all four on the counter. "Now you know old Devnar knows better than to mess with you. I owe you a life debt," he responded, leaning heavily against the counter. "You tell Devnar what you want, and I'll get it for you."

"You owe me three life debts, you old thief," Creon grunted out, moving closer. "I don't need parts, I need information. I know if anyone talked you would hear about it."

Devnar nodded. "What information do you need? There is much talk going on. This have anything to do with the disappearance of a certain hot-headed, stubborn cat prince?"

Creon's lips twisted at Devnar's description of Vox. "You aren't still upset with him, are you? He did save your life from that Bovdean assassin."

"Yeah, he did, but I've got cat claw marks across my ass from him grabbing me and pulling me under that damn shuttle. The missus wasn't happy with me. She thought I had been to the pleasure house and got caught by a Sarafin warrior working over his woman. Took me almost a month to get her to quit throwing things at me," Devnar snorted out angrily.

Creon shrugged. "Be thankful it was your ass he grabbed and not something else. What have you heard?"

"I heard your uncle has decided he wants control of the Valdier star system, preferably without the current royals alive, that is except for a beautiful Valdier princess. I never heard the name, but he did say something about she should have been his instead of his brother's mate. I am assuming you will know who he was talking about?" Devnar asked, rubbing two of his hands together while one of the others scratched his ass.

"You heard this from him directly?" Creon asked, staring into the beady black eyes.

One hand came up to rub the back of his thick neck. "Well, not exactly from him. I heard it from a man who was talking to another man who was working on a ship that heard a couple of the crewmen on board the *Mortar*, one of the warships your uncle is known to use, talking about it," he responded with a shrug.

Creon fought the urge to grind his teeth together in frustration. "What else did you hear?"

"The *Mortar* was taking a hot-headed prince and two of his men to the Antrox mining asteroid between the Quillar moons of Bosca and Dorland. They were going to have the Antrox work him until they sent notice that he was to be terminated. They were giving the damn insects three times the credits just to keep him." Devnar grinned, if one could call the twist of his thick lips a grin. "I heard he killed three of the security force members guarding him before they knocked his ass out again. The captain ordered him and his men to be kept sedated until they were turned over to the Antrox. I bet his furry ass is royally pissed!" Devnar's belly rolled again. "Do you get it? Furry royal ass! Damn, sometimes I'm good."

Creon shook his head in disgust at the Toluskin's obvious enjoyment of Vox's situation. "Have you heard anything else?" he asked, ready to be done with the Toluskin and get back to the ship.

"Just for you to watch your back, dragon," Devnar said, suddenly very serious. "Your uncle has a new weapon the crew was bragging about that can kill a Valdier warrior, his dragon, and his symbiot. That is a weapon a hundred star systems would pay a king's treasure of credits for."

"Have you heard what the weapon is?" Creon asked tersely.

Devnar was shaking his head. "Nope, the bastard is keeping it close to his chest. The crew doesn't even know what it is, just that it works."

"Thank you, my friend," Creon said, turning to leave. "You only owe me two life debts now. Your help is appreciated. Watch your own back until this is settled," he added with caution before he turned back toward the door again.

Devnar called out as Creon reached the doorway. "You just tell that damn cat shifter that my debt to him is paid. I would rather owe you than him."

Creon nodded his head in agreement before he walked out of the door. He turned the opposite way from which he'd come. He wanted to know who was following him, and he wanted answers to what his uncle was up to next. He strode down the crowded street, stepping off a narrow walkway before ducking into a covered doorway. His eyes scanned the crowd, focusing in on a dark-green-and-brown-scaled reptilian species often hired for their skills as an assassin.

There! His dragon hissed out in anger.

You know what to do, my friend, Creon muttered darkly.

Yes! His dragon growled out, licking its lips in anticipation.

CHAPTER SIXTEEN

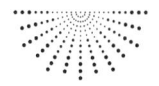

*C*armen grinned at the merchant, who was trying to catch her attention with a large collection of brightly colored beads. She laughed when he put his small hands together as if begging for her to come shop at his stand. She kept her eyes scanning the crowds and stands in the marketplace. One of the older warriors who worked in the food service area on board the *Horizon* had become friends with Cal and he promised to escort Cal and Mel to the market so they could meet up.

Harvey saw them before Carmen did. The huge gold symbiot bounced up to Mel, circling the boy over and over before sitting down so he could bend down and rub on him. The boy kept his head down, and a huge hat covered his head. Carmen still hadn't seen Mel's face. The boy was extremely shy. He never came close when she came to visit, preferring to stay with the small pactor that he was caring for or hidden in the maze of huge crates stored in the repair bay.

She didn't know who was more surprised, her or Cree and Calo, when their two symbiots suddenly rushed to the boy who was kneeling down. Both symbiots brushed up against him, pushing for some of the attention he was giving to Harvey. She watched as the boy, who kept his head tilted down, rubbed his hands up and down both symbiots affectionately.

"Carmen, it is good to see you," Cal said with a wide grin and a soft southern drawl, drawing her attention back to him. "Zuk has been showing us around. We left the ship as soon as it docked so we could get a few things Mel and I needed. Have you eaten? Zuk was saying there is a good place not far from here."

"No. We've been exploring. Isn't this just totally mind-blowing? I mean, I saw alien movies back home, but to see them in real life is like… so different than I was expecting!" Carmen said as she watched several creatures that were obviously women walk by them, staring at her with just as much interest as she had staring at them.

"If you permit me, my lady, it would be a pleasure to escort you, Cal, and Mel to grab a bite to eat," Zuk said politely making sure he had Cree and Calo's permission as well.

"Thank you, Zuk," Carmen replied, looking over to where Mel was still kneeling with the three symbiots surrounding him. "Cal, do you think Mel would mind if we joined you?"

Cal turned to look hesitantly down at his grandson before he turned back and stared at the two men behind Carmen. "Yeah, Mel will be fine. Just make sure that those two stay back or it might spook him. He doesn't like being out here and is jumpy as hell as it is. Maybe your gold friends there can sit with him. They seem to have a calming effect on the boy."

Carmen smiled in understanding. "That would be fine," Carmen replied in relief.

The small group moved slowly through the marketplace, down the street and finally up two levels. Mel followed behind them all with Harvey and the twin werecats by his side. He made sure to keep a wide distance from Cree and Calo, who kept turning around and frowning back at him when he dragged his feet too much. Carmen felt sorry for the boy. The huge hat and obvious overlarge clothes overwhelmed his small figure.

"Cal, has Mel has always been this way?" Carmen asked quietly, not wanting the boy to hear her.

"Naw, just since we were taken," he replied gruffly. "It's been especially hard on him. Being taken away from his world at such a young age. The only thing he found comfort in is taking care of those damn mine creatures."

"Maybe I can talk to Creon about taking you back to Earth," Carmen said hesitantly. "I can't promise anything, but he might agree when all this is over to return you and your grandson. If not, you are both welcome on Valdier. It is truly an incredible world, and I'm sure you would be welcomed."

Cal looked back at Mel, who was falling further behind again. He started when he saw Calo walk toward his grandson. He frowned when he saw Mel jerk back until Harvey and Calo and Cree's symbiots surrounded him protectively. Calo said something quietly to Mel before turning sharply with an angry expression on his normally cheerful face and marched back to stand behind Carmen in stiff silence.

"We would appreciate anything you can do," Cal said sadly. "Mel and I both will never forget your kindness," he added, looking at Mel one last time before following Zuk into the small eating establishment he had told them about.

They were seated at a large rectangular table near the door of the small bar. It reminded Carmen of some of the open cantinas back home in Mexico. There was a circular bar in the center of the room.

All different types of creatures sat drinking and eating around it as well as around the widely spaced tables. Carmen puzzled at first why the tables were so far apart until she saw the barmaids moving around taking orders and serving drinks. The smallest one had to be almost four feet wide and six feet tall. They each wore sheer scarves over what looked like a two piece that barely covered their multiple breasts and lower region. They had a dark, scaly, red skin with long, green hair. Their faces were flattened with only two small slits where their nose was, no lips to speak of, and tiny black eyes.

Carmen knew she was staring and had to force her eyes back to the images on the table. "If you wish to order anything just touch the image," Zuk said with a smile. "If you are not sure what something is I can help you."

Cree looked down at the far end of the table where Mel sat. He frowned when he saw the twin bands of gold peeking out from around the boy's slender wrists briefly before he pulled his jacket down over his hands again.

"What do you want to eat, boy?" he called out harshly.

Mel's dark green eyes peeked up at him briefly before he lowered his head again and slumped in his seat, as if he was trying to disappear into it. Cree's jaw clenched, and he looked at his brother who was staring in stony silence at Mel. Cree shook his head briefly at his brother when he turned to look at him.

"I'll order for Mel," Cal said briskly. "The boy doesn't eat much."

"He needs to eat more," Calo bit out gruffly. "He is too small for his age as it is. How will he become a strong warrior if he doesn't start eating? Maybe Cree and I can work with him on developing his strength and fighting skills."

"That won't be necessary," Cal responded. "Carmen is going to ask her mate if he will return us to our world. Mel will be fine the way he is once we get home."

Both men turned to glare at Carmen before they looked down angrily. "Perhaps that's for the best," Calo finally said in a quiet tone. "If you don't mind, I am not hungry. I will patrol the area outside," he added, standing up.

Cree stood as well. "I will take the back. We will leave our symbiots with you. If you need anything, just call out. We will be close."

Carmen frowned at the two brothers as they quickly left the bar. She glanced down and was surprised when she saw Mel's eyes following the men. She was definitely missing something, but she couldn't quite figure it out. She was about to say something when one of the servers appeared with their food. She looked down at the breads, cheeses, and fruits in relief. She recognized many of them from the warship and Valdier.

She looked up when she heard Zuk chuckle. "I didn't think you would care for some of the more traditional fare of the residents here," he said, pointing to his own dish that looked like a combination of cooked worms and strips of a mauve meat.

Carmen pressed a hand to her stomach as it suddenly rolled in distress. "I need to visit the little girl's room," she whispered, turning pale.

Cal looked at Carmen in concern. "Are you feeling okay?" he asked anxiously.

"I'm fine," she choked out. "Bathroom?"

Zuk pointed toward a narrow corridor. Carmen threw him a grateful, if shaky, smile before hurrying off to the bathroom. She sighed in relief when she saw an emblem she recognized from her studies and pushed the door open. She made it to the toilet just in time as her stomach rebelled.

She braced her hands on the wall until she felt like she had expelled everything that was going to come out. She shakily wiped a hand across her mouth as she straightened up. The light went over the bowl of the toilet and the contents disappeared. She stumbled over to the device on the wall and waved her hands in front of it. Another light appeared and swiped over her hands. She just needed something for her mouth now. Taking a chance, she leaned forward and opened her mouth in front of the light sensor. Sure enough, the light focused on her mouth, cleansing it.

With relief, Carmen opened the door only to find herself facing two slender purple females standing outside the door. One of them sprayed something in her face. Carmen vaguely felt the other one grabbing her as she began to collapse. Her first thought was a sense of disbelief that this could be happening before she sent out a brief call for help as darkness descended on her.

∽

Zuk and Cal were talking quietly when Harvey suddenly shifted into the shape of a werecat and hissed loudly in distress. The two creatures sitting next to Mel immediately moved in closer and began shimmering in a variety of colors as they sensed the danger that Harvey had reacted to. Zuk ordered Cal to stay with Mel as he stood quickly, yelling out for Cree and Calo.

Harvey was moving through the tables, ignoring the curses as he knocked several over, spilling food and drink everywhere. He moved rapidly toward the corridor where Carmen had disappeared down. He paused to scent the air around the door; his loud sound of distress was so high-pitched, glass shattered.

"What is it?" Calo asked as he broke through the crowd of patrons in his way.

Cree moved in quietly from the back entrance. "Marastin Dows," he said, bending down and picking up the empty container of anesthetic gas.

Calo's curse filled the air as he looked around. "They didn't take her out the front," he said harshly.

"Or the back," Cree said. "They must have beamed her to their ship. They must be working with someone with the Spaceport authority. They never would have been able to beam out otherwise."

The Spaceport prevented all species from using any type of transport beam unless it had been authorized. They had shields in place to prevent it from being used. It would make it too easy for assassins, thieves, and would-be criminals to use it to escape, leading to mass chaos. The Marastin Dow did not follow any rules, believing they were above any type of restrictions. Cree pressed his comlink and informed the *Horizon* of the situation. They would not be able to reach Creon or Ha'ven until the men turned their comlinks back on. They had not wanted to be distracted or overheard by someone tapping into their communications device.

"Get a security team to the authority tower. I want all ships locked down. No one is allowed to leave until they have been searched thoroughly," Cree bit out rapidly. "Creon's mate has been taken by the Marastin Dow."

Calo was already pushing through the crowd following Harvey, who was communicating with the thin, gold bands on Carmen. "Zuk, take Cal and his grandson back to the ship immediately," Calo called out as he rushed out of the bar.

Cree paused a moment in front of Zuk before he followed his brother. His eyes were glued to where Mel stood next to his and his brother's symbiots. He called to his symbiot to stay with Mel. He finally forced his eyes away from the small, hunched figure.

"I will hold you personally responsible for their safety," he muttered before he called to his brother's symbiot to follow him as he rushed out after his brother.

He knew his brother's symbiot could find Calo, who was following Harvey through the crowded streets. It looked like the huge gold creature was heading away from the docking bays and into the rougher living areas of the spaceport. He picked up speed until he could see his brother up ahead. He stopped suddenly when he rounded a corner and found his brother standing in the shadows as Harvey moved stealthily up the side of a tall building, stopping periodically before continuing onto the next level.

"This is not like the Marastin Dow," he said quietly from behind his brother.

"Why would they bring her here?" Calo asked, watching as Harvey climbed over the balcony to another level.

"I don't know, but they are dead, so it won't matter," Cree bit out as he moved forward to follow Harvey.

Calo and Cree climbed stealthily while Calo's symbiot transformed into a large flying creature and swept up to land on the top of the building next to Harvey. They pulled themselves up and over the top level of the building. The door at the top was ripped open, revealing the dark stairwell. Both brothers called forth their dragons so their eyesight was enhanced enough for them to see in the darkness. Calo's symbiot split in half, then divided again. The largest portion was in the shape of a small werebeast while the two smaller portions formed armor over the brothers.

Calo nodded to his symbiot to follow Harvey, and they moved into the darkness. They had to find Carmen. Both brothers felt the weight of their failure to protect her. If anything happened to her, they could never live with the dishonor of failing to protect their prince's mate.

~

Carmen lay still as she slowly regained consciousness. She heard the soft murmur of feminine voices in the room. They sounded like they were frantically trying to convince someone of something. She didn't get the feeling they were angry, just… desperate? She frowned and let her eyes open so she could see where she was at. She jerked in surprise when she saw a pair of dark brown eyes looking down at her with worry.

"Can you understand me?" the voice asked in a rusty voice.

"Who are you? What are you doing here?" Carmen asked huskily as she stared up into the distraught face of a very human male.

The man smiled nervously down at her. "My name is Ben Cooper. Are you okay? I'm sorry about what happened. I didn't know that Evetta and Hanine would do this," he said quietly as he pulled a chair up near the bed she was lying on.

Carmen's eyes flew to the two purple-skinned women standing behind him. One of them was biting her lip while the other looked at Ben with a look of worry. One of the women said something to Ben softly before disappearing into the other room.

"Why... why did they kidnap me?" Carmen asked, confused.

She pushed herself up into a sitting position so she could get a better look at the room around her. It was dim, with only a couple of small lights on. The walls were dirty and worn, but it looked like the place was being kept as clean as possible with the shabby furniture and fixtures. The walls and floor were a dull gray. The furniture was sparse with only the single bed and a small table and chair in the room she was in. The outer room did not look much better. She could see another beat-up-looking table and four chairs in it.

"Where am I?" she asked hesitantly, looking closely at the man in front of her.

He had long, light brown hair and dark brown eyes like hers. He looked to be in his early- to mid-thirties and, if she had to guess, was about six feet two inches. He was thin, though, as if he hadn't eaten well in a long time.

"In the apartment we are renting temporarily," he replied quietly, looking behind him and holding out his hand. "This is Evetta. She is my wife," he said gently as his fingers closed over the slender purple ones. "My brother and I were kidnapped from Earth almost fifteen years ago. We were sold as slaves several times before the freighter we were on was raided by the ship Evetta and her sister were on five years ago," Ben said before he pressed a light kiss into Evetta's palm. "We had convinced every species since we were taken that my brother, Aaron, and I couldn't be separated, otherwise we would die. Evetta and her sister were working as engineering and programming specialists on the ship that hijacked ours."

"I saw Ben," Evetta said hesitantly, looking at Ben with a soft smile. "His touch, his voice made me feel things I have never felt before. I would give my life for him. He is my husband," she said proudly as she smiled down at him.

"We've been on the run ever since we were able to escape two weeks ago. Aaron was wounded in the escape. He needs help. Evetta and Hanine were searching for a healer who would work for cheap. We don't have a lot of credits, and we have to be careful who we approach," he said tiredly. "I am too unusual to go out. It would have sent a red flag up immediately."

Evetta looked at Carmen. "My sister and I saw you. You looked like my husband and his brother. We thought you would know how to heal my sister's husband. He is in much pain. You travel with the Valdier. Their gold is magic. You will use it to heal him," Evetta said with determination. "My sister's husband cannot die."

Carmen looked back and forth from Ben's tired, haggard face to the determined look in Evetta's face. "Let me take a look at him. I might not be able to do much, but the healer aboard the *Horizon* can help him," she said, rising up off the narrow bed. "I'll do everything I can to help you," she said, placing her hand on Ben's arm in encouragement. "You, your brother, and your wives are welcome to leave with us when we go. We have two other humans who were also taken. I am hoping my mate will return them to Earth," she added.

Evetta carefully removed Carmen's hand from Ben's arm before pulling him closer to her. Ben smiled down at his wife, wrapping a tight arm around her waist. He murmured something in her ear that seemed to make her feel better as she relaxed against him.

"I appreciate the offer. We would be happy for the transportation to somewhere safe, but neither my brother nor I can return to Earth. As you can imagine, Evetta and Hanine would stand out, and I won't leave her," Ben said in a quiet, determined voice.

Carmen's lips curved into a small smile. "I know exactly how you feel. Let's take a look at your brother," she said.

Ben turned and walked out into the other room. There was another narrow bed along the wall, and a pale, sweaty male lay on it. He opened his pain-filled eyes to stare at her. Hanine was using a damp cloth to wipe his forehead. He had a bloody bandage wrapped tightly around his chest.

"Please, help my husband," Hanine said slowly. "He is in much pain."

"I'll see if I can help," Carmen said gently. "I will need to contact my friends. He will need more than I can do."

"No!" Hanine said, rising to stand in front of Aaron. "You help! You are same as him! You know how to fix him."

"I'm not a healer, Hanine," Carmen said gently. "I will do everything I can to help him, though. Please, trust me. I would not hurt you, your sister, or Aaron and Ben."

Carmen knelt down next to Aaron when Hanine finally stepped to one side. She brushed her hand over his forehead. It was hot. He was running a high fever. She moved her hand down to pull the bandage back. A ragged hole in his side showed he had taken a deep cut to his right side. It was about three inches long, and she would guess almost as deep. The edges were red, hot, and swollen, and a light pus oozed from the wound.

"It's infected," she said as she pulled the cover further back.

Please, you have to help him, she said softly to the gold bands around her wrists.

She felt the bands shiver in denial. They did not want to help those who had taken her. She saw the image of Harvey coming for her.

Please, he is like me, she begged. *They only took me because they were desperate. I would have never known about them otherwise. We have to help them. Please, for me.*

The gold sent a sharp heat of unhappiness before it slowly dissolved and flowed onto the man lying stiffly on the narrow bed. It moved rapidly over him, cleansing the wound and drawing out the poison before it reformed just as quickly and wrapped itself back around Carmen's wrist with a shake.

The wound wasn't healed, but the infection was drained, and the skin didn't look nearly as angry. She picked up a clean piece of cloth and laid it over the wound. She turned to Hanine who was watching her with doubt and worry clouding her dark eyes.

"It is too small and his wound is too bad for it to heal it completely. It was able to draw the infection out and clean the wound. He needs additional healing that my symbiot can't do," Carmen said, standing up and turning to Ben and Evetta.

"No!" Hanine said, drawing her laser sword. "You make it heal him! I want him healed!" she cried out angrily.

"He is too badly injured for it to completely heal him," Carmen insisted as she stared into the wild eyes of Hanine. "Hanine, I know what it is like to lose someone you love. If you let me contact my people, he can survive. Please. It is the only way."

"It is a trick," she said, raising her laser sword. "You can heal him if you wanted to, but you think to trick us and turn us in. My husband will not die!"

"Hanine," a weak voice whispered. "She is right. I could tell it did what it could, love. Trust her," Aaron said, looking up at his wife. "For me…for us. Trust her."

Before Hanine could reply, the door to their small, dingy apartment shattered, and a very furious golden werebeast stood in the doorway. It reached out, wrapping tentacles of gold around Hanine's arm that held the sword and pulled her roughly toward it while another section of gold flowed to form a shield in front of Carmen.

Aaron roared out weakly from where he was lying. Ben thrust Evetta behind him, ignoring her cry of outrage as her sister was pulled down and under the huge gold werebeast. Moments later, Cree and Calo stormed into the room with their laser swords and pistols drawn. Cree raised his arm to fire at Ben.

"Cree! Don't you dare!" Carmen yelled out at the top of her lungs. "Harvey, let Hanine go right this instant! I mean it. *Now!*"

Cree paused, but didn't lower his arm. Harvey had his mouth open, ready to pierce Hanine's throat with the dagger-like teeth in his mouth. The tips of two of his teeth had drawn just a small amount of blood as Hanine struggled fruitlessly under the mammoth creature.

"Calm down," Carmen said in a sharp voice. "Harvey, let me out."

The gold shield around her slowly dissolved, reforming into several small flying dragons that hovered around her like gnats around a piece of ripe fruit. Carmen shook her head in aggravation, but didn't say anything, knowing that the gold symbiot was just trying to protect her. She took a step toward where Hanine now lay quietly on the floor.

Carmen shooed Harvey back as she reached her hand down to help Hanine off the floor. "This is Harvey," she said as Hanine moved slightly behind her in an effort to get away from him. "Those two are the Bobbsey Twins, Cree and Calo. Don't worry about which is which. They answer to either."

"So help me, Carmen," Calo muttered in a dark voice. "What in dragon's balls is going on, and why are you protecting a couple of Marastin Dow scum?"

"Shut your mouth," Ben growled out, taking a step toward Calo. "That scum you are talking about are my wife and my brother's wife!"

Cree whistled under his breath. "You mated with one of them?" he asked with a raised eyebrow, looking at the two slim, purple women in surprise.

"Yes," Ben said through gritted teeth. "I don't give a damn what you think about it. If you can't be polite to her, then keep your mouth shut, or I'll shut it for you."

Calo looked on in amusement. "You look like a good breeze would knock you out," Calo said with a twisted grin. "Carmen, do you want to explain why Cree and I shouldn't kill them?"

Carmen put her hands on her hips and tossed her head in challenge. "Because if you do, I'll have to kick both your asses, and then I'll let Creon know you upset me. I think he might just kill you for that alone," she retorted sarcastically. "Evetta and Hanine saw me and knew I was human like Ben and Aaron. Aaron needs immediate medical attention. They thought I could help him since we are the same species. Now, quit being such an ass and help me get them back to the *Horizon*."

"You realize that the Marastin Dow are not to be trusted," Cree said skeptically, looking at both women.

Carmen flipped her middle finger up at Cree. "Go to hell, Cree. I trust them. If I categorized every Valdier the same way you are the Marastin Dow, I wouldn't trust any of you."

"You are comparing a Valdier with a Marastin Dow in the same breath?" Calo asked in disbelief as he sheathed his sword and his pistol. "There is no comparison!"

"Yeah?" Carmen asked as she folded her arms across her chest. "One word—Raffvin."

Both men blanched at the name and muttered a few unpleasant words under their breath. "Fine, but you get to explain this to your mate and Ha'ven when they find a couple of Marastin Dow sc— females on board their warship," Calo growled out, looking at Ben, who took another threatening step toward him when Calo almost insulted Ben's wife and her sister again.

"This has to be the strangest voyage I've ever been on," Cree muttered under his breath before he called the *Horizon* and warned them to prepare for some new passengers.

"We need to get him to the *Horizon* without drawing too much attention," Carmen said in a voice filled with worry. "Ben and Evetta are worried there might be some Marastin Dow still looking for them."

"Hanine has that covered," Evetta said quietly before she nodded to her sister. "Take us to their docking bay, Hanine."

Hanine lifted a computer slate into her hands and touched a series of commands. "Hold on," she said with a smile before she brushed her finger over it again.

As everything shifted around her and faded, Carmen's last thought was, *So much for avoiding beaming anywhere while I'm pregnant.*

CHAPTER SEVENTEEN

Later that night, Carmen sat on the bed trying to learn the Valdier language from an information slate Calo had gotten her, but she was having trouble concentrating. Aaron was doing much better. Tandor had assured Hanine her husband would fully recover.

Carmen had giggled when Hanine had thrown herself into his arms and sobbed. He held her, awkwardly looking around for help at the small group in sick bay. None of the Valdier had ever seen a Marastin Dow act with such joy and relief before.

Ben had wrapped his arms around Evetta and held her tightly as they both cried with relief. It had taken a while for Carmen to convince the security officer on board the *Horizon* that none of their new passengers were a threat. He didn't believe her until he saw both women sobbing uncontrollably in the medical unit.

Her mind drifted to Cal and his grandson. Zuk had made sure both were safely returned to the *Horizon*. There was something strange about the boy, but she couldn't put her finger on it. Maybe it was his age. He had sat away from everyone and didn't eat much.

Harvey and the other two symbiots had stood guard as if knowing he needed extra protection or support. Carmen thought back to

Samara, the girl who worked with the horses at Trisha's dad's ranch. Animals reacted the same way with her. They seemed to know that she preferred their company to humans. Ariel was like that to a certain extent. Carmen suspected animals just knew Ariel was a sucker that could be conned out of anything when it came to them.

She smiled when she heard Creon enter their living quarters. She slid from the bed and walked to the door. He was deep in thought and didn't realize she was watching him. She saw him wince in pain as he removed his sword sheath strapped across his back. She hurried forward and helped him remove it without saying a word. He paused to look down at her bent head as she focused on undoing the fastenings holding it on.

"I missed you today, *mi elila*," he said huskily, brushing her hair behind her ear. "You have had a very exciting day from what I have heard," he added gruffly as he touched her hair. It was getting longer and slid easily through his fingers.

"I missed you, too," she whispered quietly. "You need Harvey to come heal you. You have a long, narrow cut about four inches long and about half an inch deep along your left shoulder," she insisted as she ran a finger along the outside edge of the cut skin.

"There were two assassins instead of the one," he sighed heavily. "I must be getting old. I would never have made such a mistake before."

"Perhaps it's not that you are getting old, but that you are getting distracted… by me," she said with remorse.

He put a finger under her chin and forced her head up so he could look her in the eye. "Never think that. It was my error, and it will not happen again. The assassin they sent normally works alone. I did not anticipate their desire to kill the assassin as well as myself," he insisted sternly. "This had nothing to do with you. There are many things going on right now. We leave for the asteroid belt between the Quillar moons of Bosca and Dorland. That is where we believe Vox has been taken."

Carmen nodded before calling for Harvey. She continued removing Creon's clothing as the gold symbiot moved over his skin, healing the cuts and bruises. She didn't say anything, knowing he would fill her in on what had happened and the new information he had learned when he was ready. Scott had been the same way. It was as if they needed to have it neatly organized in their brains before they could share it with anyone else.

"Ha'ven told me that Trelon rescued Cara," Carmen said as she gently pulled him behind her toward the bathroom. "Or, I should say, he rescued the poor Curizans who took her. I guess she had escaped and reprogrammed their ship," she said lightly.

Creon muttered a dark curse. "There is nothing poor about them. I hope my brothers killed the lot of them."

"My, you are feeling a little bloodthirsty, aren't you?" she teased before sobering. "Kelan killed N'tasha. She said that she had killed Trisha." She placed her hands on both of his cheeks when he groaned in horror. "Let me finish. She said she had killed her, but she didn't. Trisha was taken by another group. Kelan has gone after her. Many of the men on board were there under duress. Raffvin has their families imprisoned and was forcing them to help. Trelon has sent a crew to rescue the families."

Creon closed his eyes. Now, the only one still unaccounted for was Trisha. He prayed to the gods and goddesses she would be safe until his brother could reach her. He had sent a brief account of what he had learned to Ha'ven, but he had not had time to meet with him before they departed.

"Trisha will be fine," Carmen said with confidence. "Not only was she trained by our military back home, but her dad is one of the best survival trainers in the world. He taught her to hunt, track, and fight in ways no one else knows. If anyone can escape, it will be her."

Creon opened his eyes and pulled her close to him. "Bathe with me," he said huskily. "I need to hold you close for a while."

Carmen stepped back and slowly began to undo her shirt. She burst out in giggles when he groaned impatiently and just ripped it off her. She twisted in an effort to save her pants, but he was too fast for her.

"If you keep doing that I won't have any clothes to wear," she giggled breathlessly.

"That sounds good to me," he groaned, wrapping his big hands around her waist. "You still need to gain more weight. I cannot wait until you are rounded with our younglings."

"What is it with you and seeing me plump?" she complained. "Most guys want slim, trim girls back home."

"They are idiots," he responded, sliding his mouth along her shoulder. "It is more fun to have something to hold on to when I am driving my cock into you."

She shivered at the image that formed in her mind. "So, are you saying you don't like me as I am now?" she asked, looking over her shoulder at him with a raised eyebrow.

Creon paused and tilted his head back to look at her carefully before replying. "That is one of those questions I heard my brothers talking about," he said, looking a little nervous. "They warned me there were certain questions a human female asks that should never be answered."

"Like?" she asked, fighting the need to burst out laughing as he fought to figure out a way out of the mess he had made at commenting on her weight.

"Like… like 'Does this make my butt look big?'" he said in aggravation. "Why would that bother her? I would love it if you had a big butt! I wouldn't be able to keep my hands off it. I have a hard enough time as it is, but if it was bigger…" A low growl escaped him as his dragon agreed.

Carmen twisted in his arms and wrapped hers around his neck, pressing her breasts into his muscular chest. "Well, in that case, I think you need to show me how much you like it," she whispered.

A long moan escaped as he picked her up and stepped into the showering unit. "I always wanted to try this," he groaned out as a warm, heavy mist of moisture surrounded them.

"Put your arms above your head," he growled out as he set her down. "I want to touch every inch of you."

Carmen nodded, breathless at the hunger in his voice. She could feel her pussy pulsing with need. She turned so her back was against the wall of the bathing unit. A long, metal bar ran around the top, probably for the males to grab onto should anything happen to the ship while they were in it.

She had to stand on the tips of her toes to reach it. This stretched her body out. She wrapped her fingers around it tightly and hung on as he began soaping her down. A soft moan escaped her as he started with her hair, massaging the soap into her scalp.

"It is growing longer," he murmured, enjoying how her eyes closed and her body shook as he touched her. "I would like for you to let it get longer. I want to be able to wrap my hands in it as I take you from behind."

Carmen's eyes flew open. Her eyes had turned to dark brown with gold flames in them as she and her dragon heard both their two-legged and four-legged mates express their desires. She arched toward him, impatient for his hands to touch her in other places.

"More," she breathed out.

"My impatient little kitten," he whispered as his rough hands moved down over her shoulders and up her arms. "I liked it when you meowed at Ha'ven, Cree, and Calo. I want you to do it for me."

Her eyes blazed as his hands moved over her fingers and started the slow path toward her breasts. "I'll fucking purr if you touch me how I want you to," she stated, leaning forward to nip his jaw.

He thrust forward, grinding his cock against her. The hard, thick length was trapped between their bodies, and she could feel it throbbing. His hands reached out and cupped her breasts, his finger and thumb seizing her nipples between them. He pinched them hard, enjoying her loud gasp at his roughness. He had always been tender, careful when he made love to her. Tonight he wanted to take her rough and hard.

"Yes," she answered to his softly spoken words. "I won't break. I need you to take me, claim me…possess me. Don't hold back."

"If you get frightened or don't want me to do something, you will tell me?" he asked, fighting the primal urge to take her at her word.

"Only if you do the same when I take my turn," she said with a sassy grin. "Because let me tell you something," she added in a husky tone. "I plan on taking you every way I can."

The challenge and promise in her words fired his blood to boiling. His dragon was bouncing around inside him, panting. He could feel the male's restlessness as the scent of his mate in heat filled the air despite the heavy mist.

"Oh, dragon's balls," Creon groaned as his body jerked painfully.

His hands became rougher as his desire grew. He latched onto one of her nipples, sucking and nipping it until it stood swollen and pink before attacking the other. Her loud cries egged him on as he moved down her body to the sweet moisture of her clit. He slid two thick fingers across her swollen cunt, enjoying how she opened like a bloom to him. He tugged on the soft, curly blond hair that protected her. When she groaned, he tugged again, a little harder. She lifted both of her legs up and wound them over his shoulders.

"Eat me," she demanded, looking down at him on his knees between her legs.

Creon's eyes widened at her heated demand. He liked a woman who told him what she wanted. He felt her cross her ankles behind his back. He spread her swollen lips as she tilted forward, exposing her swollen vaginal channel to him.

"Fuck me!" she cried out desperately. "Now!"

He leaned forward and nipped her engorged nub with his teeth. "You will be fucked when I say you can be fucked," he retorted in a deep voice. "You need to learn who is in charge."

Carmen's head bowed so she could watch him as he began sucking on her clit. It was so swollen it was painful at first, but she relished it. Her arms shook from holding up her body, but she couldn't let go. The discomfort added to the pleasure as he worked her with his tongue and teeth. The sharp nips followed by the wash of his tongue over and over pulled cries from her, begging for him to give her relief from the waves of desire building up inside her.

"Oh!" she cried out, her head falling backward as she felt his tongue sliding up inside her along with his fingers. "I'm coming!" she panted out just as her body jerked, and a long, keening whine broke from her.

Creon milked her orgasm, sucking until she melted. He wrapped his hands around her waist and helped her move her legs from around his shoulders. Even with her legs back on the ground, he had to support her as her arms fell uselessly by her sides.

"I think you've killed me," she whispered, leaning against his chest. "I can't move."

His chuckle echoed around the bathing unit. "No, my little kitten. I haven't killed you...yet. This is just the beginning."

Carmen leaned back against the wall, hoping that she wouldn't disgrace herself by becoming a puddle on the floor. "The beginning?" she asked in disbelief.

"Oh yes," he said, tilting her head to the side. "My dragon has a need to release some of the dragon fire burning inside. Trust me, this is only the beginning," he murmured before he bit down and breathed the fire burning in his veins into her.

Carmen's body jerked and shuddered as flames raced through her. She felt the immediate clenching of her pussy and the throbbing need before it began to beat heavily inside her. She leaned forward as her teeth began to elongate.

Mate want to be horny? her dragon responded with determination. *We show him what horny is! Two can breathe this fire.*

Oh shit, Carmen thought as she bit down on Creon's shoulder and began breathing her own dragon fire into him. *You and your mate are going to kill us!*

Maybe, but it fun way to die, her dragon giggled as she felt the hot waves building in her mate's body. *Yes, very fun way to die.*

Creon's loud curse filled the shower unit as he pulled back, swiping his tongue over the mark on his mate. He commanded the showering unit off. Carmen was still attached to him, breathing dragon's fire hot enough to burn the balls off a dozen Sarafin warriors. His body was already on overload from before. Now, it was scorching him from the inside out.

"Gods, Carmen," he groaned out in desperation. "You have to stop!"

Unfortunately for her, or him depending on how you looked at it, she couldn't. Her dragon was determined to expel every last drop of dragon's fire into her mate. She felt her body being lifted and slammed against the wall of the shower, her legs gripped and pulled apart, but she still couldn't pull away. Creon's thick, hard cock was swollen to almost twice the size of normal from the feel of it as he pushed it into her as far as it would go. Still, it wasn't far enough. He pulled out and slammed into her again and again, going deeper and deeper until she released him with a gasp.

"Mine!" he growled out, his pupils narrow slits of burning gold flames. "My mate!"

Carmen clung to his shoulders as he pounded into her over and over. She watched in fascination as black scales rippled over his bare chest, up his neck, and over his cheeks. Her own arms were rippling with white, red, pink, and purple scales in answer to her mate.

Creon's eyes locked on her breasts as they bounced up and down with the force of his possession. His teeth lengthened just a little before he bent over and sank them into her right breast. A scream erupted from her as he breathed, marking her as his again. He never slowed down. His cock pushed through her slick channel until she could feel the tip of his cock against her womb. Each stroke seemed to be telling her she was his, she was his, she was his.

Her body reacted violently, tightening around him, making it almost impossible for him to pull out. As she strained to pull away, his body jerked and a loud moan filled the air as he came hard and deep inside her. Hot waves of his seed washed through her as he filled her with every bit of his essence. Only when his body had spent the last of it did he release her breast, running his rough tongue over the tender flesh.

They were both panting and weak. His arms tightened protectively around her when he felt her shiver as the cooler air of the room washed over her still damp skin. He didn't bother pulling out of her yet. He was still too swollen. Instead, he forced his shaky limbs to step out of the showering unit. Grabbing a couple of towels, he carried her —still straddling his waist—to their bed while awkwardly trying to run a towel over her back.

"It's okay," she slurred sleepily, rubbing her nose against his neck while her arms hung limply over his shoulders.

Creon chuckled. She didn't realize she was making a soft, rumbling noise in her chest. His little kitten was purring. He sat down on the bed before stretching out with her on top of him. He would pull out of her in a little while.

She feels too good to leave just yet, he thought tiredly as he pulled the covers over both of them. *I'll pull out in a few minutes.* That was the last thought he had before sleep claimed him.

CHAPTER EIGHTEEN

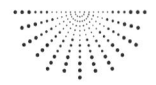

The shudder of the warship woke them both. Creon's arms were still wrapped tightly around her, and she was still sprawled over him. She lifted her head in confusion before her head cleared. She stared down at him for a moment before rolling off him and scrambling out of the bed.

"What's going on?" she asked as she began pulling on clothes.

"It sounds like the *Horizon* is receiving fire," he bit out quickly as he dragged his own clothes on.

"Ha'ven, what in the hell is going on?" Creon growled out into the comlink.

"Well, if you would get your sorry ass up to the bridge you would know," Ha'ven replied sarcastically. "Two damn Marastin Dow pirate ships are attacking a short-haul supply freighter. One of the bastards thought they could take us on as well. I guess the cloaking device is working too damn well. I'm ready to disengage it just so I can watch those bloodthirsty pieces of shit…"

"Why don't you just blast the hell out of them?" Creon said, strapping his sword around his waist and grabbing Carmen's hand to pull her with him as he charged out of their living quarters.

"One of them is docked to the freighter and the other is too close,"

Ha'ven replied with a snort. "If you were here, you could see for yourself."

"I am here," Creon said as he and Carmen stepped onto the bridge. "Disengage the cloaking device. Let them see who in the hell they are dealing with. If that doesn't scare them away, send a squadron of fighters and disable both of their ships. We'll kill them one by one if necessary."

Carmen watched the two strange-looking spaceships locked with another one. The two smaller ships were long and narrow with a wider stern than bow. The freighter was almost twice the size, but was built with a boxier design for room, not speed. Lights were flickering on and off on the freighter. It was almost comical observing the two pirate ships once the *Horizon* disengaged its cloaking device revealing it to be a Curizan first-class warship. The pirate ships actually bumped into each other as the one docked tried to move away from the freighter.

"Marastin scum," Ha'ven growled out, before he looked at the frown on Carmen's face. "Excluding the two in medical, of course," he added hastily. "They may be mean bastards, but most of them are cowards. They only attack those weaker than they are or whom they outnumber," he said in disgust. "Open communications with the freighter and see if they need assistance. I imagine as fast as those cowardly pactor dung left they didn't get all their crew back on board."

"This is the *Horizon*. Do you need assistance?" Ha'ven asked as soon as a communications link was established.

"I'm sorry we can't come to the phone right now but if you would like to leave your name and number after the beep we'll be happy to return your call as soon as possible. *Beep...*" a husky female voice said —followed by a long string of cursing. "How the bloody hell am I supposed to know who the hell the *Horizon* is? You just ordered me to sit here and not move, damn it!" There was a muffled voice in the background before the woman's voice hollered back, "Well, if you don't want me pushing the fucking buttons, then don't put me where I can reach them!"

Ha'ven looked with amusement at Creon who was struggling not to laugh. "I repeat, this is..." Ha'ven started to say.

"I know who in the fucking hell you are," the voice said in frustration. "I heard you the first time. We are just a little busy at the moment, and there's a big pussy pissing me off right now. Will you just leave a friggin' message, and I'll have him call you after I declaw his ornery ass?" the husky voice replied before she began shouting. "Vox, I swear you need to be neutered! If you get blood on my handbag, I'll do it with the first dull knife I can find. Do you have any idea how much I paid for that damn thing?"

The sound of a loud roar echoed harshly through the communications link. "Bob! Look out behind you, sweetie. There's another ugly purple guy coming up through the hatch. Fred, be a sweetheart and give Bob a hand. Lodar baby, I think Fred might have a little cut on one of his heads. There is blood all down the side of it. When you get a chance can you look at him? Tor darling, why can't you just zap their asses out into space? I thought you knew how to do things like that. What did you say, Lodar? I couldn't hear you because a certain hairball was making too much noise when you spoke. Oh yes, dear, I'll tell Fred you'll see him as soon as you finish fighting. Fred, honey, Lodar is busy, but he'll see you as soon as he is done killing the bad guys. Vox, damn it, you are totally on my shit list! You got blood on my skirt, you jerk! Go kill someone on the other side of the room. I can shoot the bastards near me! I don't need your help!"

Ha'ven had given up trying not to laugh. "I think we have found our missing hairball," he said when he could catch his breath. "I'm just not sure who he needs rescuing from, the Marastin Dow or the female who is manning the communication's console.

"I heard that, honey," the husky voice replied with a Midwestern drawl. "I would place all bets on that bossy, arrogant, demanding…" A loud roar interrupted the female's description. "Well, if you don't like what I have to say about you, then you can just dump my *big* ass back on my planet!"

"Uh-oh," Creon murmured. "He didn't say the right thing when he was asked."

Carmen elbowed Creon in the stomach to quiet him. "Hi there, my name's Carmen. I'm from Wyoming," she called out, giving in to a hunch that she had discovered another missing Earthling.

"Oh, hey, darling—" The woman's voice changed to excitement. "My name is Riley St. Claire. I'm from Denver. What are you doing out here? You don't know how nice it is to hear another girlfriend way out in the Twilight Zone! I hope you've had a better time of it than I have." There was some muttering too soft for Carmen to understand before they heard the woman reply. "No, Bob. I didn't mean you, you gorgeous tub of Jell-O. I was referring to that annoying pile of cat…" This time when her voice faded, it was because a very irritated male voice was responding.

"By Guall's balls, Riley, I'm going to spank your ass until it is bloody red if you don't stop giving me a hard time," the deep voice snarled out.

"Don't you mean my *big* ass, you moron?" Riley replied sarcastically.

"Female, I am going to…" The voice died off as a loud curse filled the air above the sound of laser fire. "You shot me!" The deep voice roared out in astonishment.

"But not where I was aiming for," Riley snapped back. "So help me, Vox, you better stay away from me until my temper has cooled, or I won't miss where I'm aiming for the next time I shoot you."

"Vox, do you need assistance?" Creon called out.

"Yes! I need you to come and—" Vox growled out before he groaned. "Come on, Riley. I didn't mean anything when I said you had a big ass. I like big asses. I— Shit. Will you quit shooting at me!"

Carmen put her hand over her mouth to try to stifle the giggles escaping her. The men on the bridge, including Creon and Ha'ven, didn't bother trying to hide their amusement. It was obvious when they heard Vox's long line of curses followed by threats of what he was going to do to all of them.

"Come get us off this piece of worthless Trillian shit," Vox snarled out. "There are ten of us on board. You can kill any number over that."

"A shuttle will be dispatched immediately," Creon said with a chuckle. "It is good to hear your voice, my old friend."

"Yeah, well, your uncle isn't going to like to hear it. That piece of Valdier royal ass is mine! He'll wish he had never messed with this Sarafin prince," Vox bit out harshly.

"Yewww, the big putty cat is hissing again," Riley's sarcastic voice sounded behind him. "Watch out—the next thing you know you'll be shooting hairballs."

"Riley, so help me, I'm going to wring your neck when I catch you!" Vox snarled out.

"Tor!" Riley said in a singsong voice. "Vox is being mean to me again."

"Don't you listen to a thing she says. I am not being mean to her! What did I ever do to deserve a mate like this?" Vox groaned out before the communications link was cut.

Carmen turned to look at Ha'ven who had a bewildered look on his face, as if he had never heard his friend talk like that before. He looked at Carmen with a raised eyebrow. All she could do was shrug her shoulders and smile innocently.

"It must be a human thing," she replied, not bothering to hide the grin on her face.

∼

Carmen sat relaxing with Cal and Riley down in the repair bay, drinking coffee and laughing as Riley explained how she ended up in outer space and with five mates, four of whom were not allowed anywhere near her by one "hot-headed-stubborn-frustratingly royal prissy cat." A soft giggle escaped from behind some of the cargo crates where Mel, who still refused to come out whenever anyone was there, hid.

"So, who is the scarecrow?" Riley asked, looking over the rim of her cup at Cal.

Cal's face scrunched up in confusion. "Scarecrow?"

Riley jerked her head toward the cargo crates. "Yeah, little Miss Priss. Does she think I have cooties or something?"

Carmen frowned for a moment before understanding dawned on her. She felt so stupid. Of course! Mel wasn't Cal's grandson. Mel was his…

"Granddaughter," she said softly, looking with compassion at Cal. "That is why she stays hidden and doesn't talk."

Cal let out a deep sigh before he nodded reluctantly. He glanced at the door to make sure that Cree or Calo were not in the repair bay. He glanced at both women sitting across from him for a few seconds longer before he called out.

"Melina, come here," he said gruffly. "It's okay, honey. They won't tell anyone."

The slim figure slowly emerged from behind the crates. The huge hat that she normally wore was in one slender hand. She was wearing the oversized clothes she favored and was twisting one of the ragged edges nervously between her fingers. She walked toward her grandfather with slow, cautious steps before kneeling on the floor next to him.

She had the biggest, greenest eyes Carmen had ever seen. She smiled shyly at her before turning to look at Riley with wide eyes. Carmen watched as Cal tenderly brushed his hand over Melina's dark brown hair.

"You can speak, girl. They won't tell on us," he assured her, looking sternly at Carmen and Riley to let them know he would not accept anyone else knowing about his granddaughter.

"Hey," Melina said in a softly accented voice. "It's nice to finally get to talk to you."

Carmen leaned forward, looking at Melina with concern. "Hello, Melina. If you don't mind my asking, how old are you?"

"I was twenty-one last week," Melina said with a sad smile. "Gramps and I have been counting the days since we were taken so we could keep track of how long it's been."

Carmen glanced at Cal and asked the question that was bugging her. "Why?"

Cal looked down sadly at his granddaughter. "The Antrox use women as a way of controlling the men. They don't give them much choice. If they knew my granddaughter was a woman, there's no telling what would have happened to her. It was easier passing her off as a boy. The trader who sold us to the Antrox couldn't tell the difference, and those insect creatures just accepted Mel as being a young boy, not old enough for the heavy work in the mines yet but old enough to keep for other duties," he explained.

"I saw some of the other women being sold to traders who would come to drop things off at the mines," Mel said quietly. "We were afraid they would sell me, especially if they knew I was a woman. I worked with horses at a farm near our home and was always good with animals, so I worked with the pactors. They aren't much different from mules in the way they act. Gramps thought it would be good if I acted like I couldn't speak and was not all there in the head," she continued, touching her temple with the tips of her fingers.

"When the mines ran out, the Antrox decided I was too old to do much. Mel overheard them and hid in the tunnels where they couldn't find her. She knew the tunnels backward and forward from the years of running errands. They couldn't find her so they left us behind," Cal said. "When the men on board the *Horizon* showed up, I had to take a chance. We were down to less than a week's worth of food and water. Mel and I decided it would be best if we continued pretending she was my grandson with a handicap. It's kept the men on board from looking at her," he added.

"I don't want them looking at me," Mel said forcefully. "I saw what the males did to some of those women," she said, flushing as she looked at Riley. "No offense, ma'am."

Riley laughed and shook out her heavy mane of blond, curly hair. "Darling, those insects didn't know what to do with me! I had those bastards shaking in their long underwear!" she said with a wink. "I don't think they were too happy with the trader who dropped me off at their place. Once we get home things will be better."

Carmen looked startled at Riley. "Home? I thought you had five mates with four of them not counting?" she asked with an amused grin.

Riley snorted in a very unladylike manner. "I just said I'd take the five hemorrhoids so they wouldn't end up on someone's plate for breakfast, lunch, or dinner. But like all good hemorrhoids, they have continued to be a pain in my ass, and it is time for them to pass on and be flushed down the nearest toilet, as my dear Grandma Pearl would say," she said with an exaggerated sigh and one hand clenched over her heart as if she was making the ultimate sacrifice.

Mel giggled and glanced at her granddad. "That sounds just like something you would say, Gramps."

"Unappreciative little whippersnapper," Cal said affectionately.

The door to the repair bay opened suddenly, and Cree walked in. Mel immediately slammed her hat on her head and jumped to her feet, heading for the crates again. Carmen watched Cree's face darken as his gaze followed Melina. A look of strain tightened his mouth into a straight line before he tore his gaze away to look at Carmen.

"My lady, your mate wishes to see you," Cree said carefully. He cleared his throat before he looked at Riley. "Your mate as well, Lady Riley. Lord Vox said, quote, 'Tell her to get her beautiful ass to our living quarters now.'"

Riley snorted and tossed her head in dismissal. "Tell him, quote, 'My beautiful ass is quite comfortable where it is, and he can shove his...'" Cree choked on a cough as Riley continued to tell him what he could repeat to Vox. "Oh, never mind. Tell him I'll be there when I'm damn-well ready."

Cree bowed stiffly before glancing toward the crates where Mel was hiding. "Yes, Lady Riley. Carmen?" he asked.

"I'll come with you. See you later, Riley. Cal," Carmen said with a smile. "Bye, Mel," she called out as she stood up.

Cree's eyes searched the darkness before he turned and escorted Carmen out of the repair bay. Carmen laid a gentle hand on his arm to stop him. Cree was surprised at the compassion he saw in the human female that had changed so much since his first meeting with her.

"We Earthlings are not always what we appear to be," she said, looking into the golden flames of Cree's eyes in concern. "We don't give up our hope of returning home easily. Cal and Mel want to return to Earth."

Cree stiffened before he shrugged. "Why should I or Calo care if the old man and the boy want to return? It would be better off for all if they did."

Carmen opened her mouth to repeat her comment about all not being as they appeared but thought better of it. From the closed look on Cree's face, it was obvious he did not want to discuss it anymore. She glanced at the door to the repair bay with a frown. Things could become very complicated if he or Calo found out that Mel was actually Melina.

CHAPTER NINETEEN

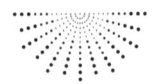

Several days later, Carmen stared out the viewport in the lounge area aboard the *Horizon*, lost in thought. Her life had changed so much in such a short time. She gently brushed her fingers along Harvey's smooth head. The gold symbiot could sense her emotional distress and had stayed close to her all day. She let her fingers caress his head, needing the touch to help calm her.

She was no longer nervous about being in space, which was a good thing considering they were going to be away from Valdier for several more months. That didn't mean she was ready to jump into one of the small shuttles any time soon; she was just more comfortable on the larger warship. There was plenty to do on board to keep her busy.

She and Creon worked out each day at different times due to his work schedule. Sometimes when they couldn't meet up, she would coax Cree or Calo into a sparring match by baiting them. Most of the time when he was working, she studied the history of Valdier and worked on learning their language. She also chatted with her sister a few times. Their relationship was slowly improving. It wasn't quite what it had been before Scott's death, but it was better than it had been in the past three years.

Creon had stopped by during a brief break in his work to tell her that Kelan had found Trisha. She had been taken to a hostile moon known for its dangerous inhabitants. He had reassured her that Trisha was unharmed and safe aboard the *V'ager*. She didn't know all the facts about what happened, just that Trisha and Kelan were safe and they were headed for Earth.

He and Ha'ven had also talked with Mandra and Adalard, Ha'ven's younger brother, as well. They had met up with an informant and were heading to an isolated moon on the outskirts of the Curizan star system. The *Horizon* was on its way to meet up with them. It would take a couple of days at full speed.

She had sadly said good-bye to Riley yesterday. One of the Sarafin warships had met up with the *Horizon*, and Vox, Riley, and the rest of the crew from the freighter, minus Bob and Fred, transferred over to it. Vox's warship was traveling beside the *Horizon* to Raffvin's hidden base. The Sarafin king was not about to let a chance at retaliation slip through his fingers.

Riley had been going to stay on board the *Horizon*, but Vox had refused to let her. She didn't go quietly. In fact, Carmen was pretty sure everyone within three star systems could have heard her.

On Vox's side, there was a lot of cursing, followed by a wide variety of threats that Riley blew off. Riley, on the other hand, was more into throwing a few wild swings and anything else she could get her hands on. Carmen decided she was in desperate need of a few pointers after she belted "Fred" upside one of his heads and her fist got caught in "Bob's" gelatinous body. She suspected that was one of the reasons those two unusual aliens decided it was safer to stay aboard the *Horizon* rather than transfer with the others.

Vox finally had to tie Riley up and throw her over his shoulder before they all departed in a hurry. She had tried to help her new friend, but Creon had caught her and pinned her down when she went after the huge cat shifter.

She raised her hand and laid it against the cool, clear glass, staring with unseeing eyes at the darkness on the other side. It mirrored the way she was feeling on the inside. She closed her eyes against the depression that was threatening to take her down its dark, cold path again. She had been down it so many times over the past three years.

She had hoped that she was finally able to resist it, but the dark hold of pain and grief appeared not to be done with her yet.

"What troubles you, *mi elila*?" Creon's soft, concerned voice came from behind her.

Carmen wiped at her face self-consciously, trying to make sure she wasn't crying. "Nothing," she said, glancing quickly over her shoulder at him with a forced smile before turning back around to face the dark cloak of space.

His dark frown showed she had not been very convincing. He walked toward her. Once he was standing behind her, he wrapped his arms around her, drawing her closer to his warmth. They stood like that for several minutes before he brushed a light kiss against her ear.

"Perhaps you have been overdoing it lately?" he suggested. "Between your studies, your visits to Cal, and working out, you have not had much rest," he said.

She shook her head. "I'm fine," she said distantly.

"You forget you are also carrying our younglings," he insisted. "This will take much out of you, as well."

Carmen leaned back in his arms and wrapped her hands over his. "How would you know that?" she asked with a small, sad smile as her head rested against his chest.

"I asked *Dola*," he confessed sheepishly. "I wanted to know everything there was to know about a female who was with young. She told me it was different for each female, and even each youngling, but that there are some things that happen frequently to all females during their breeding time."

"Like?" she asked curiously.

He moved his hands down to cover the slight rounding that was appearing under her loose shirt. "Like you would become tired more easily. You might become emotional at times. If you do, she said I must always agree with you," he added teasingly before continuing. "You will go through a period when you might become sick all of a sudden," he said, resting his chin on the top of her silky hair. "She also warned that it might be worse for you because our species do not carry as long as yours does."

"Well, that explains why I was puking my guts out earlier," she mused before her shoulders slumped. "I want to go home, Creon," she whispered.

Creon's arms tightened. "We will return to Valdier as soon as we have killed Raffvin. We will be joining Mandra and Adalard in a few days. With the combined force of Curizan, Valdier, and Sarafin warships there is no way he can defeat us," he assured her.

Carmen bit her lip and shook her head. "I want to go home. Not to Valdier but to Earth."

Creon's body stiffened, and his arms tightened around her. "Your home is now on Valdier, Carmen. You can never return to Earth," he said in a soothing voice.

Carmen lowered her head so he couldn't see the tears forming in her eyes in the reflection of the glass covering the viewport. She made to step away from him, but his arms tightened, refusing to let her go. He reached down and tilted her head back far enough to look into her glittering eyes.

"Why is it so important for you to return? Your life there is no more," he said with quiet frustration.

She closed her eyes briefly before opening them to look up at him sadly. "It will always be a part of my life," she whispered before pulling away to walk toward the door leading out of the lounge area.

Harvey brushed up against him as he followed Carmen, leaving threads of gold that wound up his arms. Images of Carmen and another man burst into his mind. The scenes flashed rapidly. He saw her laughing with the man who must have been her first mate. She was very young, and the boy was holding out an ice cream for her. He was small and had a black eye and a missing tooth. The scene flickered to years later when the boy was standing grinning at her with flowers in his hand this time. The next showed the two of them dancing slowly with multicolored lights swirling around them. He could see the look in the younger man's eyes. Love shone brightly as he awkwardly rocked back and forth.

The scene changed to the man holding Carmen. She was weeping softly near what appeared to be fresh graves. He was holding her protectively near his body while others stood around talking. It was the last scene that finally broke through his resistance.

The scene of the slightly older man lying on the ground, bleeding. His eyes were filled with grief as he stared at Carmen with love, regret, and acceptance. His lips moved, and Creon knew what he was saying without hearing them. He had told her he loved her and was sorry. The image changed to a man standing over his body and pulling the trigger while Carmen's anguished screams filled the humid night air.

∽

Creon muttered a curse before he quickly strode after her. He had been nervous about telling her about Kelan taking Trisha back to Earth. He had even debated about telling her but decided he wanted no secrets between them. He had talked to Ariel for a little while last night after he and his brother had talked. She had asked how her sister was doing. She was worried as it was coming up to the anniversary when her first mate and unborn child had died.

"Watch her carefully," Ariel had warned him. "She gets very depressed as it draws closer. She…" Ariel's voice died away as she bit her lip and looked down.

Creon could tell she was trying to control her emotions. "She…" he prompted.

Ariel looked up, and he could see the tears streaming down her cheeks. "She almost took her own life the first year. She overdosed on the sleeping and pain pills the doctors gave her. I was worried when I couldn't get hold of her. Something told me I had to find her immediately. When we found her, she"—Ariel took a deep breath before she continued—"she was lying on the stone bench in front of their graves with a serene smile on her face, as if she knew it wouldn't be long before she was with them.

It was freezing outside, and she didn't have a jacket on. She had swallowed almost a full bottle of the pills. Paul, Trisha's dad, was with me when we finally found her. He carried her back to the car, and we rushed her to the hospital. She spent a little over a month in the psych ward. When the docs released her, she left the country. She barely talked to me for the next year and a half. Even now, she is distant. She doesn't trust me any longer," she said, crying softly. "I love her so much, Creon. She's all the family I've got left, and I didn't want to lose her, too."

He had thanked her for helping Carmen through that difficult time of her life. He had reassured her he would take care of her and not let anything happen to her sister. He also shared that Carmen was expecting their young.

"Perhaps this will help her," he had added. "I plan on filling her life full of happiness."

"I hope you do," Ariel had said with a sniffle. "She deserves it. I'm glad she has you as her mate, Creon."

"Not as much as I am glad that she has you as her sister," he had replied with feeling. "Watch over my hardheaded brother, little sister. You have truly blessed our family with your gentleness and love."

Ariel had laughed. "Mandra may not agree with you on the gentleness part, but I sure have the love part covered. Take care, Creon, until we meet again."

∽

Creon decided as he followed Carmen out of the lounge that it had been too long since their dragons had been out to play. Maybe a little distraction would help. He would do anything to help her get through this difficult time. He knew the longer they were together, her pain and grief would eventually fade to a more bearable level. He did not expect it to ever go completely away any more than his own pain would, but he knew he could heal as long as she was by his side.

He jogged up behind her, sweeping her off her feet. He ignored her startled squeal as he continued down the corridor at a brisk pace. He knew of a large storage bay that was relatively open. There would be plenty of room for their dragons to move without fear of damaging anything.

"What are you doing?" she asked breathlessly, looking up at him with those beautiful brown eyes of hers.

"I want to have fun," he said with a mischievous grin.

"Creon, I really don't feel like fooling around right now," she murmured, laying her head on his shoulder. "I would rather be alone for a little while, if you don't mind."

He chuckled. "Don't you know that as the mate of a Valdier prince, you will never be alone again? If Harvey is not with you or a part of him is not on you, you will always have your dragon. And soon, you will have two very stubborn little ones who will demand your attention. I want to have fun before they come along to take your attention away from me!" he exclaimed with an exaggerated pout of his lower lip.

"You are being a little juvenile, aren't you?" she asked with a sigh. "That pout is right out of a two-year-old's instruction manual for getting his own way."

Creon raised one of his eyebrows at her in indignation. "I am a Valdier dragon prince! I am never juvenile. I am gorgeous, sexy, loving, adorable, delightful, handsome, sexy…"

"Full of shit?" Carmen giggled as he passionately declared all of his attributes.

He wiggled both eyebrows up and down as he walked through the doors of the storage bay. "Totally! And did I mention sexy?" he asked with a grin as he gently set her down.

"I believe you did. A couple of times," she responded, looking at him with a somber sigh.

He smiled down at her and gripped both of her hands tightly in his, drawing them to his lips. "Play with me. Please," he asked quietly.

Carmen looked into his serious eyes. She suddenly knew that he was aware of what was bothering her. Tears filled her eyes and overflowed. Her quiet sobs grew until her body shook from the force of them. He pulled her into his arms and held her tight.

"Let it out," he murmured soothingly. "You have held it in too long. Let the tears wash the pain away and soothe your grief. He was a very fortunate mate to have someone like you in his life. I am glad I am being given that gift now," he said quietly stroking her back up and down. "Soon, our younglings will fill your arms. They will never replace what you have lost, but I hope that you will let me and them fill your heart so it can help you heal as you have helped to heal me."

Carmen listened to his softly spoken words as she sobbed out for the lives lost at too young an age. She knew life wasn't fair, but damn it, did it have to hurt so much? She closed her eyes and breathed in the heady masculine scent of Creon. It pulled at her, calming her until she lay quietly in his arms.

He wrapped one arm tightly around her waist and the other around her head, rocking her back and forth slowly. "Close your eyes for a moment," he said. "I want to show you something."

Carmen drew in a shuddering breath but did as he asked. "What now?"

"Look deep inside you to where your dragon is," he said in a hushed voice. "Let her show you what she is protecting for us."

She drew in another breath and focused inward. It was difficult at first as her mind felt like it was beaten and bruised. She forced herself to relax as Creon continued to whisper quietly to her, urging her to look deep. She gradually made out the shape of her dragon curled deep inside her.

The small, delicately built dragon lifted her slender head and looked at Carmen with flaming golden brown eyes. Her scales glistened and appeared to glow as she became clearer in Carmen's mind. Her wing was lying slightly away from her body as if she was having problems closing it all the way.

Carmen's breath swooshed out when her dragon lifted her wing to reveal why she couldn't pull it closer to her body. The two little sparks were more defined now. As she reached out to touch them, warmth flooded her. The sparks grew brighter and moved in excitement.

Now, you get to watch them while I get my mate for a little while, her dragon snorted. *They have too much energy like you! Always moving and playing! I not get no sleep.*

Before Carmen could react to her dragon's statement, she felt the tingling over her body as the change came over her. Vaguely she was aware of Creon taking a step away from her as she transformed. Her body twisted and turned, tingling before warmth flooded her and her dragon took control.

Creon watched lovingly as Carmen's body transformed into her dragon. Beautiful white, red, pink, and purple scales rippled and flowed over her skin in a glowing display of brilliance. Her long wings burst outward, expanding until their transparent white membranes stretched out above and behind her. Delicate claws formed with elegantly shaped pink nails peeking out from under her. Her head elongated until the beautiful curves of her jaw, snout, and forehead formed. Her small ears twitched back and forth as she looked around the storage bay.

"You are so beautiful, *mi elila*," Creon said, walking toward his mate.

He reached up to run his fingers over her delicate ear before sliding it along her jaw. He rubbed his fingers along her lower lip, using pressure to turn her head toward him. He smiled as she lowered her head and affectionately rubbed it against his chest. He continued stroking her and murmuring sweet words of love and need to her.

"You have helped to heal me, Carmen," he said quietly as his fingers caressed her smooth scales. "You healed me when I thought I was beyond redemption."

Carmen looked at him puzzled. She gently nudged him with her head, wanting him to continue. Creon looked into the dark golden brown eyes of his mate and sighed. His face softened with love as he stared into her eyes.

"The Great War changed me, making me harder and…darker. I changed greatly from the carefree young dragon I was before it began. We later learned that the war was started by a small group of Sarafin, Curizan, and Valdier royals who wanted to take control. They began small, raising dissension and unrest within their own clans. They called for radical changes. They wanted to restrict certain clans from having a say in the ruling of their worlds. They began making and changing laws to suit themselves. The non-warrior class was pressured to produce more while receiving less. Restrictions were placed on those who believed differently than they did. As the unrest at home grew so did the tensions between our star systems and the Sarafin and the Curizan." He paused as she pressed her head into his shoulder and sighed heavily.

"I guess you understand what I am talking about," he replied gruffly before continuing. "The Valdier had always been more reclusive because of our symbiot relationship. We were not sure how it would react to other species or what would happen if one was captured and taken. Those fears were realized when one clan accused a group of Sarafin warriors of attacking their village and capturing both the warriors and their symbiots. It wasn't until four years into the war that I found out differently. Ha'ven and I were in a fierce battle on one of the moons we use for mining the crystals. We had each become separated from the rest of our warriors during the battle. The tunnel we were in collapsed, trapping us. Ha'ven was pinned under some of the debris. When I moved in to kill him, he said for me to go ahead, but that the Curizans would never give in to the cowards who would murder innocent women and children." He stopped as he stared into the emptiness of the storage bay.

Carmen lifted her head and rolled onto her side. She pulled one of her wings around to grab him and pull him closer to her belly. She snorted to let him know she wanted him to rub her belly while he continued his story. The act of such innocent, caring pulled a smile from him.

"You like me stroking you, don't you?" he asked with a chuckle as he moved to sit down on the floor next to her and began running his hand up and down her soft belly. He sighed and continued his story. "I didn't know what he was talking about. I dug him out with the demand I wanted to know what he meant. One thing led to another, and for the first time, two members of the royal families from each star system sat down and talked. It took four bloody years with countless loss of life for us to face one another and only then because we were trying to kill each other," he shook his head in regret.

"So many fine warriors lost their lives for the greed of a few. Needless to say, instead of killing Ha'ven he became my best friend. We worked together after that and began piecing together the facts until it became clear who was behind everything. The only thing we weren't sure of was what part the Sarafin had played in the war. We needed to meet with a member of the royal family of Sarafin. That is not an easy task when you are friends with them, much less enemies. It just so happened that we caught up with Vox at the same time as an assassin did. I ended up saving his furry ass. He had been shot with a poisoned dart. The assassin wanted it to look like the Curizans had killed him.

Ha'ven captured the assassin. Once it became evident that the war was just a cover for what was really going on back on each of our planets, we made plans to bring the traitors down." He stopped stroking her and sat very still until she nudged him with her head again. "We thought we had succeeded until…until the woman I thought I loved betrayed everything that I believed in."

He looked with anguish at Carmen. "Aria was beautiful on the outside, but cold as ice on the inside. She was a member of a royal family on Curizan. I met her not long after Ha'ven and I became friends. We became lovers, and I made plans to bind my life to hers even though I knew she was not my true mate. My dragon tolerated her, but my symbiot couldn't stand her. It would leave whenever we were together. For over a year, she led me to believe she loved me as much as I loved her. It was only when Ha'ven was kidnapped and tortured—"

He let out a long breath. "She had planned it all using information she had been getting from me after we made love. Vox suspected her immediately, but I refused to believe someone so beautiful and passionate could betray me like that. It was only when he caught one of his warriors returning from her bed and tortured the truth out of him that I finally began to believe him. She came to my bed that night dressed in nothing but moonlight," he explained in a quiet voice. "She was beautiful, but for once I saw her for what she truly was, a cold-blooded bitch. I forced her to tell me where Ha'ven had been taken before I killed her," he said in an emotionless voice.

Carmen raised her head and looked at him steadily. She let out a deep growl and a snort before she pushed against his shoulder a little harder than before. He gazed into her eyes waiting to see the horror for what he had done. Instead, she blew out a small puff of hot air and raised one curved eyebrow before shaking her head.

He smiled. "I should have known you wouldn't be upset, my bloodthirsty little mate," he chuckled drily. "We rescued him, of course. But not before he had been beaten and tortured badly. It took him several months to recover. He forgave me long before I forgave myself," he said with a sigh.

Carmen realized it had taken a lot for the proud Valdier dragon prince to admit this dark time of his life to her. She loved him even more for having the courage to listen when he could so easily have ignored his doubts. She loved him for fighting to save not only the lives of his people but for forming a friendship with the ones who were once his enemies. And, she loved him for sharing with her his life, for good or for bad, and loving her for who she was…the pain, the grief, and the dream of a new life.

She rolled over, wrapping her wings around him and lifting him up until he lay on her rounded tummy. She cradled him against her body while rubbing her head against his. He chuckled as she rocked back and forth.

"How about I let my mate spend some time with you," he whispered in her pointed ear. "He wouldn't mind doing some rolling around with you either."

She slowly opened her wings so he could slide off her. In seconds, his larger black body was towering over her. His dark golden eyes flaming as they took in her exposed belly. A low, rumbling filled the storage area as he moved over her. He wrapped his long tail around hers, pulling her lower region up sharply as he slowly mounted her. His loud groan shook the walls as he slid deeply into her.

Now, I'm definitely having fun, he thought as he began rocking faster.

CHAPTER TWENTY

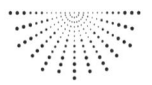

Two days later, Creon was fuming. They had arrived at the outer rim of the asteroid belt protecting the moon base Raffvin had built. Reports were coming in on what had taken place earlier in the day.

His brother's and Adalard's forces had led an attack on the base. Raffvin had been present, but from the reports, he had made plans to leave for another unknown base. This had forced his brother to make the decision to proceed in the hopes that the *Horizon*, with her added forces, and Vox's ship, the *Shifter*, could back them up should they need it. He understood the need, but he was also worried when he received word that Mandra had been seriously injured.

"Damn his hard-headed stubbornness! He should have waited for us! We were within a day's travel," Creon growled out as he slammed into the bridge conference room where Ha'ven was talking to Adalard. "He could have been killed, and we would have lost both him and my mate's sister!"

"Calm down, Creon," Adalard said calmly over the holovid. "We didn't have much choice. Bahadur intercepted a transmission that he was pulling up to move to another base. We had him cornered and out powered. We all agreed to take him out."

"We'll discuss your decision later, little brother," Ha'ven said grimly.

"I'm not that little anymore, Ha'ven," Adalard growled back. "You can't boss me around like you used to, big brother."

Ha'ven's eyes flashed, but he held his tongue. He knew he was out of line riding his younger brother's ass, but it worried him how close he had come to losing him lately. Between the assassins Raffvin had sent to kill his younger brothers and this battle, he was at his wits' end. He was surprised his mother had not tied Adalard up and stuck him in the dungeons under the palace for safe keeping.

"How is he?" Creon asked more quietly.

"He will be fine. The healer has him sedated right now. He had a hole in his chest, but it will take more than that to kill him. His mate is unbelievable!" Adalard said with a grin. "Bahadur has been trying to sweet-talk her away from him, but she won't budge. Your uncle had changed his symbiot to pure negative energy," he continued more soberly. "That was the weapon he had perfected. Somehow, his essence was enough to contaminate it. Ariel was given a stone by an unusual species on the moon where we met up with Bahadur. That is a story for another day. The stone absorbs negative energy. She was able to use that and her unusual way with the symbiots to hold his symbiot off long enough and pull enough of the negative energy away so that part of Mandra's symbiot was able to defeat it. What is left of his symbiot is very weak. Ariel has been spending time with it as it is very distressed."

"What of Raffvin?" Ha'ven asked, looking at his younger brother intently, noting the new scar on his face. "Were you able to kill him?"

Zebulon spoke up as he came into view. "No, he got away. He took a Curizan fighter. We are tracking him at the moment, but the signal is very weak. He was wounded. Without his symbiot to heal him and help protect his dragon, he will be greatly weakened. We believe he is going after Vox."

"Well, tell him to turn his ass around!" Vox said as he joined in on the holovid conference. "If he hadn't been such a coward, I would have saved him a trip off the moon."

"What in the galactic balls is going on, Vox?" Adalard said as he jerked back from the screen. "Are you torturing one of your men again?"

Vox sighed and rubbed his aching head. "No, my mate is mad at me again. She is singing something about bottles of drinks on a wall. She has been at it for two solid days now!" he growled out, throwing a look over his shoulder. "Riley, how was I to know you liked that piece of cloth so much? I thought it was alive when I saw the fur on it! How was I to know it was fake?"

"You could have asked before you shredded it, you furry moron! My sainted sister gave me that jacket for my birthday! Until you take me back to Earth I am going to make your life bloody hell!" she hollered back before she began singing off-key again.

Zebulon and Adalard's laughter echoed over the holovid. "I thought Ariel was bad! How did Vox get so lucky to find a female like that?"

"Obviously you are not sitting where I am!" Vox growled out in a low voice.

He winced when something flew through the air and struck him in the back of the head. "That's it, I'm telling Lodar and Tor you are being mean again!"

"Oh gods! Now they will be mad at me, too," Vox groaned out. "I need to go calm my mate before she starts another mutiny on board. I thought my crew was going to place me in a detention cell for killing her jacket. I thought the thing was attacking her! How was I supposed to know the fur was for decoration? Keep me posted on what is going on," he muttered defensively before he logged out quickly.

Creon shook his head in disbelief before turning back to the task at hand. "We need to regroup. Unless your tracking is successful, my guess is Raffvin will find a place to hide until he can recover. I think it would be best if we plan for that time," Creon said tiredly. "Mandra needs to recover. I suggest he return to Valdier where he and his symbiot can heal faster. I also have a favor to ask of my brother's talented mate. I have a young pactor that is lame and needs care. An old human man and his grandson were found at the Antrox mines when we were searching for Vox. I would appreciate it if the animal was transferred to the *D'stroyer* where it can be taken back home and cared for. The boy has become very fond of it and would be heartbroken if it was disposed of," Creon said before looking at Ha'ven. "I plan to take my mate to Earth before we return to Valdier. There is an issue there that I need to take care of personally, and she has family she needs to say good-bye to one last time."

"What of the old man and the boy?" Ha'ven asked. "Do you plan to let them return to their world? From what I have heard, it might not be a good idea."

Creon nodded his head. "The old man swore he would not say a word, and the boy is mute. No one would believe them anyway. It is important that I travel there," he said with quiet determination.

"I will continue tracking Raffvin. I can leave as soon as we have a fix on where he is heading," Bahadur said.

Ha'ven nodded. "Adalard, I want you to come aboard the *Horizon*. It would be better if you traveled with Creon," he said.

"No," Adalard bit out. "I know what you are trying to do, Ha'ven. I am meeting up with Jazar. He thinks he has discovered where two additional bases are hidden. We need to strike before Raffvin's forces discover we have their locations."

"When did you find out this?" Ha'ven demanded. "Why wasn't I told immediately?"

"Jazar has been very busy. Let us just say he took advantage of your desire to send him to the furthest spaceport in the star system," Adalard said with a crooked smile.

Ha'ven cursed under his breath. He had sent his two brothers on different missions in the hopes of keeping them safe. Instead, they were neck deep in the middle of the trouble Raffvin and Ben'qumain had started.

"I need to return to my home," Ha'ven said with an apology. "My brothers and I will continue to search for Raffvin. I will coordinate everything with your brothers and Vox and his brothers," he said in apology.

"It is much appreciated," Creon murmured. "If this was not so important, I would wait, but my mate needs this to finally heal and accept her life with me."

Ha'ven reached out and squeezed Creon's shoulder. "You deserve this happiness, my friend. Never doubt that."

Creon smiled at the man who had become like a brother to him. "Thank you."

"If this is the part where you two start hugging and kissing, I am out of here," Bahadur said sarcastically.

Creon flipped his middle finger up at the holovid. "I learned this gesture from my mate. It means 'fuck you,' Bahadur." Creon chuckled.

"Only in your dreams, dragon prince. Only in your dreams," Bahadur laughed back before bidding them farewell to go check on several of the warriors who had been injured during the battle.

"I will join my brother and yours on the *D'stroyer* before heading home," Ha'ven said, getting up. "Safe journey, Creon. Take good care of your warrior kitten."

Creon smiled as Ha'ven walked out the door. "Oh, I plan to, my friend. I plan to."

~

Creon quietly entered his and Carmen's living quarters late that night. Ha'ven, Adalard, Bahadur, Zebulon, and he had discussed plans for taking out the rest of the Curizan bases that Ha'ven and Adalard's half-brother had created before Zoran killed him. They wanted to eliminate all of Raffvin's defenses in an effort to corner him.

He sighed tiredly. The healers had worked on Mandra for most of the afternoon until late into the evening. They assured him he would heal. It would take a little longer due to his symbiot not being able to help him.

The golden creature had split in half so a part of it could remain with his mate. Creon learned that Ariel had escaped from the detention cell his brother had confined her to with the help of the symbiot. He was thankful she had escaped, otherwise he would more than likely be mourning the loss of both of them.

Raffvin's symbiot was a formidable enemy. It had the power of the royal blood behind it. With Mandra's symbiot being cut in half, it was stronger than most but would have been no defense against his uncle's more powerful one. He would have to remember to question Ariel more on the stone she was given. It might be necessary to see if they could find more or at least discover what properties it had that allowed it to absorb the negative energy. He was sure his brother Trelon and Cara, Trelon's mate, would be fascinated by it.

A smile curved his lips as he thought of the extraordinary women that his brother Zoran had discovered. Each one was strong and powerful in their own way. Abby's gentle strength, protectiveness, and caring made her the perfect queen for their people.

Cara's energy matched her inquisitive nature. The things she had invented were helping to improve their warships already. Trisha's ability with what she called "guerilla" warfare was unbelievable. He had talked to Palto and Jaguin about her. All four of his best trackers were amazed at her abilities. He had also talked to Kelan about what happened on the moon orbiting Quitax. Her ability to survive on such a hostile moon while being hunted was worthy of any warrior. The fact that she was pregnant when this happened was nothing short of incredible. Now, listening to what his mate's sister, Ariel, had done in the middle of battle left him in awe.

These women might be smaller, more delicate, and more fragile than many of the females inhabiting the ten known star systems that he had traveled to, but they held a quiet strength and dignity that made them fiercer than any warrior. They had a passion for life and an abundance of compassion and loyalty that would make any mate proud to call them theirs.

His thoughts turned to his and Carmen's time in the storage bay. She had fought to protect those weaker, and it had cost her dearly. He had decided then and there they would travel to Earth. When she had broken down and cried, as if each tear was pulled from the very essence of her being, it had torn at his heart.

The pain and grief trapped for so long in her slender body shook him to his core. He had seen many, many things, but what she had witnessed broke through even his staunch belief in what a warrior could survive. To watch helplessly while his mate's life was taken in front of him would have driven him mad with grief and pain. The images of her memories sent from his symbiot burned into his soul with a raging need for revenge on the man who had taken so much from her.

He walked quietly to the counter where an assortment of refreshments were and poured a drink. He let his gaze roam the spacious interior of their living quarters before walking over to the viewport. It wasn't anywhere near as large as his living quarters back on Valdier, but it was larger than the other living quarters on board the *Horizon*.

He knew there was an excellent possibility that Carmen would give birth before their return to Valdier. From what he learned from his mother, human females carried their young for nine months while a Valdier female carried for five. He knew Zoran's mate, Abby, was due any time and Trelon's mate would not be long after that.

He stood staring out at the richness of space. He had spent a great deal of his adult life in space but now he found he wanted more. He wanted a place where he could watch his younglings grow and run and play. He wanted a place where he and Carmen could fly in their dragon forms whenever they wanted or lie in a meadow of purple grass and listen to the sounds of the river and creatures of the forest around them. He wanted a home.

Slender arms wrapped around his waist from behind, and he could feel her cheek as she laid it against his back. He lifted one of his arms to hold her close. They stood like that for several long minutes before he pulled her around so he could wrap his arm around her, laying his palm over her stomach as he drew her back against his chest.

"What are you thinking about?" she asked him quietly, staring at his reflection in the glass.

Creon raised his drink and took a sip before he answered. "I was thinking that our younglings will more than likely be born in space or perhaps even on your world," he said softly.

Carmen jerked in surprise. "You mean…as in on Earth?" she whispered in surprise.

He set his drink down on the small round table near the viewport and wrapped his arms around her, pulling her closer as he rested his head on hers. "Would you be upset?" he asked. "It's what you wanted, isn't it? To return to your world at least one more time."

Carmen turned so she was facing him. "Why?" she asked suspiciously. "Why would you take me now when you were so adamant before?"

"I am going to kill the man who hurt you and your first mate," he said with quiet conviction. "I have seen what he did. How you survived such loss I will never know, and if it is within my power, you will never have to face again. But know this, I will be the one to kill him. It is my right as your mate to seek justice."

Carmen shook her head. "What if something happens to you?" she asked with a catch in her voice. "I couldn't go through that again, Creon. To lose you..." Her voice faded as fear for him overrode her desire for revenge. "Killing him will never bring Scott or our baby back," she said, looking up at him with tears in her eyes. "But loving you and having you in my life give me something I never expected to have again. I can't take a chance of losing you."

Creon chuckled. "Carmen, I am not human. I am not easy to kill. He has hurt more than just you. He will be brought to justice for hurting you, your first mate, and your unborn child. But, I will also stop him from hurting others. Plus, I want you to have a chance to say good-bye. You deserve that closure before you can rise up completely out of the ashes to be reborn again, my beautiful phoenix."

Carmen didn't say anything. Instead, she leaned into Creon's warm body and hugged him tightly to her. She snuggled closer, wishing she could always remain this close to him. A slight fluttering in her stomach caused her to jerk back in shock. Her hands flew to her stomach as the fluttering continued.

"What is it?" Creon asked in concern.

"The babies," she whispered in awe, looking down at her hands pressed tightly against her stomach. "They are moving."

Creon's face broke into an eager grin as he pressed his hand over hers. Carmen moved her hand so she could press his against her slightly rounded abdomen. A moment later, his face lit with a huge grin as he felt the slight movement under his palm.

"They will be strong warriors like their father!" he exclaimed with pride.

You better tell mate they be strong warriors like their mommy. They only have one head on them, her dragon muttered tiredly. *They kick like you too.*

Carmen's eyes grew wide. She bit her lower lip, trying to hide the giggle that was threatening to escape. Her eyes glowed with mischief as she looked up into Creon's face.

"Well, according to my dragon," she giggled, "you better start thinking in shades of pink instead of blue. She says they are going to be just like me. How do you feel about having a couple of rough-and-tumble little girls?"

The smile on Creon's face faded along with all the color in it. He swayed dizzily as the fact that she was having little girls sank in. He groaned and pulled her closer to him.

"I never… It has been so long since a female…" He was having trouble breathing as the thought of what having two beautiful daughters would mean. "Dragon's balls!" he roared out suddenly. "I'll kill any warrior who so much as looks at them," he growled out. "I will have to get Cree and Calo… No, they are too young. I'll have to find some older warriors who are mated… I'll build us a home surrounded by the highest walls… Maybe I can…"

"Creon…" Carmen said gently. "Creon…"

"What?" he asked, looking down at her with a wild, dazed look.

"They aren't even born yet. I think we have time before the warriors start coming to ask them out on dates," she said as she smiled patiently up at him. "Years even."

"Years?" he asked blankly.

"Years," she replied, brushing a kiss over his lips. "Make love to me," she whispered.

"Years?" he asked again, doubtfully.

Carmen giggled and grabbed his hand to pull him toward their sleeping quarters. "Years," she assured him as she dragged him toward the bed.

CHAPTER TWENTY-ONE

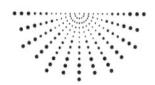

It had been four weeks since they left the *D'stroyer* and Vox's warship, the *Shifter*. She was beginning to show more and more each day. She had to cut back on some of her workouts.

She spent more time stretching and just walking the warship than she did kicking Cree and Calo's ass now. They were told to stay near her at all times as she began to "blossom," as Creon called it. He was constantly trying to get her to lie down and rest. Cree and Calo had been just as bad. She knew the two warriors had to be sick of being her babysitters, because she was thoroughly sick of having them as her twin shadows.

"I think you should take it easy today," Creon said as he finished getting ready so he could report for duty. "Your ankles were swelling a little."

"They are supposed to swell some! I'm pregnant. I am sick of being in here. I want to go visit with Cal and Meli— Mel," she corrected quickly. "They are both excited about returning to Earth soon. I think they are both as sick of being cooped up in the repair bay as I am of being in here."

"There is no reason for them to remain there all the time," he said, looking at her with a frown. "We will be near Earth by the end of the week."

"I think they are just more comfortable being by themselves," she said, rubbing her stomach absently when the twins decided to kick at the same time.

"I wish we had been able to see Kelan and Trisha before they left," he said as he came to lay a calming hand over hers. "It sounds like they were having problems getting some of the warriors back off the planet. Several warriors found their true mates, though they appear to be having some minor difficulties with them."

Carmen raised her eyebrow. "Let me guess," she said drily. "The guys forgot to ask before they decided to claim."

Creon shifted uneasily from one foot to the other. "We don't always have much choice. When our dragon and our symbiot find our mate, it is a little overwhelming. We get around to asking later," he added defensively.

"No, you get around to telling, ordering, and demanding later," she added, daring him to tell her differently.

"Yes," he added as his hands moved up to her fuller breasts. "But, you love it when I am like that. Now before you go, remember you have your comlink and that Cree or Calo are with you. Just in case…" he added before he crushed his lips to hers to still the protests he could see forming on her lips.

∽

She was so going to get Cree and Calo back at the first opportunity she got after she delivered. Cree was snickering and making fun of her walk as she moved down the corridor. He was so going to be toast. She might even have to think up some things to do before she had the babies. Maybe she should talk to Cara about how to modify their cleansing unit or something.

Another thing she noticed was the bigger she got, the more protective and annoying Creon became. She could barely go pee without him wanting someone to be there with her. If she heard one more "in case of" she was going to scream. It had finally gotten to the point that she spent most of the day down in the repair bay with Cal and Melina. Since the pactor had been sent to a new home on the *D'stroyer* with Ariel, Melina had been feeling depressed.

"Cal?" Carmen called out as she entered the repair bay.

"I'm in here, Carmen," Cal said, walking out of his and Melina's living quarters.

"Are you all right? You look a little pale," Carmen asked with concern.

"I'm fine. The soup I had for lunch isn't agreeing with me, is all," Cal said with a gruff snort. "God only knows what was in it. I quit even trying to figure it out years ago. Figured if I knew what was in the food I'd probably starve to death. I worry about Melina, though. She is real picky about what she eats."

Carmen laughed. "She isn't the only one. You should have seen the warriors trying to figure out what to feed my sister. She's a vegetarian. They had never heard of such a thing before. The only thing they could think to feed her was fruit. She was so sick of it by the time we got to Valdier I wasn't sure she would ever eat any of it ever again," Carmen replied as she moved to the chairs they had set out.

"Hi, Carmen," Melina said quietly after she made sure that no one had followed her into the repair bay. "How are you doing? Have you talked to the girls that took you back at the spaceport?"

"Yes, I stopped on my way down here," she answered. "Evetta and Hanine are helping the engineers and programmers on board the *Horizon* with some things. Hanine shared how she was able to bypass the shields on the spaceport, and Evetta is working on identifying some of the programming the Marastin Dow use to overtake the freighters. Aaron is almost as good as new, and he and Ben are training with some of the warriors. I think they are going to settle on Curizan when we get back. Ha'ven mentioned a village that would welcome them all."

"That's wonderful," Melina said, pushing a strand of dark brown hair back behind her ear. "I was able to listen in to some of their conversations. Ben and Aaron were from Kansas. They worked on one of the big farms out there."

Melina turned to her Granddad who was sitting quietly. "Gramps, why don't you go lie down for a while? I think you should get the doc to come look at you. You weren't feeling good last night either," she said with soft concern.

"I don't need no doctor, but I think I will go lie down for a while," Cal said, getting slowly to his feet. "Carmen, you stay and take care of my granddaughter. She needs some girl time."

"I will, Cal," Carmen said smiling up at Cal. "I hope you feel better."

"Thanks," Cal said with a genuine smile. He turned to look at Melina. "I love you, girl. Don't you ever forget that."

"I won't, Gramps," Melina said, standing up to help her granddad.

She took a step toward him as he suddenly stiffened and grabbed at his chest. She barely had time to grab him before he collapsed to the floor. Her cry of fear echoed loudly in the repair bay.

"Gramps!" Melina cried out as she frantically rolled him over onto his back. "Carmen, he's not breathing! Gramps!"

Carmen yelled for Cree as loud as she could as she moved over to where Cal lay on the floor. She bent over him, listening for a heartbeat, and feeling for a breath. She didn't feel or hear either one. She climbed over him and began doing CPR.

Melina moved to his head and tilted it back, waiting for Carmen's signal to breath for him. The doors to the repair bay opened, and Cree rushed in. He saw Cal's prone figure and immediately called for medical assistance. He knelt down next to the elderly human male, and quickly assessed his condition. There was no pulse, and his skin was turning a light shade of blue. He glanced up at the man's grandson and froze.

Dark curls tumbled over Melina's shoulders and down her back. She was whispering frantically for her grandfather to be all right, begging him to please not leave her alone. She ran her small hands over his cheeks.

"Please, Gramps, don't leave me," she cried softly. "Please don't leave me here alone. We're going to be home soon. We'll go back to the farm. I'll do the cooking and cleaning, and we can go visit mommy, daddy, and grandma's graves on Sundays after church. It will be just like before. I bet that old hound dog is still coming around looking for scraps. Please, please, please, don't leave me."

Melina looked up into the stunned eyes of Cree. "Please help me," she whispered. "Please make him better."

Cree stared into the stunning green eyes filled with desperate fear and pleading and knew he was totally lost. He would have moved all the stars in the galaxy to do what she begged, if he had the power to do so, but he knew there was nothing to be done for the old human. His essence had already left his body.

"I... There is nothing that can be done to save him," he said, gently reaching out to touch Melina's cheek in comfort. "He is gone."

Melina scrambled back before he could touch her. Hatred, pain, grief, and despair burned in her vivid green eyes. She jumped to her feet when he rose to stand over her grandfather's body. Carmen sat on the floor next to Cal, holding his hand and bowing her head.

"No! You don't want to help him," she cried out, looking down at her grandfather as tears overflowed down her cheeks. "I've seen what your gold creatures can do. They could save him if you told it to."

Cree shook his head, taking a step toward her. "No, Mel..." he said in resignation. "Even our symbiots cannot heal what age has wrought."

Melina's cry of pain filled the repair bay. When Cree took another step toward her, she turned and fled to the crates, scrambling between the narrow slits where he could not touch her. The doors opened again to admit Tandor and several other medical staff. Creon followed closely behind them.

"Carmen," he called out desperately.

Carmen looked up as he called her name. Silent tears fell gently down her cheeks. In the far recesses of the crates, Melina's jagged sobs filled the air. She carefully laid Cal's wrinkled hand on his chest.

"Good-bye, my dear, dear friend," she said quietly before letting Creon help her to stand. "It was a heart attack, I think."

She turned into Creon's arms and sobbed as Tandor nodded his head briefly to confirm what she suspected. "He died instantly. There would have been nothing we could have done to save him. It just gave out," he confirmed.

Carmen buried her head in Creon's shoulder and sobbed quietly as the medics placed Cal's body onto the portable med bed. Tandor looked over to the crates where Melina's sobs could be heard. He shook his head sadly.

"I'll see to the boy," he said.

"Woman," Cree said quietly, his eyes glued to the crates before he turned to look at Creon and Tandor. "The boy is a woman. What is her name?" he asked, looking at Carmen now.

Carmen raised her head and looked with tear-filled eyes toward the crates where Melina's sobs were growing quieter. "Melina," she replied softly. "I'll stay with her. She shouldn't be left alone."

"Melina," Cree repeated softly as the door opened and his brother walked in. He looked at him in silent determination. "*Her* name is Melina."

Calo's stride slowed as what his brother was saying sank in. His eyes immediately went to the crates where only an occasional whimper could be heard. His face tightened in concern and resolve. He looked at his brother and nodded once. They were in agreement.

∼

It had been a little over a week since Cal had passed away. Melina refused to leave the repair bay. It had taken days to finally get her to come out from the crates where she had created a hidden den. She had quietly piled bedding and the few things that belonged to her grandfather into the narrow opening. She only came out when Carmen was alone. Several times Cree and Calo had tried to remain, but she wouldn't even respond to Carmen if she sensed they were anywhere nearby. Both of their symbiots had divided and slipped into the narrow crack between the crates. The men were frustrated because they couldn't even move the crates apart for fear of crushing her under them if they did. Their only contact was with their symbiots that had become her constant companions. The men went several times a day to leave food and drinks for her, as well as, fresh linens and articles of clothing.

Carmen was waiting for her to finish with her shower. She had sworn Carmen to not let anyone, especially those two warriors who wouldn't leave her alone, into the repair bay. Carmen turned when the door opened, and both men entered with a defiant and determined look on their faces.

"No," she said, shaking her head and crossing her arms. "Don't make me have to kick your asses!"

"Lady Carmen, please," Calo said in a strained voice. "You do not understand. She is our mate."

"Don't you think she has enough to deal with?" Carmen asked as she let her hands slip to her hips. "She just lost her last family member, she is about to return home after being gone for the past four years, and you think having not one but two mates is supposed to help her feel better?"

Cree's face tightened. "We have no choice," he growled out. His fists clenched tightly at his side. "She has us now. We will care for her."

"No," said a voice from the doorway. "I want you to leave me alone. I'm taking Gramps back so he can be with grandma and my folks," Melina said in a defiant voice. "I'm going home."

"Melina," Cree choked out harshly. "You are our mate. We have claimed you," he said as his eyes moved to the twin bands of gold wrapped around her wrists and her neck.

"Our dragons and our symbiots have claimed you, as well. You are our true mate," Calo said, taking a step forward.

Melina determinedly shook her head. "No," she said softly, looking at the men with sad eyes. "I'm going home and will forget this ever happened to me. I'll live my life back home in Georgia. I can't be your mate," she said, bowing her head until her hair hid her face.

"Melina," Cree and Calo said at the same time.

Melina just shook her head and darted to the crates again before they could stop her. Their loud roars of frustration echoed around the repair bay. When the sound died down, Carmen could hear Melina's soft sniffles as she cried.

"Give her time," Carmen encouraged both men quietly. "She needs to bury her grandfather. Give her that before you do anything. Give her time to say good-bye."

"What if…" Calo asked hoarsely, looking at the crates.

Carmen laid a hand on each man's arm. She waited until they turned to look at her before she said anything. She needed them to understand what she was trying to tell them.

"She needs closure," she whispered sadly as tears burned in her own eyes. "We have to say good-bye and accept there is no going back, only forward. Trust me. I'm speaking from experience."

Both men stared down at her intently before their eyes moved back to the crates and the soft whimpers. Pain flashed through both men's eyes before understanding and resignation followed. They each nodded their reluctant acceptance.

"Just know this," Cree spoke in a voice filled with resolve. "She will not be remaining on her world when we leave," he said before he nodded to his brother.

Carmen watched as both men turned and left. Her heart went out to Melina, but she also understood the men had no choice. To leave her behind would be a death sentence to not only the men, their dragons, and their symbiots, but also to Melina who, unbeknownst to her, had already accepted the men's claims if the way she gently rubbed the gold bracelets wrapped around her wrists were an indication of how she felt.

CHAPTER TWENTY-TWO

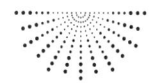

"It was nice to see Trisha and Paul again," Carmen said as she sat in the living room of Paul's ranch house. "Even if it was only on a holovid screen."

"They have their hands full," Creon replied. "At least two of the warriors remained behind only because Kelan knew we were coming," he said, moving closer so he could brush a kiss across her lips. "It was very nice of Paul to have set up this house as a base for us," he continued as he sat next to her, pulling her onto his lap.

"We'll still have to be careful," she whispered. "If the government finds out about aliens landing in the middle of Wyoming, I don't think they are going to be very happy with you."

"We will be very careful," he promised. "We cannot deny our warriors a chance at finding their true mates. This is a rare chance. They will be very careful not to ruin it for others."

Carmen laid back against his arm, pulling his other hand around to cover her belly. She was definitely showing now. There was no denying or hiding that she was pregnant. She played with his fingers as she thought about what still needed to be done.

"Who remained on the planet?" she asked huskily as she ran her fingers lightly over his hand which was making very arousing circles on her belly.

"Jaguin and Gunner are still here," he replied distractedly. "They are two of the best trackers on Valdier and know how to disappear when they need to."

"Trisha said that there were several other women on board that were not being very cooperative," she said as she gripped his hand and moved it higher so it was closer to her breast.

"Kor and Palto are returning to Valdier with their mates. Two men who were with Trisha also found mates, as well as several other warriors. Kelan gave each warrior time to search before he was forced to return. Jaguin has yet to find his mate, but Gunner has found his," he murmured before he pushed her back into the cushions of the couch. "I would rather talk about my mate. Do you have any idea how long it has been since we have made love?"

Carmen giggled and acted like she had to think hard for a minute. "Let me see—oh yeah!" she said, snapping her fingers. "I think it was this morning." She laughed as she wrapped her arms around his neck.

Carmen reached up to press a kiss against his lips when her cell phone buzzed out with the ringtone she had set for her contact. She jerked back and stared at Creon silently for another ring, before she pushed against his shoulder, forcing him back as she scrambled to reach for the cell phone on the end table.

"Speak," she said tersely.

"He'll be at this location in two days," the voice said on the other end. "Watch your back. I've uploaded additional information about the compound. This is the last time I can help you," the voice growled out on the other end. "I think he is on to me." The line went silent.

Carmen turned to look at Creon with cool, clear eyes. "We have him," she said stonily.

Creon nodded grimly. "You will do exactly what I say, Carmen, or I will tie your ass up until I get back," he replied sternly.

Carmen's eyes softened, and she let them drop to her swollen midsection. "I won't let him take this away from me again," she said quietly. "When this is over—"

"When this is over," he said gently, brushing his knuckles down her cheek before continuing. "Then this world will be a little safer for others such as yourself."

"Love me," she whispered.

"Always," he replied as he pushed her back down into the cushions once again.

~

Gunner and Jaguin looked on in silence as the symbiot transport glided over the terrain. They had returned late last night to Paul's ranch. Both wore grim expressions when they were asked about their mates.

"Mine is safely aboard the *Horizon*," Gunner stated. "I hope," he added in a low voice. Jaguin added under his breath, "I have not been successful in finding a mate."

Creon had recruited them to help with protecting Carmen on the mission to find and eliminate Javier Cuello. Cree and Calo had not returned with Melina yet. They had traveled with her to bury her grandfather in the family plot back on the small farm that they had owned outside of Clayton, Georgia.

"Carmen is your first priority," Creon was telling both men. They were traveling in Harvey who had formed into a sleek jet. Jaguin's symbiot and a smaller section of Gunner's symbiot would travel along with them. Half of Gunner's symbiot had remained on board the *Horizon* to "protect" his new mate. Carmen suspected it was more to keep an eye on her since he seemed just a little stressed at the moment.

Creon grinned at Carmen briefly over his shoulder. "You caused the same headache for me, in case you don't remember," he reminded her quietly.

"Who? Me?" she teased back with a nervous smile.

He raised one of her hands to his mouth. "Yes, and I would do it all over again to have you by my side," he added softly.

Carmen's eyes shimmered for a moment before she blinked rapidly. "You've turned me into a wimp! I never used to cry," she muttered, pulling her hand free and rubbing her eyes.

"It is the hormones, according to *Dola*," he teased. "You will be back to kicking everyone's ass, including mine, after the girls are born."

"You can bet your ass on that," she grunted out.

"How much further?" Gunner asked, looking at the holovid image of the compound that Javier was hiding at.

"We should be there in another thirty minutes," Creon said.

JD, the informant Carmen was supposed to have met months ago, hadn't let her down. He was an undercover agent with the DEA. He had been close friends with her former boss, Kevin.

He had worried when she didn't show up months ago that Javier had found out she was after him and had put a hit out on her, especially when Kevin couldn't tell him where she was either. Carmen had told him a story about being hurt in a kidnapping. She stayed as close to the truth as possible without mentioning her unexpected meeting with aliens and being on another planet.

JD had sent her a complete map of the compound in Colombia, where Javier was currently hiding. He could only tell her that Javier would be at the compound in two days' time. He didn't know how long he would stay, as the government was cracking down on the cartel. The governor he had tried to kill was now the president of the country and was not a forgiving man when it came to someone trying to kill his family, especially his son.

"After we land in the compound, I want both of you to cover Carmen. They have weapons that can shoot long range. I've given you some of Ha'ven's toys. The shields will protect us from their weapons. Kill any who fire on you," Creon said grimly. "Carmen, you will stay behind me. They will not see Harvey until he shifts into a different form. Jaguin and Gunner's symbiots will take out most of the guards. Hopefully, we will enter before Cuello is aware we are there."

"Why didn't we just beam in?" she asked quietly, rubbing her stomach which was knotted with nerves.

You not like beaming, her dragon growled out, annoyed that she was even doing this. *You let me out if you get trapped. I make bad guys crispy.*

You are so bad, Carmen replied softly. *After this is over, how about I talk Creon into going flying when we get back home. Paul showed me some nice secluded places we could have some fun in.*

You promise? her dragon rumbled in delight. *I have my mate? All me?*

All you! I promise, Carmen swore with a giggle.

I still want to burn bad guys, her dragon grumbled.

"No," Creon's voice was deeper than it normally was as his dragon answered his mate. "I know what she wants. It is too dangerous. Do not let her out," he said fiercely.

"I won't," Carmen responded. "At least, not here."

Creon's eyes shifted to her at the sound of the slight purr in her voice. Black scales rippled on his arms in response to his mate's teasing suggestion. He was about to answer when he felt a slap on the back of his head.

"What?" he snarled at Gunner who was sitting back in his seat.

"You pulled me away from that stubborn ass…my mate, so the least you can do is have a little sympathy on me," he grumbled out in a pout. "I was almost to the point I think she was going to talk to me instead of trying to kill me."

"Yeah, well, you are still ahead of me. At least you found your mate," Jaguin bit out as he turned to look at the brightly lit compound coming into view. "Do you think he has enough lights on? This place could be seen from the *Horizon*," he complained.

No sooner had the words escaped from his mouth that the lights flickered and went out. Jaguin and Gunner grinned. Their symbiots had arrived ahead of them and prepared a landing party. Harvey floated unseen above the ground. A doorway dissolved, and Jaguin and Gunner stood. They nodded their heads and dove out the doorway, shifting as they fell into their dragons. They moved in silence through the compound, helping to take out any armed guard. Gunner breathed a glowing blue fire ring that faded quickly to show it was safe to land.

Harvey set down in the center of the burned ring. The doorway appeared again, and Creon helped Carmen down. Jaguin and Gunner were waiting for her and quickly took up their stance on each side of her as Creon led the way.

Harvey shifted into a huge werecat. An invisible shield protected the small group as they moved toward the house situated in the middle of the compound. Creon waved his hand, and the door disintegrated. He quickly pocketed the device Ha'ven had given him.

"Cool toy," Gunner murmured. "I hope that damn thing doesn't work on us."

Creon grinned and shook his head. "No, only wood," he said, nodding to the pieces of metal hanging from the door and the pieces on the ground.

A young slender girl came out of a side room. Her eyes widened, and her mouth opened to scream, but no sound came out. She looked at the door further down the hallway, then back to the small group of strange beings coming in through a door that was no longer there. Her dark eyes looked hopeful as she glanced back to the door.

Carmen locked eyes with the young girl whose eyes moved to Carmen's rounded waist before they rose to stare at her in silent understanding. The girl pointed at the door and raised four fingers, then two more and the shape of a woman. The girl pointed to the four fingers and nodded. Then pointed to the two and shook her head vigorously in denial. Carmen raised her finger to her lips and nodded her understanding. The girl moved aside as the group walked silently down the hallway.

Creon reached for the device before realizing it would not work as the door was solid metal. He looked to Harvey, who snorted and moved forward rapidly. In seconds, the door was lying flat on the floor and gold tentacles wove around the room, holding three men in place where they were sitting and the fourth by his ankles in the air.

Creon moved to stop Carmen from entering the room when he saw what the men were doing, but she pushed past him. Her eyes darkened in distress as she saw one young girl around Melina's age stretched out on a T-shaped rack. Her shirt was pulled down around her waist. Bloody stripes crisscrossed her back where the man standing had been whipping her. Her head hung down, a long, pale braid of blond hair was hanging down in front of her.

"Cut her down," Carmen demanded immediately as her eyes went to the other girl.

She stared at the other girl who was tied up in a kneeling position. She had blonde hair, as well. Her hair was shorter, but not by much.

She had dark bruises across one side of her face, and her eyes were dazed as if she might have a concussion.

"Who are you?" Javier demanded in Spanish from where he was trapped in his seat.

Carmen stepped out from around Creon's left side so she could be seen by Javier. She knew he recognized her the minute he saw her. She turned to face him. She felt frozen inside until the moment her eyes locked on his. The fire of rage began burning uncontrollably inside her as hatred, pain, and grief rose. Memories of Scott looking at her before Javier shot him, the months of pain from recovering from her own wounds, and dealing with the loss of her husband and child.

"You!" he snarled, fighting to break free. "I have looked for you for the past four years!"

"You should have looked harder because I wanted you to find me," Carmen said in a voice devoid of all emotion.

She looked at the two women. Jaguin was gently holding the body of the girl who had been whipped. His symbiot was circling her in distress, trying to wrap around her. Jaguin cradled her bloody body, trying to be careful of her ravaged back.

"Why?" she asked as Gunner gently lifted the other girl up when she couldn't stand.

"She looked enough like you that I could make her pay for what you did to me!" he bit out in rage. He looked at the gold threads holding him. "What is this? What type of weapon is this? I have never seen anything like it before," he said, suddenly realizing that he was in a perilous position.

"You hurt her because she looked like me?" Carmen asked, swaying slightly. "You hurt an innocent girl because she reminded you of me?"

Creon wrapped his arm around Carmen's waist. "Gunner, take Carmen with you and return to the *Horizon*."

"No!" Carmen said sharply. She pulled away from Creon and stared at Javier. "What I did to you?" she bit out harshly, taking a step toward Javier. "What did I do to you?"

"Let me go and I will show you," Javier demanded coldly.

Carmen waved her hand. Creon bit back a curse and told Harvey to release the man but to be cautious. Javier pulled a cane that was leaning against the desk toward him. He stood awkwardly and moved slowly around the desk. Once he was on the other side, he pulled his pant leg up enough for Carmen to see he was wearing a prosthetic leg.

"You took my leg when you stabbed me," he bit out harshly. "You disfigured me for life!"

Carmen looked at him with cold eyes. "You killed my husband and baby. You left me for dead. Do you really think I give a damn that you lost a leg? You took everything I cared about in this world away from me!"

"You seem to have found something in this world to replace the man and child you declare was taken from you," Javier snarled out, nodding his head toward her rounded belly.

Carmen smiled coldly. "Yes, but there is one big difference," she said quietly.

"And what is that?" Javier asked with a sneer.

"They are not from this world," she said as she let the wave of change sweep over her. Brilliant shades of white, red, pink, and purple scales rippled over her as she let her dragon have her way.

Crispy? her dragon asked hopefully.

Extra! Carmen said firmly.

Creon's muttered oath followed his orders for Jaguin, Gunner, and their symbiots to return with the two injured women to the *Horizon* while he took care of the men and his mate. Creon shifted, breathing fire at the same time as Carmen did. Their combined fire engulfed Javier, freezing the look of horror and terror on his face for the briefest moment in time before ash floated down where he had once stood. Creon turned to the other men as Harvey released them, one at a time. Small mounds of ash were the only testament to their existence.

He turned to his mate who had raised her head and roared out as the last of her grief poured out of her. Gently, he moved his black body closer to hers. He snarled out to Harvey to create an opening large enough for them to fly through.

In seconds, a huge hole opened the back wall out into the dark. Creon pushed his mate with his wings and tail, nipping at her to force her to follow him. He knew she was trapped in the past. He needed to bring her away from this place and take her into her new future.

Slowly she responded, moving toward the opening. The closer she got, the faster she went, as if she was ready to face the new beginning that awaited her outside of the walls of the compound. Her wings swept the ash of the men up and away until nothing remained of their existence.

Soon they were both airborne, followed closely by Harvey. He would let her fly as far and as fast as she wanted. When she tired, he would hold her and guide her. He would never let her fall or flounder again.

Neither one of them saw the young girl standing in the remains of the compound alone, a look of wonder and a small smile of relief on her face. Miracles really did exist she thought as she crossed herself. She was free!

CHAPTER TWENTY-THREE

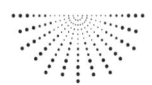

*C*armen flew into the night, her wings stretched wide as she soared. She raced the winds, touched the clouds, kissed the moon as she flew up as high as she could before exhaustion began to set in. She had reached the Yucatan Peninsula before she began to slow down.

As she floated along the coastline, sandy beaches called to her. She moved away from the lighted towns to a small dark cove. The waters were calm as she glided inches above them. The stars and moonlight reflecting like diamonds on the surface. She could make out the glowing multicolor shades of her scales against the brilliant white light of the full moon. She let the tips of one of her front claws touch the surface, making ripples behind her as she flew.

You are beautiful, mi elila, Creon said as he swooped protectively down next to her.

He hurt those women because of me, Carmen mourned softly. *How many has he hurt over the past four years?*

Hush, my little warrior kitten, Creon said as he followed her down to the satin white beach below.

Carmen touched down first, folding her wings against her side as she turned to stare up at the full moon. It looked close enough to touch. She raised her head and let out a mournful cry at the thought that others were harmed because of her. Creon's midnight black shape touched down. In the darkness of night, it was impossible to see him except for the glow of his golden eyes.

Do not blame yourself, Carmen. You have no control over what that man did. He was evil. Do not take his deeds as your own. You are the light to the darkness, he said as his larger shape moved closer to her. *Look,* he whispered. *Look how your brightness shines, lighting up the darkness of my soul.*

Carmen looked down as he gently touched his front claw to hers. His scales shimmered for a moment before the color darkened and began to reflect the stars from the sky. She looked up into his flaming gold eyes.

Together we are one, he whispered. *It is time for my phoenix to rise up from the ashes and to embrace our life together. Will you do this with me? Will you do this for our daughters that you carry?*

Carmen laid her slender head against Creon's massive chest briefly before she drew back enough to look into his eyes again. It was time to finally say good-bye. She would never forget her old life.

It would always be a part of her, but it was time to accept her new life. She had changed just as the phoenix had until only the ashes of her old life remained. Out of those ashes, she had a choice as to how she wanted to live her new life. She wanted one with no regrets.

I want to go home, Carmen said quietly.

To Wyoming? Creon asked hesitantly.

Carmen looked up at the moon and the stars again. *No,* she said softly into the wind. *To Valdier.* She looked at him with flaming golden brown eyes. *To my new life with you and our children.*

You are mine, Carmen. Forever, Creon whispered.

The huge male moved behind the smaller female. He would take her again tonight. He would claim her under the stars and the moon of her planet, on a sandy beach. He would roar for all to hear that a Valdier dragon prince had found his mate in the most unlikely place with the most beautiful female he had ever seen. She was delicate, fragile, strong, and brave. She was stubborn and loyal and compassionate. She was the light to his darkness. She was his perfect mate, and he loved her more than life itself.

The slender female dragon lowered her head in submission until the larger male nudged her with his head. *Look to the stars as I take you, my beautiful phoenix. Look to the stars and home,* he murmured as he slowly mounted her from behind.

When she raised her head to the stars, Creon bent over her biting down and breathing the dragon's fire of his male into her. He embraced the fire as it burned through them both. He welcomed the fire that would ignite in both of them as they came together as one again and again.

Carmen's hoarse cry shattered the silence as the huge male caged her within his wings, holding her and taking her with long, strong strokes. She rocked back against him as he gripped her wings at the shoulders with his front claws, rising up on his hind legs and wrapping his tail tightly around hers to hold his balance as he pushed deeply into her over and over. He released her neck as her jagged coughs broke along with the waves on the surface. Her body milked his over and over, pulling him deeper into her and holding him trapped as she swelled around him.

The loud roar of the male as he climaxed shook the trees, scaring the native birds and animals living along the isolated coast. His roar could be heard for miles and many residents along the coast would swear they saw and heard the ancient god, Quetzalcoatl, as he roared his claim for all to hear that night.

∽

Carmen fell into an exhausted sleep wrapped in her mate's strong wings, the sounds of the waves her lullaby, the warm breeze her fan, and an endless sky of stars her nightlight. She was finally at peace. She vaguely remembered Creon coaxing her to transform back into her two-legged form before dawn. She quickly fell back into a deep, deep sleep brought on from being pregnant and too many years of stress. Creon carried her wrapped just as tightly in his arms as he held her in his wings to Harvey, who was waiting patiently for them further down the beach.

"Thank you, my friend," Creon said quietly as he laid Carmen down on the contoured bed that formed under her. "Take us back to Paul's home. We have one thing left to do before we can leave for home."

Harvey shimmered, changing colors to match the early morning light. A fisherman, coming around the cove, would later tell of the magnificent creature that had disappeared right before his eyes but not before he saw it rise up off the beach. He would later bring several of his friends and one scientist with him to show them the footprints the gods left in the sand before the waves and wind washed them away.

~

Later that day, Carmen and Creon stood in the small graveyard outside of the town of Casper Mountain, Wyoming. Scott's grave lay near his mother's and her parents. Carmen walked forward and laid several red roses on the grave and one small teddy bear. She let her fingers brush over the words:

More than a husband, more than a friend, the love of my life. He rests here protecting our unborn child forever in his arms. You will forever be in my heart.

Carmen smiled thankfully as Creon helped her to stand up. He held her tenderly, giving her time to say good-bye. She squeezed his hand before turning and taking a deep breath as she looked up into the brilliant blue sky.

"I'm ready to go home," she said calmly. "I'm ready to live again."

Creon didn't say a word. He didn't have to. He could see the sense of peace in her as she let go of her past. He wrapped his arm around her and turned toward Harvey who was waiting for them. They would be leaving this afternoon for Valdier. Carmen wanted their children to be born in their home there, if possible. It would be close if they were to make it back in time, but she was determined that their girls would know their home world.

Creon had talked with Trelon. He told him about using the symbiots with the crystals plus the sound waves Cara had perfected. He cautioned that it had to be done in the right order and at the right frequency, otherwise it made the symbiots act like a bunch of Valdier warriors having a drinking contest.

He had given the task to the Marastin Dow females, of all people, to set up. They were both amazing in the engineering department. His chief of engineering would oversee them. He had received word as they were coming here that Cree and Calo had returned to the warship. Nothing was said about whether Melina was with them or not. He figured he would find out soon enough. He couldn't imagine them leaving without her, but if she absolutely refused, they might not have had a choice as he had sent word to them that they were departing today.

There was still much to do. His uncle was still in hiding, but he had no doubts that he would reappear. Ha'ven said that three more rebel bases had been found. Jazar and Adalard were taking care of them.

Vox was going through his own star system. One of the bases had several Sarafin warriors who refused to name who they were supporting. With the might of the three royal houses working together instead of at war with each other, it was only a matter of time before they discovered who else was behind the rise of the rebellion.

Creon helped Carmen into Harvey, making sure she was comfortable before he ordered Harvey to take them to the *Horizon*, which was orbiting on the other side of the moon. Carmen didn't look back as they rose up in the air. She looked up into the sky with a smile and held out her hand to him.

"Take us home, Creon," she said.

EPILOGUE

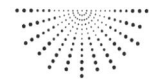

Carmen groaned as she finally rolled out of the bed. In the past almost eight weeks she had blossomed until she looked like she had swallowed a couple of watermelons, a few cantaloupes, and maybe a few honeydews. They had arrived on Valdier late—or should she say early—this morning. She felt like she had just gotten to bed when she woke up full of energy.

Oh hell, she thought as she waddled over to the dresser in the master bedroom of their living quarters at the palace. *Let's just add a couple of pumpkins as well.*

You think you have it bad, her dragon complained. *No room for me in here! I pressed into little ball.*

I know, Carmen said as she rubbed her back. *Right against my kidneys with those two little devils who think it is their personal punching bag!*

"Where are you going?" Creon asked anxiously as he walked out of the bathroom.

Carmen let her eyes roam up and down his tall, muscular form with a sigh of envy. "I wish I looked as good as you do," she groaned.

He hurried over to her and wrapped his arms around her. "You are the most beautiful thing in all the star systems," he said huskily. "The rounder you grow the more your beauty shines through. There is not a warrior on all of Valdier that does not envy me."

Carmen snorted. "You obviously haven't been listening to what they are saying!" she retorted.

His face darkened dangerously. "Who has insulted you? I will gut them and roast their corpses over an open pit," he demanded.

"Oh no, you don't!" she snapped back with a chuckle as she imagined Cree and Calo slowly turning on a spit. Not that she had seen both of them at the same time lately. "I get that privilege when I'm not the size of a compact car," she said with a gleam of mischief in her eyes.

"Who has insulted you?" he asked in a deceptively persuasive voice.

"I've got it under control. The Bobbsey Twins know the only reason they can beat me right now is because I am too big to toss their asses around. So far, they owe us two weeks' worth of babysitting!" She giggled huskily. "Trust me, that is more than payback when they have to change a few diapers!"

He picked her up gently and walked back toward the bed, determined to make her lie back down and get more rest, but she tightened her arms around his neck. "No! I have a hard enough time getting up from a sitting position. There is no way I want to struggle up from lying down again," she said desperately, looking at the bed with horror.

"You need to rest. You have only had a couple of hours sleep," he said stubbornly—plus he needed to go kick two of his warriors' asses.

"So have you," she pointed out. "I'm fine. You finish getting dressed, then I'll get a quick shower. I want to go see Abby's little boy, Cara and Trelon's twins, and Trisha's baby too. Oh my god, can you believe all of us are having kids at the same time? Well, except for Ariel," Carmen said with a sad smile.

"Do not be so sure of that," Creon said as he gently set her back on her feet. "Mandra had a huge grin on his face, and it wasn't from beating any of the warriors' asses."

"Really?" Carmen said excitedly. "Are you sure?"

"Yes," Creon laughed. "He let on that they are expecting a boy. But don't say anything yet. He said Ariel swore him to secrecy until she was sure. She refused to believe him when he told her he had planted his seed in her."

Carmen rolled her eyes and started to say something sarcastic when her face twisted in pain. She grabbed her stomach and drew in a deep breath as she felt a sharp kick followed by a popping. Warm water began flowing down her legs and pooling around her.

"Are you well?" Creon asked, looking at her carefully when she drew in a shuddering breath. "Maybe I should call Tandor to come take a look at you."

Carmen nodded her head. "Yes, I think that might be a good idea," she panted as waves of pain started coursing through her.

Creon swallowed hard and paled as he followed Carmen's hands, which were wrapped around her stomach. "Carmen, you are leaking," he said hoarsely. "Are you supposed to leak?"

Carmen glared at him, but couldn't say anything as another contraction gripped her. She let out a long moan of pain and bent over. Creon reached for her, wrapping his arms back around her again.

"What is it?" he asked frantically. "What is happening?"

"Babies," she moaned out as she struggled to turn and make it back to the bed. "Now!" Another contraction, harder than the one before, swept through her.

"Ouch!" Creon yelped as she squeezed his hand. "That hurt!"

"Yeah," she panted. "It does."

Creon thought it in his best interest not to correct her on what he meant. He helped her into bed before he turned to rush out of the room. He stopped only because of her desperate cry.

"Creon!" Carmen called out hoarsely.

"What?" he asked in a panic, his eyes darting back and forth between the door and Carmen, who lay panting on their bed.

"Put some pants on before you bring everyone in here," she instructed before she moaned long and loud. "I need you! Now. The babies. Now."

"What?" he asked again, falling over face first as he got tangled up trying to pull his pants on. He grabbed his comlink and fumbled with it, trying to activate it. "Help! Carmen, babies, now, help!" he yelled hoarsely into it as he climbed back to his feet, jumping up and down to get his pants the rest of the way up.

He barely got them partially fastened before Carmen let out a guttural cry of pain. He reached for her, pulling her damp nightgown up to see if there was anything he could do. He saw the head of one of his daughters cresting just before his eyes rolled back in his head and he fell to the floor. Carmen looked down on the floor and let out a loud scream as their first daughter pushed through. Within moments, Morian was next to her as well as Tandor and several of the other healers. Three of them and Morian tended to Carmen as she delivered their first, then their second daughter within five minutes of each other. The other healer ordered two warriors who were looking very pale to help him carry Creon out into the living quarters where they quickly deposited his unconscious body on the couch before they disappeared out the door again.

"What? Where? Carmen?" Creon muttered as he slowly came to several minutes later. He lay on the couch for a few seconds before he remembered. Rolling, he grunted when he hit the floor again before cursing when he hit his head on the low table in front of it. "*Carmen!*" he yelled in a panic, trying to get up.

The healer reached out and gripped his arm. "*Carmen!*" Creon yelled again as he jerked away unsteadily. "*Carmen!*" he called out frantically when he didn't get a response.

He rushed back to their bedroom. Carmen lay propped up against the headboard of the bed. A tiny, bundled figure in her arms nestled against one breast. He moved forward, only to stop when his mother stood up and turned with another small bundle in her arms.

He stepped forward, entranced by the small gurgling sounds. His mother held out the small bundle she was holding. Instinctively, his hands reached out, and he carefully pulled it toward him. His eyes widened when he saw the thick black hair covering the tiny head.

Brilliant brown eyes stared up at him, and a tiny fist waved in the air as if searching for something. He raised his hand and held out his smallest finger. The tiny hand gripped it eagerly, pulling it into her tiny mouth and sucking on it.

"She's beautiful," he whispered in amazement.

His eyes lifted to Carmen's. Tears glistened in his eyes as he lo[oked] at his beautiful mate. He slowly walked over to her and sat down n[ext] to her. She gently pulled the tiny mouth away from her breast an[d] burped her before holding her out for Creon. He pulled his finger away from his daughter's tiny mouth, frowning with worry when she whimpered.

"Let me feed her as well," Carmen said softly, holding out the tiny bundle now full and sleeping.

Creon carefully laid his fussy daughter down against Carmen before carefully lifting the soft, sleeping infant. She had hair as white as Carmen's. She opened her golden eyes briefly to stare at him. She opened her mouth and yawned, smacking her tiny mouth several times before she closed her eyes again in contentment.

He lifted his eyes when he felt his mate's hand brushing along his cheek. He felt the cool, dampness from his tears. He had so much to live for. He would do everything in his power to protect his mate and his daughters from harm.

"I know," Carmen whispered tiredly. "Together. We will protect them together."

"What would you like to name them," he asked quietly.

"Spring and Phoenix," Carmen said, looking at their daughters. "Both mean new beginnings, rebirth, hope, life."

He looked at the pale figure laying in his arms. "Spring," he murmured softly. "I like that. Phoenix looks like she is enjoying her meal."

Carmen blushed as her eyes moved to Morian who was cleaning up the room. Morian chuckled as she looked at Creon and Carmen with their new daughters. She had made the right decision when she decided it was not her time to leave this world.

Her sons would need help, and her daughters would need to band together when the men became too protective. She felt a blush rise as she thought of the dark eyes of a certain human who had returned with Kelan and Trisha. His look had been… Morian shook her head. She was too old for such fanciful thoughts. She must have misunderstood. She had only met him briefly. But still, he… She released a soft sigh.

"...uld you need me," Morian said as she quietly ...ens in the small crib set up near the bed.

"...," Carmen said tiredly as the after effects of too ...u with having the babies pulled on her.

...e over and took Phoenix out of her arms. "Sleep, child," ...tly. "They will wake you when they are hungry again."

...on held Spring tightly against himself for a moment before he ...ood up and laid her gently down next to her sister. They turned almost immediately toward each other, touching just a little before settling down again. Creon stood over them, gazing at them in awe. Everything about them was perfect. He looked back at Carmen who was asleep still sitting up.

"Go to your mate, Creon. She needs you now more than your daughters," Morian encouraged.

Creon looked down at his mother. He bent down and brushed a kiss across her forehead. His throat was tight, but he felt he needed to tell her how much her help meant to him.

"Thank you, *Dola*, for everything," he said quietly. "You saw the pain and grief inside my mate before I did. Without your guidance I don't know if I would have seen it in time. Your guidance and love has made me a stronger, better warrior," he said with quiet conviction. "Her love fills my life to overflowing."

Morian brushed a kiss against her youngest son's cheek. "Just as your father and you and your brothers have filled mine."

Carmen's soft sigh caressed the air. "Go to her," Morian encouraged again.

Creon didn't need any more encouragement. He gently lifted his mate and laid her back down until she was lying comfortably before he crawled in next to her. He wrapped his arms around her tightly and pressed a kiss to her silky hair.

"You are not the only one to rise from the ashes, my beautiful Phoenix," Creon whispered tenderly. "I have risen alongside you. Together, with our daughters, we will begin a new life."

Continue the journey with:
Paul's Pursuit

Sacrifice, impossible dreams, and the ultimate predator...

Paul Grove loves two things in the world more than anything else: his daughter Trisha, and roaming the mountains and forests of Wyoming, but after Trisha and her friends disappeared, the tracks he found made no sense, the clues left behind unlike any he'd ever seen before, and when his daughter returns - with a warrior from another world - Paul realizes he has to return with her to her new home or lose her forever.

Check out the full book here: books2read.com/Pauls-Pursuit

Or read on a sneak peek into 2 new series!

A Warrior's Heart
This novella is free.

Only the most ruthless Marastin Dow are allowed to live, and Evetta and Hanine have killed enough of their own to stay alive, but they desperately want a different life. When they meet two human brothers fighting for their lives, the sisters are in agreement: this alliance could be their only chance.

Check out the full novella here: *books2read.com/A-Warriors-Heart*

Choosing Riley
Sarafin Warriors Book 1

Readers' Crown Finalist! A brash, kick-ass heroine with a hidden vulnerability and an arrogant king forced to be a slave...

Check out the full book here: books2read.com/Choosing-Riley

ADDITIONAL BOOKS

If you loved this story by me (S.E. Smith) please leave a review! You can discover additional books at: http://sesmithfl.com and http://sesmithya.com or find your favorite way to keep in touch here: https://sesmithfl.com/contact-me/ Be sure to sign up for my newsletter to hear about new releases!

Recommended Reading Order Lists:
http://sesmithfl.com/reading-list-by-events/
http://sesmithfl.com/reading-list-by-series/

The Series

Science Fiction / Romance

Dragon Lords of Valdier Series
It all started with a king who crashed on Earth, desperately hurt. He inadvertently discovered a species that would save his own.

Curizan Warrior Series
The Curizans have a secret, kept even from their closest allies, but even they

are not immune to the draw of a little known species from an isolated planet called Earth.

Marastin Dow Warriors Series
The Marastin Dow are reviled and feared for their ruthlessness, but not all want to live a life of murder. Some wait for just the right time to escape....

Sarafin Warriors Series
A hilariously ridiculous human family who happen to be quite formidable... and a secret hidden on Earth. The origin of the Sarafin species is more than it seems. Those cat-shifting aliens won't know what hit them!

Dragonlings of Valdier Novellas
The Valdier, Sarafin, and Curizan Lords had children who just cannot stop getting into trouble! There is nothing as cute or funny as magical, shapeshifting kids, and nothing as heartwarming as family.

Cosmos' Gateway Series
Cosmos created a portal between his lab and the warriors of Prime. Discover new worlds, new species, and outrageous adventures as secrets are unravelled and bridges are crossed.

The Alliance Series
When Earth received its first visitors from space, the planet was thrown into a panicked chaos. The Trivators came to bring Earth into the Alliance of Star Systems, but now they must take control to prevent the humans from destroying themselves. No one was prepared for how the humans will affect the Trivators, though, starting with a family of three sisters....

Lords of Kassis Series
It began with a random abduction and a stowaway, and yet, somehow, the Kassisans knew the humans were coming long before now. The fate of more than one world hangs in the balance, and time is not always linear....

Zion Warriors Series

Time travel, epic heroics, and love beyond measure. Sci-fi adventures with heart and soul, laughter, and awe-inspiring discovery…

Paranormal / Fantasy / Romance

Magic, New Mexico Series
Within New Mexico is a small town named Magic, an… unusual town, to say the least. With no beginning and no end, spanning genres, authors, and universes, hilarity and drama combine to keep you on the edge of your seat!

Spirit Pass Series
There is a physical connection between two times. Follow the stories of those who travel back and forth. These westerns are as wild as they come!

Second Chance Series
Stand-alone worlds featuring a woman who remembers her own death. Fiery and mysterious, these books will steal your heart.

More Than Human Series
Long ago there was a war on Earth between shifters and humans. Humans lost, and today they know they will become extinct if something is not done….

The Fairy Tale Series
A twist on your favorite fairy tales!

A Seven Kingdoms Tale
Long ago, a strange entity came to the Seven Kingdoms to conquer and feed on their life force. It found a host, and she battled it within her body for centuries while destruction and devastation surrounded her. Our story begins when the end is near, and a portal is opened….

Epic Science Fiction / Action Adventure

Project Gliese 581G Series
An international team leave Earth to investigate a mysterious object in our solar system that was clearly made by someone, someone who isn't from

Earth. Discover new worlds and conflicts in a sci-fi adventure sure to become your favorite!

New Adult / Young Adult

Breaking Free Series
A journey that will challenge everything she has ever believed about herself as danger reveals itself in sudden, heart-stopping moments.

The Dust Series
Fragments of a comet hit Earth, and Dust wakes to discover the world as he knew it is gone. It isn't the only thing that has changed, though, so has Dust...

ABOUT THE AUTHOR

S.E. Smith is an *internationally acclaimed, New York Times* **and** *USA TODAY Bestselling* author of science fiction, romance, fantasy, paranormal, and contemporary works for adults, young adults, and children. She enjoys writing a wide variety of genres that pull her readers into worlds that take them away.

Printed in Great Britain
by Amazon